THE ENDORIAL ARCHIVES
THE STAR KEY

By

Daniel J. Wright

First Edition: 2026

Paperback ISBN: 979-8-218-87079-9

FOR THE STARLIGHT THAT
GUIDES AND INSPIRES ME.

FOR THE DRAGON THAT
ENCOURAGES ME.

FOR THE WILLOW TREE THAT
SHADES ME.

FOR THE MONKEY THAT
KEEPS ME ON MY TOES.

FOR THE MOON THAT
BRIGHTENS MY NIGHT.

FOR THE FOX THAT
KEEPS ME CUNNING

Listen to the soundtrack composed

by Daniel J. Wright for this book

on Spotify:

Contents

FOREWORD

Truth unaltered. Memory eternal. From the first spark to the final silence, we remember.

Grand Universe Archives, Official Release 98467-GUA

It is the solemn duty of the Grand Universe Archives to safeguard records of events that have defined existence across realities. This volume, *The Endorial Archives: The Star Key*, is the inaugural official account from Archivist Endorial, chronicling the life of Lienad. Despite an unremarkable origin, Lienad's trajectory exemplifies the universe's unpredictable forces.

This record has been fully verified under Codex Protocol 17.4, through meticulous primary extraction, dimensional corroboration, and artifact cross-referencing. In accordance with GUA principles, the documented events remain substantively unchanged, representing our commitment to faithful truth.

The Council's decision to release this record beyond our central archives underscores its profound relevance for all readers. This work initiates Archivist Endorial's anticipated series chronicling Lienad's evolving impact.

Readers are encouraged to approach this account with the understanding that history often unfolds through the determined actions of individuals facing profound uncertainty.

In honor of remembrance and vigilance, this account is respectfully presented. For the benefit of all readers, regardless of where they are from, a pronunciation guide is included at the end of this work. We at the G.U.A. recommend that those who may read this start by familiarizing themselves with the guide.

Authorized by:

Tolen-Bran
Senior Archivist
Grand Universe Archives

Prologue

If you can read this text, let me first start by applauding you—this already proves you are capable of greatness. I say this because you are clearly able to auto-translate my writings from Entonichian to your native tongue.

My name is Endorial, a member of the Grand Universe Archives Reconnaissance Division. For those unfamiliar, the Grand Universe Archives is the most extensive collection of written works in existence. Anything that has ever happened, since the dawn of time, can be found within its tomes. It is located within the void between the dimensions, with connections to everything there is. The G.U.A. was formed when the universe was created, tasked with the mission of maintaining all knowledge of every sentient being. All Archivists are a special type of species, able to leave our physical shells and attach inside the mind of another. The G.U.A. is broken down into a variety of departments to ensure our tasks are completed to the highest degree.

The Reconnaissance Division is a special task force

that records the data that is compiled. Each of us is assigned to someone, tasked with observing and recording their life. We document every thought, feeling, and action of who we are assigned from the moment we are placed with them. In fact, you probably have someone from the G.U.A.R.D. watching you right now; as well as anyone else you know. Though, to be honest, most of what we get to write is dreadfully dull, especially if we are assigned at birth. The baby phase where you don't really do anything feels like it will never end. Because of this, only select compilations are ever shared outside of the Archives. Unfortunately, those that do get shared are often disregarded as fables of fantasy. But make no mistake, what I am about to tell you is very real.

I was assigned to a man named Lienad after his previous Archivist, and all previously transmitted documents about him, mysteriously disappeared. That matter is a separate issue entirely, and is currently under investigation back at the G.U.A. Because of this, I had extremely limited information coming into this assignment. I mostly know that he leads a very dull life with a very boring routine. My initial few months watching Lienad could be summarized as such: depressingly dull. To give you an example, there was an entire week that I merely observed him eat his meals and sit on the couch. Not to mention lengthy periods where he didn't even muster up the will to bathe himself, which made me glad I could not smell him. Those months are not included here as they had already been sent as a test transmission. I begin writing this following the confirmed receipt of that transmission. But, believe me, you aren't missing much from that. I can put everything he did during that time into a single word, nothing.

This story begins on the small, and frankly unremarkable, planet Earth. In terms of Earth years, it is 2125. Humanity dreamt there would be flying cars, laser guns, and convenient space flight by this time. Unfortunately, that is not the case. Around the year 2035 a giant solar flare destroyed Earth's satellites, thereby plunging the entire planet into pure chaos. Society completely collapsed and civilization had to crawl its way back through the ashes. By the year 2125 technology had just barely recovered to what it was in the year 2019, over a full century behind where it should have been while the rest of the universe continued to move on. In a way, though, this also ended up saving them.

The Earth remained unnoticed, nothing more than a mere speck within the grand cosmos. This was a blessing because over the last five years an interdimensional war has raged on, causing severe devastation. This war was started by an unnamed terror organization led by the loathsome Krind. He has but one goal: to hold power over every dimension there is, spreading blood among the stars to obtain it. The only thing that stands in his way is the Dimensional Intervention Containment and Kill Squads, or, as they are more commonly known, D.I.C.K.S. As humorous as that may sound, I can assure you it is no laughing matter; war seldom is. The D.I.C.K.S. dedicate themselves to finding and exploiting all enemy weaknesses. Turning defectors, eliminating threats, and extracting all intelligence they can. They are also the only reason there are select humans that have still made their way across the stars. Despite all their efforts, the darkness continues to spread.

As this story starts, the universe is a war-torn and dying cosmos, where hope is but a fleeting illusion. While they say things usually get worse before they get better, I only expect them to get even worse. Though I cannot say for sure, as this story was written in real time—and this is merely an introductory section for this transmission in case the G.U.A. decides to release it... I just don't believe in excessive optimism.

1

<u>The Dreary Start</u>

In his blacked-out room, chilled by the struggling air conditioner, a shrill digital alarm tore through the silence. Lienad rolled over on his lumpy mattress and smacked the off button. Blinking at the blurry clock, he thought it read "HELLO." After rubbing his eyes, he realized it was just 6:15 AM.

"Great," he sighed aloud to himself. "Another worthless day to be mindlessly wasted."

It had been over a week now since he had lost his job. Most people would get stressed about this, but he found solace in no longer dealing with the stupidity of humanity day in and day out. Having to listen to everyone's problems—and

then expecting him to give a damn. If they wanted a therapy session they should have gone to a shrink, not their grocery store cashier.

However, this had cast him into the existential crisis of what to do with life now—which could easily be seen by the ever-growing pile of crusted dishes in his kitchen. He had no friends, no love life, no family, and not even so much as a goldfish. Lienad had never really thought about what he really wanted to do, he just simply passed through life. He never truly felt like he belonged. Not just with people, but existing in general. As far back as he could remember, it was always as if he wasn't supposed to be here. Every so often, he would even dream that he was really someone else. In these dreams he still looked the same, but his mind was different. Those dreams were the only times he ever felt right. Sadly, they very rarely happened.

He made his usual bland breakfast—eggs, bacon, buttered toast, and lightly sweetened black coffee. Then, he sat in his robe and pretended to read the newspaper by staring blankly at the front page. However, if he had been paying attention, he would have noticed that today's headline read:

"Mysterious Happenings, Is the End Near?"

Granted, had he read it he still wouldn't have cared.

He then put the newspaper down and reached for his laptop. Apathetically he skimmed through the online job boards. The list seemed increasingly dreadful the further he scrolled. Warehouse, restaurant, clerical work, grocery—all of them just seemed like an even bigger waste of time than doing nothing at all. As he went to shut down the laptop, he quickly noticed a posting that read:

```
"Are you tired of aimlessly living a de-
pressing life? Can't seem to find interest in
ANYTHING? Ready for something other than just
another dismal job to fill your time? Then we
may have the solution for YOU!"
```

Normally, he would just chalk this up to being yet another scam to fool the weak-minded—but this time he felt curious. As he clicked on the link, a thunderous boom from outside startled him, making him hit the table and knock over his coffee—which poured all over his laptop.

"GODDAMMIT!" he yelled, as his laptop zapped and crashed.

Finally, something had given him even the slightest hint of interest and now it was just gone. He became irate at the burning smell coming from his sparking laptop. So, he did what any rational person would do, he hurled his laptop at the wall. Then he cleaned up the disaster that was his laptop—or, as he saw it, the shattered remains of his only chance at changing his bleak life.

After the breakfast debacle set the tone for his day, he decided to get dressed—even though he had no real reason to do so. He opened the door to his closet and stood there, staring at the slightly varying shades of gray button-up shirts and multiple pairs of black slacks; how endless his options were. A few moments passed until he made the obvious choice, a gray button up shirt with black pants.

Looking into the mirror, brushing his medium length brown hair, he decided it was time to change his style a little bit. He un-tucked his shirt and left his hair slightly messy, although this was hardly a real change. He grabbed his briefcase, which contained a notepad, three black pens, and a few copies of his tiny resume. As he grabbed his keys and headed for the door, the phone began to ring.

"It's probably a bill collector," he thought, "if it's really important they will leave a message."

Had he decided to answer it, he would have known it was definitely not a bill collector. It was, in fact, especially important—and they would not leave a message. He went outside and started his car. It was a black sedan with above average wear and tear on the slate grey interior. He sat there, having no idea where to go. At a crossroads, Lienad hesitated. Go back inside and waste another day—or just drive and see

4

what happens?

Normally, he would have chosen the former. He was, after all, neither one for chances nor one to exerting any type of energy he deemed unnecessary. For some reason, though, today he chose to drive out into the world. It could have been confidence gained from "changing his style", but probably not. Regardless of the reason, he made a different choice than normal.

As he was driving through his town, which was about as interesting as a gray-scale photo of snow, he noticed a few "Now Hiring" signs. All of which were, of course, for industries he had no desire to work in. Lienad began to feel as though today was just a waste and that leaving the house had been a stupid decision to make—and in this case, he was right.

He began to turn the car around and head home. As he was doing this, he noticed a billboard that seemed as though it was meant for him. He was right because, little did he know, it was. It read:

Lienad, I am trying to reach you. Stop wasting your life and come to me!

When he looked back at the road, he slammed on his

brakes, trying to stop at the last second from hitting a woman that was waving at him. When he stopped, he rushed out of the car to see if she was alright—but there was no one there. This didn't make sense, he vividly remembered her. Beautiful black hair, skin like snow, lips of roses, and eyes of the ocean. Who was she? Where could she have gone? He had many questions, but there were no answers to be found.

As he was trying to figure out what had just happened, he remembered the sign. Quickly turning his head looking for it, he saw it had changed. The billboard was completely different. Now it read:

Place your ad here. Call 800-654-4578

He was so confused. The disappearing beautiful woman and the billboard that was directed at him—wasn't real. Being the logical man that he is, Lienad's first thought was aliens. Realizing how crazy of a notion that was, he decided it was just a mixture of sleep deprivation and depression causing mild hallucinations. I had no reason to believe his hallucinations were the work of any intergalactic species—nor do I believe they were just hallucinations.

He decided to start driving home to get some rest. He tried and tried to stop thinking about it, but no matter what there was always some little voice in his head constantly

reminding him about it.

"But what if it was some crazy cosmic power doing this?" he asked himself.

"It's not, that's a crazy notion, drop it already," he responded.

"Why not?"

"ENOUGH," he screamed aloud to himself, "It's not a big deal, I'm just exhausted; that's all. There is nothing else going on here, end of story. Let's just stop thinking and talking about it already."

Luckily, talking to yourself is completely normal. Responding, however, is not—even less so to argue. It was a good thing that no one saw this, they would probably consider him to be hysterical and in need of help. Still, Lienad was glad that he had won the argument against himself, as if there was any other possible outcome. His drive home continued. Turning onto his street, Byrd Street, his car began to shake and sputter. He looked at the dashboard—his gas light was blinking. As soon as he pulled into his driveway, his car ran out of gas and died.

"Well, that's great," he sarcastically expressed aloud, "Just another thing to add to an already perfect FUCKING day."

He parked, pulled the emergency brake, and trudged inside to rid himself of this wretched day. At this point he felt

it would have been better to have just stayed home, and he was right.

"Well," he sighed with little effort, "Maybe tomorrow will be better."

Personally, I doubt that it would be.

✲⁎8 ✲⁎

2

The Aliens

On Earth, the consensus about aliens is quite divided. Are they real? What are they like? Are they green? Et cetera. Everyone has their own opinion about them, and almost all of them are wrong. If you are not a human on Earth reading this, feel free to skip this section. Chances are, you already know everything I'm going to say here. If you are a human reading this, there are a few simple facts that I can tell you about alien life. They come in all shapes, colors, and sizes. There are nice ones, lazy ones, evil ones, and many more in between. They most certainly exist—even humans are considered aliens to other species. I can also tell you that many in the intergalactic community find this term to be very derogatory and offensive. But I don't really care, and neither should you. They get offended by everything, and it is

ridiculous.

While this information may not seem important to the tale at hand, I can assure you that it is essential information for you to have throughout this story. Now, did aliens cause any of the events that happened to Lienad on Earth? Well, that is a yes and no answer—mostly no. The main reason I tell you this is not because of what has already happened in Lienad's life on Earth, but what will happen to him as events unfold. Another reason aliens are important is that humans usually turn to a few things for events they cannot explain. If something good or bad happens, they usually relate it to a religious deity. If it is something that simply cannot be explained, they claim it to be either aliens or magic.

Lienad was only different in the fact that he did not believe in religious deities. But he did believe in the possibility of both aliens and magic. Which is good because they are both very real and especially important. I felt it would be important to explain now, so you could be prepared to accept their existence.

You may wonder how aliens came to be on Earth, which is an easy question to answer. Aliens have existed on Earth since the planet was formed. This is a truth that has been hidden in plain sight throughout all human history. Even something as simple as birds is proof of alien life. Many believe they evolved from dinosaurs, which couldn't be further from the truth. Most bird life on Earth is a de-evolved form of the species Heagowl from the planet Tesheraf. There are other signs as well. Stonehenge? Yes, that was aliens. The pyramids? You got it, aliens again. Lizard people within the Earth's governments? Yes, they descend from the Serpisapions of Pecoaphlyly. There are many more examples I can give, but it would take too long to go over them all.

While I am at it breaking this news to you, I may as well go over a few other species as well. Earth has many tales of folklore regarding things like trolls, goblins, vampires, werewolves, and more. Those are also very real. Unfortunately, I do not know how they came to exist. But I do know that Earth is the only planet they exist on. They have their own secret societies and the like all over the planet. Perhaps I will learn more about them while I am with Lienad. If I don't, then perhaps something will be released from the G.U.A. that does have more information about them.

3

The Call

It had been a few days now since the day of the changing billboard and the beautiful disappearing woman. Rather than spend an unnecessary amount of time recounting the lack of events that took place, allow me to give you a summary: nothing.

This morning started as most other days have. Breakfast, shower, get dressed, sit in the car, and go back inside. Usually things were easy, because he never really had to decide whether to drive anywhere as he still hadn't put any gas into the car. Today was not originally going to be any different. As he was getting out of his car, since he never intended to go anywhere, his cell phone began to ring. He pulled out his scratched and cracked smartphone to see that it was the local workforce office calling. Because this was most likely important, he reluctantly answered his

phone.

"Hello," he said in an exasperated tone.

"We are calling to notify you that your unemploy-ment benefits will be expiring in three weeks," the robotic female voice recited, "If you would like to be connected to a representative, please press -"

He hung up the phone before it could continue any further. Disappointed that his money for doing nothing would soon end, he knew that now he had to get a job. There was one minor problem, he still had a broken laptop, which meant that now he had to deal with people in real life—and he wasn't particularly good at that.

His car was still out of gas, so he had two options: call a cab or walk to get gas. He looked in his wallet and saw a measly twenty dollars. With the tiniest bit of hope, he looked at his banking app. Much to his dismay, but little to his surprise, there was only another thirty dollars. Clearly a cab was no longer an option, so he had to walk. The near-est gas station wasn't too far from his house, only a few blocks—maybe quarter a mile at the most. But Lienad loathed fresh air and the sun, making this a very daunting task for him. As much as he hated it, he knew there wasn't another choice if he wanted to avoid the potential home-lessness.

Along this seemingly never-ending walk, he saw so many things he hated. Children playing in their yard, mar-ried couples showing one another affection, and people

standing around a burning grill drinking beer. Granted, he probably wouldn't feel that way if he had some friends, children, or someone to love.

He really should have pretended to be interested and tried connecting with his neighbors. If he had, he may have learned some interesting facts. For instance, six houses down lived his neighbor Shaun. Living in his white colonial style house with a red door and picket fence, Shaun was an alien—a Coulkoid to be specific. This species rarely does nothing more than go to different planets and adopt their ways. There are many of them among us and we would never even guess it. This doesn't put Lienad in any danger, nor does it really affect his life, but he would have been interested to know that. As he passed by Shaun's house, he could see the gas station.

"Finally," he thought, "Almost there."

Many people believe the final stretch is the hardest part of any trek; Lienad was one of those people. It seemed like the sun was beating down harder and harder upon his exposed skin. With barely any distance left to go, he felt dehydrated and on the verge of collapse. He reached for the handle, stepped inside—and everything was fine. Lienad was so dramatic, he would have excelled in theater.

He pre-paid for some gas, filled his little red gas can, and began the horrid trip back to his house. Lucky for him, the trip back is never as bad as the trip there. Things always seem to go so quickly when you are returning from somewhere. Passing by the exact same houses, with the exact same people, doing the exact same things as they were before. He had already seen it all on the way there, so he didn't really need to pay attention this go around. Though, he really should have, because he might have noticed the strange occurrence that happened behind him. There was a woman standing in what seemed like a portal of sorts, attempting to get Lienad's attention. This was only for a moment before she was quickly pulled back into wherever she had come from.

He finally arrived back home and put the gas into his tank. As he put the gas can into his garage, so that it wouldn't stink up his car, he questioned whether he should leave the house or not. This questioning did not take long as he soon remembered that his money would stop coming in just a few weeks.

"Ah," he sighed aloud, "Off to find a job we go."

Since he really didn't feel like doing any of the actual leg work himself, he decided to go to a temp agency to have them give him a job. At least, that's how he expected it to go. He drove around, passing all the obvious **"Now Hiring"** signs once again. He could have saved a lot of time and trouble had he just gone into one of these many businesses and handed in his application. But he thought this agency might give him a better job. Once again, he was wrong.

He finally arrived at the slightly run down, brick building with a barely intact sign reading **"Temp Work"**,

it was obvious they didn't want anyone to question what they did. As he walked in, there was no greeting from anyone, which he enjoyed. As he sat down on a gray chair, that looked like it might collapse at any moment, he glanced around the room. The place was defined by dark walls, dim light, thick curtains, and stale air. Then he noticed their "mission statement" painted on one of the walls. It read:

"WE'LL FIND YOU A JOB, FOR A TEMPORARY TIME."

Credits to them for simplicity and straight forwardness, but they really could have thought of something better. It's almost as if the person that decided on that didn't really care about this agency, so they just wrote something plain and obvious for them. Which was the case.

Sitting there, listening to the clock tick, he wondered when they would call him back or if they even knew he was there. He didn't mind though; he was comfortable in there because he didn't have to interact with people. As he was settling in and making himself cozy, footsteps started to approach. Around the corner walked this very short woman. She was slightly below average height, quite heavyset, with long and unmanaged dark brown hair, and it looked as though she had never heard of make-up.

"Lienad," she said in her shrill, sharp, and nasal voice, "Come with me."

"Great," he thought, "An annoying and hideous troll."

Little did he know, she was in fact a troll, though she hated to talk about it. I can only imagine how surprised he would have been if he discovered that underneath the human skin suit was a grey troll with many large warts. Since he was unaware, he followed her back to her office. This room was barely distinguishable from the rest of the building, apart from a desk and computer. He sat down in yet another questionable gray chair, ready to begin the process of him getting a job; or so he thought.

"So, Lee, can I call you Lee," she screeched, "Do you know how this works?"

"Uh... I prefer Lienad," he stated, "Don't you just kind of give me some type of temporary job?"

"Hahahehuhaha," she cackled and snorted, "You're funny Lee, I'll give you that. What we do is place you with employers we feel might hire you. We get an interview set up and then it's your job to wow them. Does that make sense?"

"Yeah, I guess. I was just kind of hoping to do as little as possible."

"Honesty! Another good trait Lee, but laziness is not. We get the door open and it's your job to seal the deal.

Are you ready to do this?"

"I don't really have any other option."

"That's the spirit Lee, let's get started. Do you have a resume? References? Head shot? HA! That last one was a joke. But do you have the other stuff?"

"Um, I have a resume... but I don't really have any references except maybe my old boss... but then again he laid me off... so... yeah."

"That's fine Lee, now let's see that resume."

"Okay," he said while sliding over the mostly barren paper.

"Oh, golly gee wow," she exclaimed, "This is a mighty short resume. It's almost nothing but white space. How old are you?"

"Um, I'm 23," he said completely embarrassed and humiliated.

"Oh, well I guess that makes sense," she said, clearly holding back a laugh, "Here, let me grab this."

She moved around her office to a filing cabinet, barely even able to squeeze through the space she had. To give you a better understanding of her size, imagine a walrus. Her skin held back so much fat that it had the saggy texture and appearance of a walrus. This was one of the side effects of being a troll in human form—for the most part trolls are quite wide creatures. For this reason, trolls have

naturally tough skin; able to handle all the fat and stretching. Humans do not have this luxury.

From the filing cabinet, she pulled out a very thin orange folder; there couldn't have been more than 3 pages in it. On the folder was a big white label with the words: **FIRST TIME**.

"Here we have all the employers that might hire someone with your... qualifications," she was very condescending.

"What do you mean by that," his tone made it obvious he had been offended.

"Well," she began, "Someone with minimal job history, no real technical skills, and no education after high school. Basically, just like someone getting their first job."

"But this won't be my first job," he said confused, "I worked at the grocery store and got laid off."

"That's true," she agreed, "A basic job that anyone can get. Doesn't really set you that far apart from a first timer, does it?"

"Alright fine, so what are my options?"

"We have warehouse, food, construction, clerical, and grocery work."

All the things Lienad wanted to stay completely away from.

"You really don't have anything else?" he was highly

disappointed. "Anything at all?"

"Well," she paused, "We do have some janitorial work or plumbing."

"So, either I work a shit job, or I literally work with shit?"

"Sorry, but that's really all there is for your situation."

"Fine," he exclaimed, defeated, "They all suck, so just pick one and give it to me."

"Lee, Lee, Lee," she said, once again being condescending, "I already told you that we don't just give you the job. We send them your information and then they call you if they want an interview."

"And that's it?" Lienad was irritated at the waste of time this had been.

"Yes."

"You don't do anything else for me?"

"Well, if you haven't heard back in about two weeks you come back, and we'll see if anything new has come up. But yes, that's our job. This isn't temp work and other stuff—it's just temporary work; that's it."

"So basically if, all goes well, I never need to come in here again?" Lienad hoped that he would never have to be in her presence again.

"That's a harsh way of putting it Lee, but yes."

"Good, then can you please make sure they know my name is LIENAD not LEE."

"Well, you don't have to be so rude, but yes I will Lienad," she said in a very snide tone.

Glad to be done with that disgusting slob, he went out to his car to begin his trek home. Passing by all the signs for the jobs he could have just applied for himself once again. Still, he preferred the troll to do the leg work for him so he wouldn't have to. As he was pulling into his driveway, his phone began to ring.

"Wow, that beastly woman works quick," he thought, "Already getting a call for an interview."

This was not the case, and he should not have answered.

"Hello," he confidently answered the phone.

"Lienad, Lienad, can you hear me," a woman on the other end was shouting, "Lienad?"

"Who is this," he questioned, "Is this for an interview?"

"Lienad, help," she continued to shout, "We need your help, where are you?"

"Is this some kind of joke? Who is this?"

"LIENAD! Hurry."

The call was dropped, which was good because he didn't want to hear any further—but he was too weirded out to hang up himself. This was very confusing for Lienad, and it made him extremely uncomfortable. But now it was all he could think about.

"What in the hell was that?" he thought, both shocked and confused.

4

<u>The Girl</u>

It had been three days now since Lienad had received the strange call. They were three dull days of nothing more than wondering what that was about. During these past few days, he hadn't showered, left his home, or done much of anything other than stress about what happened. It consumed his mind to the point that he even forgot to make sure he was eating, not even so much as a snack. Also, if you are wondering—the answer is no. No, he did not receive any interview calls since giving the troll his resume. I personally believe she may have eaten it, but I have no way to be certain about that. Finally, after so many days of filth, he decided it was time to at least shower—if nothing else.

Lienad did his best to get back into his normal routine. Bland breakfast, pretending to care about newspapers—so on and so forth. But, as he was going to sweeten

his coffee, he noticed something quite strange. He suddenly found an abundance of forks but was missing a good chunk of his spoons. Little did he know though, this was not rare.

This is quite a common occurrence caused by a Snuln. You see, Snulns are ridiculously small creatures that share quite a few physical similarities with Pixies. They have a strange obsession with spoons. If you were to visit them, you would see mountains of spoons they have collected. No one really knows why.

They seem to also have an abundance of forks as well, thanks to the tricky little Pixies dumping them in their land; they love a good prank after all. The Pixies are notorious for stealing the forks they prank the Snuln with. So, if you ever notice a mysterious shortage of forks, that might be the reason behind it.

Luckily, the Snuln aren't too keen on forks and will leave a one behind for each spoon they steal from you. For some reason they believe this is a fair trade—my theory is that they probably don't eat much soup. Snuln and Pixies are not native to Earth, though they come here often. They are beings from a place known as The Colored Dust Dimension and use their magic to move between the different dimensions of the universe.

He brushed this off and went on about his business. As he sat down with his poor excuse of a breakfast, he opened his newspaper to begin his ritual of fake reading. He was not prepared for what he was about to see. As soon as he pulled the pages open, he saw, in big bold lettering:

"LIENAD, ARE YOU GETTING MY MESSAGES? I NEED YOUR HELP, WHERE ARE YOU?"

This startled him completely—and understandably so. He crumbled the newspaper and threw it straight into the trash. No longer feeling comfortable in his own home, he decided to shake things up and go out for his breakfast.

"Yeah," he thought, "All I need is some good old fresh air. I've just cooped myself up for too long."

He began his journey to the local Handerly's Breakfast & More. He had only gone there a few times as a kid, but all those memories were positive—so It felt like a safe place to go. As he pulled up to Handerly's he was flooded with a nostalgic feeling. The place looked exactly as he remembered it. Dirty red bricks on the outer walls, a neon sign that flickers sitting atop a tall metal pole, families filling the booths next to the window, and their family cars filling up all the front parking spaces. This familiar feeling did, in fact, make him feel safe.

He managed to find a parking spot not too far from the door, which was incredibly lucky considering how packed the restaurant appeared. Walking from his car, he could feel his stomach rumble and hear it growl. Yours

would too after not eating for a few days.

As he opened the door, he was overwhelmed with the cacophony of overlapping conversations and screaming children. But as anxious as this made him, he had already come this far and might as well see it through. He made his way through to an open booth in the back-left corner of the room. As he sat down, he noticed a tv in clear view playing the local news.

"Hey there Hun, welcome to Handerly's," the waitress had a pleasant southern accent, "My name is Aribell, and I'll be takin' care of you. What can I go ahead and get you started with to drink?"

"Hello," he said, admiring how attractive she was, "I'm actually ready to order, if that's all right."

"Well, a man who know what he wants, huh? That's my kind of man," she laughingly said, "What'll you have sweetie?"

"Coffee, black, two scrambled eggs, two strips of bacon, and a side of buttered toast," he was attempting to sound flirty, but had failed.

"You got it cutie pie; I'll have that right out for you."

As he watched her walk away, admiring the slight bounce of her rear end with every step, he began to question why he decided to sound flirty. He was sure she probably thought he was strange and was laughing at him in the back this very second. He was wrong, she didn't even notice. Still, he wondered if her flirting was genuine; could a girl like that be interested in him? She could have—but she wasn't. It was all in hopes of a generous tip.

After about twenty minutes of stressing over the situation with the waitress, his mind flipped to a different topic. He realized it had been an awful long time to wait for something as simple as what he ordered. She hadn't even brought the coffee yet. He began to look around to try and find her, but there were just too many people to try and see through. He was starting to get very irritated by this and was on the verge of causing a scene—or at least his version of one. As he was about to get up and go to the bar so he could ask for her, he saw her walking in the distance with his food.

"Finally." He thought, happy he didn't have to cause any problems.

"I'm so sorry doll, we got so caught up with a huge family order," she seemed genuine, "Just for your trouble I had them add on a side of hash browns for free."

"Oh, it's no trouble at all, thank you," he said with a fake smile, knowing that it was trouble, and that he hated hash browns.

She set the plate on the table and began to fill his cup with fresh coffee, which he was happy about because he was worried that she was going to bring him a cold cup that had been sitting there the whole time he was waiting. He was pretending to watch the news when suddenly, it

seemed like time had come to a stop. The television flick-ered and it changed to a video of a girl. As he looked closer, he realized it was the same girl he saw the other day, he could never forget such beauty.

"Lienad, I finally found you," she said through the screen, "How is the reception? Are you picking me up all right?"

He was so confused, looking around at all the seem-ingly lifeless bodies surrounding him, frozen in place.

"Lienad, this is a two-way channel," she said, grow-ing slightly more aggressive, "Can you hear me or not?"

"Uh... Um... Yes, I can hear you," he nervously stam-mered, unsure if he should respond at all.

"Good, I have been looking all over for you, I need your help."

"I... I'm sorry, who are you," he questioned, "Y-y-you need my help?"

"Who am I? Oh no," she exclaimed, "They must have enacted the PROTM. That explains why it was so hard to finally reach you."

"The PROTM? What are you talking about?" He felt a huge wave of anxiety overtaking him.

"Calm down Lienad, I'm sure you have a lot of ques-tions," She said reassuringly, "We need to meet in person, I can help you."

“There’s nothing wrong with me.”

“Listen, there is more wrong than you realize. I’ll be meeting with you soon; I’m sending a tracker through so I can physically find you. Just go home and wait for me.”

As she said this, a strange purple light came beaming through the screen, straight towards his head. Paralyzed with panic, he didn’t even bother trying to dodge it. As quick as it began, the situation ended. Everyone was back moving around; his coffee was finished being filled. He looked to the waitress; eyes filled with uncertainty.

“Did you see that, on the TV just now?”

“Oh, I know, I can’t believe it’s supposed to get up to a hundred degrees tomorrow,” She was entirely oblivious to what had happened, “I thought we were supposed to finally be done with this dang heat.”

“Oh… Yeah… I know,” he said trying to play it off as if he was calm and collected.

“Well sweetheart, do you need anything else right now?”

“Uh, just the check. I’ll go ahead and pay now.”

“You got it babe; I’ll be right back with that for ya.”

She walked away to go get him the check. He was in such a panicked state he couldn’t even think about the food in front of him. As he sat there, feeling like he was losing his mind, he decided it was just a delusion cause by sleep

deprivation and hunger. He violently shook his head rather quickly and tried to focus on eating.

"Here you go," she said while handing him his bill, "While you're still here just holler if you need anything."

She gave a cute smile and wink, then walked away. He scarfed down the rest of his food, as if his life depended on it. He rapidly drank his cup of coffee, trying to ignore how scalding hot it still was. His total due was $10.56, which, in his opinion, really wasn't too bad. In a major state of panic, he just threw the $20 bill from his wallet on the table and rushed out—he didn't even care about getting his change. He sped home, as fast as he could, to lay in his cold dark room.

With such a generous tip, that he didn't leave her intentionally, Aribell would have given him her number. She did find him attractive, but odd, and thought that this was his way of flirting with her. But he was nowhere to be found by the time she got the money from the table. Which was so unfortunate for him, as most things usually are.

He sped home, ran inside, locked the door, and went to lay in bed. Staring into the darkness of his room, cloaked by the frigid air, he began to find peace. As he comfortably drifted off to sleep, there was a loud knock at his front door; ruining any chance he had at giving his mind some much-needed rest.

5

The Hospital

Lienad laid there, unsure if he should bother checking the door. So many things over the past few days have happened—more than he was used to. He felt his heart was on the verge of exploding from the massive amount of anxiety he was feeling. He wanted to just ignore what was happening, but alas the knocks banged again. Three loud and heavy knocks, again. They seemed to echo through his head. He couldn't avoid it any further—he had to go answer the door.

Reluctantly, he slowly inched his way out of the bed. As he stood up, he felt a rush of vertigo and stumbled his way down the hallway. The hallway looked as though it just kept getting longer, until the door finally sped forward as if it was going to hit him. He stood there, in front of the door—filled his uncertainty. Slowly, he began to reach for

the doorknob. The closer his hand got, the faster his heart raced. Just as his hand was almost on the knob...

"LIENAD OPEN THE DOOR," he heard the girl from the tv screen yell.

"What," he thought, "How is this her? What is going on?"

In that moment, thoughts rushed wildly through his head. Was he dreaming? Did the stuff at the diner really happen? Did he do something wrong? The hurricane of questions made him dizzy and slightly nauseated. He turned his back on to the nearby wall and sluggishly slid down. Now sitting on the floor, he tried his best to calm his mind and drown out the sound of the banging. He placed his head in his hands and began to rock back and forth.

Suddenly, the banging came to a complete stop. He halfway lifted his head from his hands and glanced around. Nothing else was happening, everything seemed normal once again. He let out a giant sigh of relief and began to stand back up. He inched his way to the door and peered through the hole.

"Whew," he said aloud, "There's no one there. Maybe this was all just my imagination."

He turned around and was caught by surprise, the girl from before was right behind him. He was just as en-amored as he was shocked to see her. Her long black hair, blue eyes, pale skin, and red lips. Being so close to her made

his heart skip a beat. She was a little shorter than him, he was five foot ten inches so she had to be somewhere around five foot three inches. Something about her felt so familiar.

"Nope," she exclaimed, "This is all definitely real."

He stood there for a moment—the various emotions making his head spin—then collapsed to the floor. His head bashed against the tile, landing with a loud thud and smack. After what felt like only a few minutes of being out, he groggily woke up. As his eyes began to reset and adjust to being open once again, things didn't seem right. Slowly his fuzzy vision returned to normal, but the same could not be said for the area he was in. He began to realize that he was no longer in his own home. Lienad had no clue where he was. Bright lights, white walls, it was cold. He was lying on a bed, covered in plain white sheets. It was clear he was no longer in his home.

"Am I in some sort of hospital?" he questioned.

"Yes," an unfamiliar voice responded, "You are, Lienad."

"What?" he asked. "Who are you? Where am I? How did you respond when I didn't even say anything out loud?"

"All of your questions will be answered in due time, now rest."

As the "rest" echoed and faded, he drifted off back to sleep. While slipping away into a dreamland, he could hear the muffled sounds of people talking around him. The

majority of it was impossible to make out. But just before he was fully out, he heard a familiar voice. It was the girl. He was able to make out one single word: "PROTM".

6

The PROTM

Suddenly, Lienad was awake. His head felt light and fuzzy, almost like a hangover but without the splitting headache. He looked around, it was dark. He tried to make out any figures or objects in the room—but he was unable to. He began to recount everything he could remember.

"Okay, there was the girl in the TV who somehow got in my house," he recalled aloud, "I hit my head, woke up in a hospital of some sort, somehow fell back to sleep, and now I'm here in yet another strange location."

He was beyond confused at this point. He remembered the voice in the hospital and merely wished he knew what it meant. While he was trying hard to piece everything together, there was another voice.

"That's a pretty limited breakdown of what

happened," it was a female voice, "But I certainly wouldn't call myself strange."

It was her, the girl. His heart began to race, unsure of her intentions. His panic levels increased, unable to see her in this pitch-black room. He wondered if she was also blinded in the darkness. Perhaps if he sat still and didn't make a sound she would leave. Then he realized that probably wasn't the case. He figured he should say something, but what? He was at a loss for words but would try anyway.

"Who a-are you," he barely mustered, "Wh-what do you want w-w-with me?"

"You really don't remember me, do you?" her question had an obvious sadness behind it.

"No, should I?" he was overcome with another swell of anxiety.

"It's just... well," she paused.

They sat there, silent, for a few moments. The air was thick. You could feel the awkward tension from a mile away. With every passing second it got increasingly uncomfortable. Neither of them wanted to be the one to break the silence, but someone eventually had to. Suddenly, Lienad began feeling two smaller hands slowly caress his face. Fingertips gliding up near his temples, soft palms gently pressed on his cheeks. His heart began to flutter. As her face neared his, he could feel her shallow breath against his face. Then, ever so softly, her smooth lips began to lock

hold of his. They sat there, holding that kiss as if it was something long awaited and missed. For her, it was.

"Does that help you remember at all?" she asked, placing her forehead against his.

"I... well... um," he stammered, "It was nice, and I guess it felt somewhat familiar. But I still don't know who you are."

"Oh," she sounded defeated, "I guess it really is that bad. I was afraid of that."

"No, no," Lienad attempted to sound reassuring, "The kiss was great it has nothing to do with that."

"Not the kiss," she loudly exclaimed, "I'm talking about how seriously you were affected by the PROTM."

"PROTM, PROTM, PROTM," he repeated vigorously, "What is with this PROTM I keep hearing?"

She let out a loud sigh.

"Well, are you going to tell me?" His tone was very abrasive.

"No, I won't tell you," she paused for a moment, "But I will show you."

He sat there, confused, as she grabbed his hand. She squeezed his hand, and a bright red-purple light flashed. Suddenly, it was as if they were nowhere at all. Then, just as fast as it started, they were in a new location.

"WOAH," Lienad exclaimed, "What was that just now?"

"Teleportation," she sweetly giggled, "It's kind of cute seeing you like this."

He was astounded that there was such a thing as teleportation. Little did he know, it is one of the most common forms of transport over small distances through a multitude of dimensions; something he would soon find out. He looked around to try and find out where they were, with no luck. This place was like nothing he had ever seen.

Standing in a field of soft pink grass, three moons in the sky each on a different phase, in the distance he could see trees with green bark and light blue leaves; it was amazing. She began walking through the field towards this small shack that looked like an outhouse you would find on a farm.

"Wait," he rushed after her, "Where are you going?"

"There," she motioned towards the shack.

"There?" He asked. "Why are we going to an outhouse in the middle of a field?"

"Something you will soon remember is that the things we see are often far more than what they simply appear to be."

"What?" His tone was quite assertive. "What is any of that supposed to mean? I wanted an answer, not some cryptic response."

"Uh," she sighed. "Just shut up and follow me. You will see."

Seeing as how he felt he hasn't had a choice in this entire series of events, he continued to follow. How much weirder could things get? It's not like things could get worse; he thought. As they approached this rickety shack, he was not impressed. Nothing was different from his initial assessment. It still seemed like an outhouse. The girl grabbed the knob on the door and looked back at Lienad.

"Are you ready?"

"No, I don't really have to use the bathroom right now," he jokingly said, "I doubt we would even both fit in there."

"I see your bad jokes are still there," she said smirking, "Here we go."

She swung the door open, and a huge swirl of orange surrounded them. Suddenly, they were in yet another new location. This is something Lienad was getting very tired of, but it was something he needed to get used to. The room they were in now was basically a small steel box with a small camera on the wall in front of them.

"Can we please stop doing that," he was obviously frustrated, "Where the hell are we now?"

"Can you please stop talking and look into the camera?"

"No, I don't think I really—"

She cut his rant off, grabbing his neck and holding his face in front of the camera. A yellow light came on and began to scan his face.

"Retinal recognition sequence complete," a digital female voice said, "Welcome, Agent Brelain."

When she finished saying this a doorway began to open from the floor up. Peering in, he saw a room filled with what looked like the scene from a science fiction movie. Holograms, pointy eared people, people of diverse colors, he swore there was someone with tentacles, small flying creatures with a trail of sparkles. It was incredible, he had never seen anything like it. At this point he was even more certain he was dreaming.

"Alright Lienad," he said slapping his face, "It's time we go ahead and wake up."

"Stop that," she demanded, "You already are awake, either that or you are the most impressive narcoleptic in all of the dimensions."

"Dimensions? Agent Brelain? More questions but still zero answers. What is going on?"

"Soon you will have answers," she promisingly said, "Hurry, we haven't much time."

This did not reassure him whatsoever. In every movie he had ever watched, when there 'isn't much time' it meant something horrible was on the horizon. He was correct about that, and he will wish that he wasn't. She

grabbed his hand and began guiding him through the area filled with alien creatures, who all looked at him as if they knew who he was. Things had already begun to get weirder for him. As they are walking, they get stopped by a tall, quite round, being of some sort that was covered in curled spikes.

"Agent Brelain," it said in a gurgled and raspy voice, "Good to have to back."

"He's not really back yet sir," the girl chimed in, "We still have to reverse the PROTM."

"Ah, yes," he said, "Quite right. See to it that it gets done Agent Arura. We need him now more than ever."

"Yes sir, Commander Scenkid," she said with a salute.

"Alright, that's enough pleasantries," he said while returning the salute, "On your way."

"Wh-what was that?" Lienad asked as Commander Scenkid walked away.

"Who—the commander?" She asked. "He's a Sterimy. Don't worry, you'll soon remember."

"Yeah, you keep saying that."

"And I mean it, now come on," she grabbed his hand and pulled him again.

As they continued to walk, he thought about everything that has happened to him recently. Suddenly, being a cashier didn't seem so bad. Perhaps he should have been more accepting of a temporary clerical position somewhere, or even a warehouse. All those options were much more normal than this. At this point he would have even taken the janitor position. Same routine, every day. Nothing extraordinary happening, ever. That all seemed much better than what he was dealing with. It certainly would not have been better—but it would've been a lot less bizarre.

They soon approached a very strange looking door. It looked like it was made of rusted copper with an architecture that could only be described as a gothic version of cubism. The door stood at least ten feet tall and perhaps eight feet wide, though he didn't really have the ability to take proper measurements at that time. He stood there in awe, still unable to properly process everything that has been happening to him.

"In here we will begin the reversal of the PROTM," she let go of his hand.

"Can you please explain to me what in the hell this thing is?"

"Yes," she asserted, "The PROTM is the Preemptive Removal of the Mind. It is used to virtually erase all memories and knowledge from an agent and replace them with artificial memories so they can safely be returned to their home planet. It is used when an agent is at substantial risk of being taken, when an agent retires, or when humanely neutralizing an enemy."

"I see," he was still clearly unsure of what is being explained to him, "So which of those am I?"

"Well, your case is a bit special. It will be best if you just see for yourself rather than have me explain it to you."

"Fine," he said with an exasperated sigh, "I just want to finally know what is going on."

"Fair enough."

She placed her hand on the door and a neon light began to spread across it. When the door was covered in this light she removed her hand, and you could feel the ground shake. The door made loud rumble and scraping sounds, slowly revealing what was behind. It was a room with a variety of colored lights, a single computer like object directly in the center, and what looked like almost transparent bodies hovering above.

"So, what you're telling me is that my real mind is somewhere in here, floating around?" He asked—glancing around the room as he walked in.

"Yes, Agent Brelain," a new voice announced, "It is. It's been quite some time since we last saw you. I'm glad you're back."

"Huh," Lienad announced while quickly looking all around, "Who said that?"

"Ah, yes," the voice said, "Of course you don't remember yet. I am the combined consciousness. I am the combination of all minds that were, are, and will be. But

you may call me Remus."

"Um, okay then; Remus," Lienad said with a slight laugh.

"Yes, yes, very funny. Everyone gets a laugh," Remus said, "But laughing time is over. Let's get on with the reversal of the PROTM. Fair warning, this will hurt a bit."

"What all goes into this?"

"You see the computer in the middle of the room?"

"Yes."

"Just sit in front of it and leave the rest to me," Remus said with a slightly unsettling chuckle.

Unsure about what to expect, Lienad reluctantly walked towards the computer. Though he was nervous, he knew he had to go through with this if he wanted answers. He stepped in front of the computer and slowly lowered himself into the chair. As he sat there, staring into the screen, he began to feel very queasy.

"Agent Arura," Remus said, "At this point you may wish to leave. This experience is neither pretty nor fun. You may see things that you will regret having witnessed."

"No," she retorted, "I'm going to stay, I don't care what happens."

"As you wish," Remus replied with a slightly eerie tone, "Then we will begin. Agent Brelain, are you ready?"

"I guess so," Lienad quietly said with a slight nod.

"Look straight into the screen, and whatever happens do NOT look away until it is completed."

Lienad was nervous, sitting there and staring at the computer. His head began to fill with doubts about whether he really wanted to do this or not. But he knew he had to. There was no backing out now, it's not like he could just walk home. He gripped the arms of the chair tightly as the countdown began. Whether he was ready or not, here it came. Three—his heart pounded. Two—sweat poured down his face. One—he gripped the chair for dear life. And then, it began.

There was a giant flash of white light from the screen, bright enough to temporarily blind you. As the light died down you could see what looked like a movie on fast forward playing all around him, swirling into his eyes like a vortex. All his genuine memories being replanted into his brain. But as every memory entered, so did the emotions of the memory. He felt the pain of every fight he had been in, the depression of his greatest heart breaks, the plethora of times he has feared for his life, and so much more.

Arura became worried as she stood there watching. Lienad was in the chair laughing, crying, screaming, and everything else in between. Sweat poured from his body like a waterfall, puddling on the floor. His body would go through moments of severe twitching and flailing. She felt as though she was witnessing a true psychotic break. She had to fight every ounce of her being that wanted nothing more than to put a stop to this. There were even moments where she had briefly stepped forward before pulling back to watch in horror. Which was a smart move. No one truly knows what will happen if someone stops a PROTM reversal. Some say it causes the subject to become psychotic beyond belief, living with two minds in their head in constant conflict about what reality truly is. Luckily, it seemed she had control enough to not force us to learn if that claim is true.

Surprisingly enough, regardless of how intense this was for him, Lienad continued to push through. Though he thought of looking away many times, he never did. I do not know if it was intentional, but every time he had the thought of pulling away a memory with Arura was shown—the mere thought of her seemed to give him the push he needed to stick it through. As the process went further, things got both easier and harder at the same time. While his old mind began to take over, his current mind attempted to fight it. Slowly his current mind withered away. All the way until only his original mind was the one remaining.

All the lights went out in an instant and the room began to return to its normal look. When the lights returned, revealing Lienad once more, Arura felt a wave of relief. She smiled, waiting for him to turn around and face her. The air was still and deafly quiet, you could hear a pin drop from a mile away. The longer they sat, the more her

smile began to fade away. She began to worry if something had gone wrong, was he all right, was he still alive? All these questions were swarming her brain.

She stood there in a state of pure fear, unable to move. While she was in this frozen state, Lienad began to fall over. Time seemed to slow to a crawl as he fell in such a way that you could see the trail from his body. Arura began to run over to him. Right before she could reach him, he slammed to the ground. You could hear the hit echo through the chamber. She reached him, sobbing, grabbing to hold him. She rolled his face towards her.

"Don't worry sweetie pie," Lienad rasped, "Everything's gonna be all right. I'm back now."

She laughed awkwardly, tears still in her eyes. They stared into each other's eyes for a moment and leaned in for a kiss, one they had been waiting on for far too long. It was a kiss worthy of fireworks to explode in the background. Remus caught on to this and began to play a memory that was stored within him of just that. They stopped kissing and both looked up.

"REMUS," they both laughingly yelled in almost perfect unison.

"Sorry," Remus said, "It just seemed like the moment needed a little something extra."

They both looked back at each other, laughing. They pressed their foreheads against each other, closed their

eyes, and just felt in a state of pure peace.

"I can't believe you're back," Arura sniffled.

"Well believe it babe," Lienad smiled, "I'm back and I'm not going anywhere."

"Good," Arura pulled back and slapped him in the chest, rather hard in fact. "If you ever put me through that again, I'll kill you!"

"I'm so sorry love," Lienad looked down in shame. "I never should have done this without telling you. I can't imagine what I put you through."

"Well," Arura wiped her eyes, "Let's not focus on that, let's just move forward."

"Of course," Lienad winced, "After all that I'm feeling pretty worn down. Can we go get some sleep?"

"No arguments from me," she grasped his face and pulled it in for another kiss.

From here Lienad and Arura went back to their chambers to relax from all the recent strenuous events. They closed the door and laid on the bed. Lightly caressing each other's face, they tenderly kissed. I will be omitting any details of the events that transpired from this moment as they do not benefit the story line. If you know what I mean—and you find yourself disappointed—shame on you. This is not that kind of story. However, I will say that it was quite the wild night to say the least.

Now, if you are quite finished utilizing your imagination, we do have a story to get back to.

7

The Memory

There was gunfire all around, bullets zipping past Lienad as he ran. Fellow agents were falling to the ground right in front of him. Missiles launched, whistling as they flew and shaking the ground as they exploded. Nowhere felt safe—there was no shelter nearby. He ran as fast as he could, hoping that he wouldn't get hit.

Suddenly he noticed what looked like a cave in the distance. He immediately changed course for it and continued to run. As he got closer, he could hear the whistling sound of a missile approaching him from the rear. He looked back to see how close it was, and his heart sank; it was mere seconds away from impact. He tried to run even faster to get far enough away. Boom—the missile landed just behind him, close enough to hurl him forward like a rag doll. His body rolled and tumbled across the ground.

When he attempted to sit up, his vision was still blurry, and his ears rang painfully. After a few minutes, he could finally see and hear normally again. He looked around and realized he was in the cave. Hopefully, he would be safe there. He frantically patted himself down—did he lose it? There was a bulge in his pocket, he reached in and began pulling a glowing object. Just before it was all the way out, he heard Arura screaming his name and the ground started to violently shake. Suddenly, he woke up.

"Lienad," Arura yelled, shaking him. "Are you alright?"

"Mmm," he said with a groan, "What is it love?"

"You were violently shifting in your sleep—sweating and grunting too," she said, her voice filled with genuine concern. "I had the hardest time getting you to wake up. Are you feeling alright? That seemed like a nasty nightmare,"

"Yeah... yeah... no, I'm fine," he said sluggishly. "It just... it must be a side effect of the PROTM reversal. Maybe I should go speak to Remus about this."

"It's only 0230. Are you sure you don't want to try and get a little more sleep, sweetie?" she asked, lightly rubbing his back.

"As much as I want nothing more than to lie here

with you until the end of time…" He turned toward her and brushed his fingers across her cheek. "It's probably best I get this figured out so I can actually sleep peacefully."

"Yeah…" she pouted. "You're probably right."

He leaned in, held her face, and kissed her.

"I love you," he said while staring into her eyes.

"How much?" she asked.

"There is no love stronger in any dimension than mine for you," he said. "Not even a god is greater than my love."

"I love you too," she said with a smile and a giggle.

"Now as much as it pains me, I must go for now," he slowly began to move away.

"I understand," she said, hesitating as she let go of his hand.

He got up and started walking to the door. Just as he was about to leave, he turned back to Arura and watched as she nuzzled back into the bed. He wanted to crawl back into bed with her—but he knew he couldn't.

"I'm sorry," he thought, "I wish I could tell you what's going on, but it's best you don't know. Please, forgive me."

He closed the door and began walking to see Remus. It was a quiet walk through the halls, everyone was in their rooms most likely asleep since it was the middle of the night. Lienad tried not to think too much during the walk—his mind already brimming with anxiety over what was to come. Finally, he stood in front of the PROTM room. He raised his hand to the door, hovering without touching it, and just stood there—unsure whether to keep going down this path.

"Come in, Lienad," Remus said. "I've been expecting you."

"I... I don't know—" Lienad began aloud, before being cut off by Remus.

"No, don't speak. Just think, and I will hear you."

"Oh, um, well, I just don't know if I want to keep on. I feel this will lead to more pain than it's worth. How does this work? How can you hear me?"

"You and I are linked now—ever since you went through the PROTM. If you think with intent toward me, I will hear you. Lienad, you do not know what I know—and you only realize half of what you think you know. If you do not follow this path, you will still experience this pain and more. Move forward and you will have a chance to not only stop the heartache you've seen but to also prevent that which you do not know."

"Do you really think I can stop it from happening?"

"I cannot promise you that you will stop it, but I can promise that this is your only chance to at least try.

Otherwise, there is no hope. Come inside. There is much to discuss. The longer you remain out there the greater the chance you'll draw attention to us."

Lienad stood there another moment, wrestling with his last bit of uncertainty. He closed his eyes, took a deep breath, and placed his hand upon the door so it would open. As he walked in, he noticed the room was different. There was no computer in the center; only a large, circular chair. No transparent floating bodies. No multicolored lights. Just dim red lighting surrounding the room. There was a faint shroud of mist swirling in the ceiling area. As he continued to walk towards the chair, he heard a metal lock grinding against the room and clicking into place. The silence of the room was deafening—he couldn't even hear his own footsteps. His heart pounded in rhythm with each step. He was getting closer, yet it somehow felt farther—a constant push and pull of perception—until he finally reached the chair. He grabbed the top of the chair and slid into it. It felt like sinking in. The chair seemed made of the most luxurious pillows money could buy. The level of comfort was unparalleled.

As Lienad sat there, in the big comfy chair, he knew that this decision would change the course of his life. What he did not know was just how much it would change. All he could do was hope for the best. Luckily, at this moment, he was able to relax completely in this cloud-like chair. So much so, he began drifting to sleep.

"I take it we are comfortable then," Remus said in a slightly condescending tone.

"Huh, oh, uh, yeah pretty comfy," Lienad drowsily said.

"Well, that's nice—but please stay awake. We have much to discuss."

"Do we still need to think everything, or can we speak aloud?"

"We are safe to speak in here. I have protected this room—nothing will be heard by anyone but us."

"Great," Lienad exclaimed, relieved to be allowed to speak using his voice.

"Though it doesn't make much of a difference."

"What do you mean, why not?"

"Because most of this discussion will be what you need to see, not what you need to say."

"If we aren't talking, then how is this a discussion?" Lienad was completely puzzled.

"There will be words, rest assured," Remus said. "Please, do not question these methods. Just relax and empty your mind so it will be a vessel that is filled. Are you ready?"

"I mean, I guess," Lienad uncertain about what to expect from Remus' wording, "I am still fuzzy on the details

but all right."

"Shut up about the details," Remus snapped. "You know what you need. That should be enough. Now empty your mind so that I may fill it. One last time, are you ready to begin?"

"Fine, let's do this."

"Good, in front of you there is a small orange cube on the table, eat it."

"Table? There isn't even a table in front of me," Lienad said while looking around.

"Oh? Are you so sure about that?" Remus laughed.

"Yes, I'm su—" But before he could finish, a table appeared before him—faster than he could blink. "Ah, very funny Remus. You and your games."

"I couldn't resist—you know me," Remus laughed, though he was the only one amused by his odd sense of humor.

"Anyways," Lienad uncomfortably said while reaching for the cube, "Might as well go ahead and get this over with."

Lienad slowly brought the cube to his mouth and set it on his tongue. There was no simple "getting this over with," as he had hoped for. He could feel the cube slowly melt in his mouth along with all his surroundings beginning to melt as well. Soon he was surrounded by a pool of colors flowing like water. He reached in and felt the flow—the sensation of the colors themselves. As he lifted his hand, the colors dripped down like a mess of paints. He leaned forward, deciding to dive into this colorful unknown.

His body melted into the roaring stream, dripping back together on the other side. Drop by drop, his aqueous form became solid once more. Suddenly, he was falling lifelessly through a void. He floated in darkness—yet remained visible. He blinked and was now staring at himself, outside of his normal body. Lienad watched his physical form float. He looked down at his hands and saw that he had a new form, it was glowing and blue. Unsure of what to do next, he reached forward and touched his physical body's forehead with his finger.

As the two bodies made contact, his radiant form was rapidly absorbed into the head of his physical body. His eyes snapped open; they were brightly glowing. He raised his face upwards and opened his mouth; a blast of blazing stars erupted from within, filling the empty void with all the wonders of space.

Lienad was amazed at what he was witnessing, but what did it mean? He could hardly appreciate the beauty with that question looming over him. What is any of this supposed to do to help him with what is to come? As he began to question everything, the space around him became unstable. He could feel violent vibrations as all the sky

began to get shrouded in a dark red mist. The stars began to melt away. Suddenly, he heard Remus' voice calling out to him.

"Lienad, Lienad," Remus yelled, "Clear your mind, boy—or you'll be lost forever!"

"Wh-what is this Remus," Lienad stammered, "What is going on?"

"You're within the very fabric of the universe. Here, you can see beyond everything your senses normally block. This is where you will find the answers that you seek. Start by remembering the artifact that led you to all this."

"Okay, I'll try," Lienad said as he closed his eyes tight and strained to think back on the object.

As he focused, everything around him swirled into a single point—like water down a drain. He opened his eyes and began spinning rapidly; being sucked down like an object flushed down a toilet. Faster and faster, he spun. Suddenly, the spinning stopped and there was a blinding white light.

As the white light faded, a war-torn scenery emerged. He looked around and saw that he was in the cave from his dream. He was still wearing his regular clothes, instead of the black suit he was wearing in his dream. Everything was silent—until it was as if someone unmuted a sound system at full blast. Gunfire and bombs echoed through the cave. Lienad's anxiety surged.

Lienad stood there in the cave, frozen in fear, the sound of a missile crashing close by snapped him back to his senses. He saw a figure get thrown into the cave. As he walked closer, he saw... it was himself. Everything was unfolding just like his dream. He stood there, gazing upon his currently dormant body. A strange creature began approaching Lienad's body from the vision.

The odd being was soft green, its skin radiating with an otherworldly glow. It was a smaller creature, slightly bigger than a goblin but still shorter than a human. Lienad had never seen anything like this. It had large floppy ears, blue eyes, three fingers on each hand, and a small tail. By all appearances, the creature seemed entirely harmless. At the time of writing, I'm sorry to say—this is the first known sighting of such a creature. For now, we will refer to it as "the thingy".

The thingy approached Lienad's body and leaned forward. As it reached its arm out, a brightly glowing object began to come out of its body. The thingy then placed the object inside of Lienad's Pocket. At this point, Lienad—the one watching—began growing frustrated.

"Hey!" he yelled, hoping to be heard. "What are you doing?"

The thingy perked up, as if it could see Lienad, and walked straight toward him. It walked over and stood right in front of him, making direct eye contact.

"I wondered when you'd be visiting," the thingy

said—its voice reverberating and soft.

"What do you mean?" Lienad asked. "You can actually see me? You were expecting me?"

"Of course I was," the thingy said ominously. "How else would you find out what's going on? I assume Remus is here with you. Hello Remus."

"How did you know I was part of this?" Remus asked, his tone genuinely concerned.

"I know more than you realize, Remus—and it's time for you to step away," the thingy said firmly. "What happens next is not for you to know. Please exit, at least for now."

"I'm not going anywhere," Remus boomed. "It is essential that I am here with Lienad. I must ensure he safely returns from this."

"Fine," the thingy said with a smirk. "You don't want to listen? Then I'll just have to do it myself."

Remus began to speak again, but the thingy clapped its hands—and suddenly, there was silence. Lienad and the thingy stood there for a moment, just staring at one another. The silence wasn't just uncomfortable—it was gut-wrenching.

"What did you just do?" Lienad asked, his tone anxious. "Where is Remus? Am I stuck here now?"

"Oh, don't worry at all, Lienad," the thingy said,

attempting to sound reassuring. "I've merely blocked Remus from the session. He's perfectly safe. I'll allow him back when we're done and it's time to send you home. Think of it like placing a call on hold."

This was not reassuring to Lienad in the slightest.

8

The Orb

"So, what's this all about, then?" Lienad asked.

"Yes, I'm sure you want to know, don't you?" the thingy giggled, "Do you remember what you saw when you looked into the orb?"

"Vaguely," Lienad said, straining to remember, "When I looked inside, I saw so many horrible things. I saw Arura weeping while holding one of my jackets, I saw her die while being filled with a grey sludge, I saw Krind standing tall on a mountain of bodies. There was a fight between us, but I never saw the outcome, and so many other terrible things I wish I had never seen."

"Yes, yes, I expected you would see as much, but what else did you see?"

"I-I don't know," Lienad stammered, "Was there

something specific I was supposed to see?"

"This orb is one of the most important artifacts in any of the dimensions," the thingy stated, "When you look into this you can see what truths the future may hold, you can see facts that were hidden in the past, and secrets of the present. So far you have told me about the potential futures you saw. Now tell me, what else did you see; think hard."

"Um," Lienad groaned as he tried hard to think back, "Yes, my parents, or at least their backs, as they are abandoning me. Leaving me on the steps of the D.I.C.K.S. headquarters, where I was found by Commander Scenkid. I don't know how they got there or how they left. I honestly don't even know how I know it was them; it's just a feeling that I'm certain of for some reason. Everything about them is so fuzzy though."

"Was that all that you saw in the orb?" The thingy questioned, poking at him. "Think Lienad, think."

"Okay," Lienad said as the thingy's words echoed in his head, "I saw... I saw... Krind, sitting down, talking to someone. I don't know exactly who—just some red thing with, I want to say, bones sticking out of him. I couldn't make out what he is saying. Maybe I can re—"

Lienad abruptly stopped talking because he felt everything about his environment shift. He opened his eyes, and he was standing in the vision he was trying to remember. He was next to Krind who looked like your average Gretualin, human-like build, no hair, boils all over, black skin with splotches of brown and red mixed in, and jagged teeth. His, however, were far more pronounced. As an example, most of his boils looked as though they were ready to burst at any moment. Also, his mouth looked as though it was filled with razor blades instead of teeth.

Krind, the foul beast, was talking with someone—clearly his right-hand man. He was a very dense and intellectually inept being. Like all other Bonels, he is nothing more than a brute with red skin and various bone-like protrusions throughout his body. Slowly, the sound began to fade in, Lienad could hear Krind's grumbled and throaty voice.

"Our trans-dimensional conquest is going well so far," Krind said. "What updates do you have for me, Nereg?"

"Well sir," Nereg sneered, "Our advancements have so far been successful in the Gaseous Dimension. The Smeglin are under total submission, and we were met with almost no resistance. As far as the Serpisapion's are concerned, we are whittling away at their defense at a consistent rate and should expect to have them defeated within the coming weeks."

I realize it may be best for me to stop here and explain what they are talking about. There are currently five known dimensions. They are the Primary Dimension, the Gaseous Dimension, the Colored Dust Dimension, the Ancient Dimension, and the Zenith. Each of these dimensions has their own species, planets, star systems, and more. The Gaseous dimension they are mentioning is home to four species we are aware of and only three known planets that are inhabited. Droning on too much about them will take away from the story, so I will just fill you in later as it becomes more important. For now, back to the conversation between Krind and Nereg.

"Excellent, excellent," Krind said with a most disturbing grin, "And what of the D.I.C.K.S. and their annoying attempts at interference?"

"They have not been much of an issue," Nereg laughingly said, "They have barely deployed any forces out here to try and stop us. They are basically letting us take over. I haven't heard reports of a single agent in days."

"I'm not surprised, in all my time I have never seen much care for our dimension," Krind begrudgingly said, "We must be prepared for when we move to our next dimension for conquest. I suspect they will not be as lackadaisical as they have been here."

"Not to worry my lord," Nereg chuckled, "We are near completion on the Dugsel Bombs. Once we are, I can't imagine there will be anything able to stand in our way."

"Good, keep me posted on them," Krind said as his tone began to become a more serious and solemn one, "And Nereg, I want to remind you of something. Should you, or any other these other peons, encounter Agent Brelain; you will capture him and bring him to me alive."

"Yes sir, but why is this one agent so important?"

"It is not your place to question me," Krind boomed, "But I am in the mood for a family reunion and if he will not join us then I want to be the one to kill him."

"As you wish," Nereg said, bowing his head.

Nereg's words echoed, and Lienad returned to standing in front of the thingy. After seeing this, again, he was in shock. He had no idea what to say, nor could he even bring himself to believe what was being said.

"What was that all about," Lienad said, filled with denial, "There's no way he and I are even remotely related."

"It IS true," the thingy asserted, "He is your brother."

"There is no way I can be a Gretualin," Lienad sounded offended at the notion, "I sure as hell don't look like one—and I doubt Arura would share a bed with me if I smelled like rotten eggs."

"No, you luckily don't share their rancid features," the thingy agreed, "But yet, still, you are one."

"How, this doesn't make sense," Lienad argued, "Even if it is true, why bother telling me?"

"Do you ever wonder why you were abandoned by your parents?"

"Yes, I had for most of my life and then gave up wondering because it no longer mattered."

"Oh, it does matter. It matters very much," the thingy insisted, "You weren't abandoned, you were saved."

"How was leaving me at a military establishment on a different planet saving me?"

"You are not the first of your kind, Lienad," the thingy softly said, "There were those before you and all of them were destroyed at an early age. Your parents saved you by getting you far away from Sparebryr and with people who could protect you."

"What do you mean my kind?" Lienad began to get a bit aggressive. "First I'm human, then I'm a Gretualin, and now I'm something else?"

"No, you are a pure Gretualin, just not like what we know them to be today," the thingy explained, "They weren't always this foul race of hatred and filth. You were born pure, the purest there has been in ages. It's quite rare."

"Okay, so let's roll with this idea and assume that I believe a single word of it," Lienad said—though he didn't believe what he was being told. "This still doesn't tell me why I am being shown this."

"The fact that you're the brother of the current worst inter-dimensional war lord wasn't reason enough? What about the fact that you are a pure Gretualin?" The thingy sarcastically questioned. "Look, my instructions were simple: find you at this exact point in time, show you that truth, tell you to look at the rest of what the orb has to offer, and

disappear.”

“The rest of what the orb has to offer?” Lienad asked with a curious tone while looking down at the orb. “What does that even mean?”

When he looked up from the orb the thingy was gone. It sure was serious about the whole disappear part of its instructions. But now Lienad was even more confused than before. He had this new information, cryptic instructions, and no idea of what to do. So, he did what anyone in his position would do, he pondered. As he sat there, pondering, he started to hear a faint and echoing whisper.

“Remember,” the voice said, “Remember what you saw Lienad.”

Lienad continued to sit there, puzzled. This was a lot to take in, especially so soon after the PROTM reversal. He thought about trying to call out to Remus, but wasn’t sure it would even work.

“Oh my word, this is ridiculous!” The thingy exclaimed as it magically popped back in. “Remember what you saw at the end of this memory? You know, the whole big end of days style disaster where everything in the universe crumbled into dust?”

“What are you doing here,” Lienad said, puzzled, “I thought you were supposed to leave?”

“Of course that’s the part you’re focused on,” the thingy said in a rather aggressive tone, “I didn’t think you

would figure out the next steps on your own and look at how right I was! Look at the orb and watch it again for the love of Ganel you are so dense."

"Okay, well—," Lienad began before getting cut off.

"Nope, nope," the thingy shouted, "Stop talking and just look. Bye-bye."

Just like that, the thingy disappeared into thin air; yet again. There is no point in wondering where it had gone. I don't think any of us will ever know, nor do I think it really matters. At any rate, the potential of your mind shattering aside, Lienad began to stare at the orb once more.

He stared and squinted, squinted and stared. Trying his best to really concentrate on the orb in hopes of seeing whatever it was he needed to see. He was focusing so intently his vision was beginning to get blurred. He looked away to rub his eyes and was considering giving up.

"Is this even worth it?" Lienad thought to himself.

Then, just as he was about to call it quits, Remus' words from before echoed in his mind.

"CLEAR YOUR MIND BOY."

Lienad closed his eyes, focused on his breathing, and allowed all his thoughts to slip away. Finally, when his mind was clear and at ease, he opened his eyes to gaze upon the orb. All light began to slowly fade from his view, he was being engulfed in complete darkness. When all was black, and there was nothing but complete silence, he saw a faint

white light in the distance.

The light quickly came closer to him and stopped, hovering near by at eye level. He reached his hand up to try and touch it, but his hand merely passed straight through it. Unsure of what to do next, Lienad just stared at it. Suddenly, all his surroundings changed. He was now floating amongst the stars, able to see distant galaxies and planets. Throughout all his travels to the various dimensions, he had never been to a place like this. It was as if he was looking down at every dimension at the same time.

As he gazed in awe at everything he was seeing, he slowly began to float downward. This was alarming to him because he didn't see anything around that he would eventually land on. Frantically he attempted to keep himself afloat, flailing all his limbs as if he were trying to prevent drowning in a pool. Realizing this was a futile effort, he stopped resisting, tightly closed his eyes, and hoped for the best. Shortly after this, he felt his feet softly land on solid ground. He opened his eyes, filled with anxiety about where he was now.

Lienad looked around and saw that he was in fact standing on land, which he knew for sure that he did not see before. It was as if he was now standing on a cliff, overlooking the entirety of everything. He turned around and saw he was at one end of a path that led to a strange structure atop a hill. He felt compelled to follow it up to the end.

As he walked down the path, he was so intrigued by

the terrain around him. Floating trees and rocks, no wild-life of any sort that he could see or hear, colorful wispy mists gliding around, a river that ran to a waterfall into the abyss, no sky, no moon, no sun, just endless space. It was like no place he had ever been before. As he got closer to the structure, rhythmic chanting drifted toward him.

As Lienad got closer to the door of the building, the chanting grew louder and clearer. It was in a language he didn't understand, so it didn't really matter how clear it was, he wouldn't know what was being said. He reached his hand to open the door, but it swung open before he could even touch it. Filled with painful uncertainty, he walked in.

"Hello Lienad," a strange voice said. It seemed to come from a shrouded figure in the distance of the spacious room he was now in. "I have been waiting patiently for you to finally join me here. Please, come closer."

Lienad observed his surroundings, which were for-eign yet so familiar at the same time. There were bamboo structures around the room, like something you would ex-pect to see in Chinese architecture on the Earth. In the fur-thest part of the room, near the figure that spoke to him, there was some sort of abstract statue that was hard to even describe what he was looking at. It was a culmination of various shapes and curves, almost like it made something and nothing at the same time.

There were small waterfall ponds on the left and right sides of the room. In the center of the floor was a giant colorful mural that resembled some sort of mandala. Directly above it, on the ceiling, was the same pattern with colors that contrasted the one on the floor. The walls were vibrantly colorful, but they did not look painted. Then, of course, there was the shrouded figure in the back near the statue.

"Um, I'm not so sure about that," Lienad nervously said, "Where even am I?"

"You are in the Zenith," the figure answered calmly. "If all the dimensions were a mountain, this would be the peak. Here there are no systems, no planets, and no inhabitants other than myself. We are, completely and utterly alone."

"Well, that is extremely far from comforting," Lienad said with an extremely nervous tone, "I really don't think I want to get too close."

"That is fair," the figure stated, "You are uncertain, anxious, and scared. This is a normal reaction, not many could handle this place. That is why I am alone."

"Who are you," Lienad questioned, unsure if he even wanted the answer.

"I am the keeper of all knowledge and answers to all questions," the figure stated, "I am, Neoshyt."

"So, you are a god?" Lienad asked—a pit grew in his stomach.

"No, I am not. I have existed alongside the various

gods throughout all time, but I am not one myself," Neoshyt explained, "I have no allegiance to any of them, nor do they with me. I am outside of them all, hence why I am here."

"Okay," Lienad was even more nervous.

"Calm your nerves, Lienad; no harm shall come to you here. I am a peaceful being. I watch your wars, your times of peace, and everything in between; but never do I get involved. I simply observe and learn," Neoshyt said attempting to be comforting, "You wish to know the reason you were given the orb, correct?"

"Yes, I do."

The figure began to step closer, and the shroud coalesced into tangible shape, but it was still too far away to fully make out. Lienad's heart began to race and pound herder with each step closer the figure got. Neoshyt came close enough for Lienad to see what he looked like. He looked like a thin, furless baboon. His smooth skin and odd fingers were like that of a frog. His skin had a variety of blue hues with a splash of purple here and there, almost like spots; but slightly different. He had some long crimson red hair a top his head and was wearing jewelry of a shaman. It was almost as if he were a character from some sort of video game or science fiction story.

"Lienad do not be alarmed by my form," Neoshyt said, hoping to be reassuring, "I do not always look like this. I can shape shift, and usually do, based on who I am speaking to. I decided I would show you what my true form was before I transcended the physical plane. The shroud you saw earlier is my current form. I figure that an honest, up-front approach will be the best option here."

"I'm so confused," Lienad was really freaking out at this point, "This is extremely bizarre, and I want to leave."

"Leave?" Neoshyt questioned. "I cannot send you back until we have had our necessary conversation."

"I think we have talked enough," Lienad asserted, "Send me home please. I just got my memories back and would rather spend time with Arura than be in this freak show."

"I'm sorry Lienad. As I have stated, I cannot. Not yet anyway. I must talk to you about the orb."

"This stupid orb, I don't think I even want to know anymore. I want to go."

"Lienad, this isn't about what you want to know, but rather what you need to know."

"Okay," Lienad said in an irritated tone, "Then just tell me already, this has drug on for long enough."

"I am the reason you were given the orb," Neoshyt said, "Getting you here, with me, was the purpose behind it all."

"You...were the reason?" Lienad's heart sank deep into the pit of his stomach. His mind flooded with thoughts of horrible things that could potentially happen to him

here. Mostly, though, he was worried he would never see Arura again.

"Yes, I was," Neoshyt said, blowing a light purple fog toward Lienad that began to engulf the room, "Now relax, so we can talk."

Lienad instinctively flailed his arms, trying to push it away—but it was too fast and too strong for him. He was stuck inside the cloud.

9

The Truth

As the fog began to clear, Lienad looked around and saw that the room had changed. He didn't feel like he had been teleported anywhere, but the room was different from before. The walls were no longer colorful, instead they were now a cool tone grey. The floors and ceiling no longer had a design, instead the floor was black, and the ceiling was white. The statue in the back, the waterfall ponds, and the bamboo décor were all gone. The room only had a small silver table with two big green chairs around it. On the table it looked like there was a small bowl of some type of black candy on it.

"What happened?" Lienad asked, slightly frantic.

"Oh, this," Neoshyt said while waving his arm around the room, "I transformed the room into a more

comfortable setting to speak in. Is this not satisfactory? Should I alter it again?"

"No, this is fine," Lienad stated, "I just want all of this to be over with already."

"Yes, I understand you are uncomfortable. Here." Neoshyt motioned towards the chairs, "Have a seat and let's begin."

Lienad cautiously slid into one of the green chairs. He was incredibly nervous but had to admit that the chairs were quite comfortable. He made it a point to stay entirely alert and not give in to the relaxation he had started to feel. After all, he was in a bizarre place with a strange creature. He had no idea what was going to happen next. Not that knowing would have mattered, he was trapped there with no escape until he was released.

"So," Neoshyt started, "You say you want to know what's going on."

"Um, well no," Lienad said, slightly shaky, "You said there were things you needed to tell me—I keep saying I want to leave."

"Ah, yes, that's right," Neoshyt said with an odd tone of certainty, "This is true, there are things I need to tell you. The facts of which you have no clue that are both sad and absolutely true."

"Okay, stop right there," Lienad said abruptly, "If you are going to start talking in rhymes and riddles, I am going to jump off the edge and just hope for the best. I don't want to hear that at all."

"Sorry," Neoshyt said, sounding genuinely apologetic, "It's a force of habit. All rhyming aside, this is important. I need to tell you the truth about the beginning, and the current potential for the end. What do you know about the beginning of this universe?"

"I mean, I guess the same thing everyone knows. A long time ago there was a big boom, and everything was created."

"Well, kind of," Neoshyt said, with a tone like he just didn't understand why that's all Lienad would have known, "There is certainly more to it than that. You are aware, I'm sure, that there are many different dimensions. Just so I can know where to start, do you know what those dimensions are? I don't want to seem condescending, but I need to know what I'm working with."

"Well," Lienad said doubtfully, "I thought I knew about all of them. But that is clearly not the case since I didn't know this place existed. I know there is the Primary Dimension, the Gaseous Dimension, the Colored Dust dimension, and now this one."

"Okay, good," Neoshyt had a bit of relief in his voice, "You almost know enough to have the basics covered."

"Thanks," Lienad was slightly offended.

"You're welcome," Neoshyt continued—oblivious to

the offense. "There is another dimension, one that I guess is not well known at this point. It is known as Tinacenimodinnes, but for the sake of this we can call it the Ancient Dimension. This is the current home of Ganel and Velid. I assume you have heard of them?"

"Well, yeah kind of. They are the powers believed in by some of the religions out there," Lienad was very unsure of what he was hearing, "You mean to tell me they are real?"

"Well, I'd sure hope so or nothing we currently know would exist," Neoshyt said with a slight chuckle in his tone.

"So, what does that have to do with all of this," Lienad questioned.

"Everything," Neoshyt said assertively, "It has everything to do with literally everything."

"Then by all means," Lienad stated, "Please continue."

"I'm so glad I have your permission," Neoshyt had a sarcastic and dry tone, "Ganel and Velid are the self-proclaimed 'rulers' of this universe."

"I'm sorry," Lienad interrupted, "This universe?"

"Yes, there are many dimensions in this universe and there are many different universes out there," Neoshyt explained, "Please stop interrupting. It might be easier to do this in more of a cinematic context. Take one candy from the bowl and eat it."

"Why," Lienad was extremely unsettled by the request.

"Eating one of the candies will link your mind to mine so I can show you what it is you need to know telepathically," Neoshyt stated as if this were an everyday occurrence, "It will prevent you from interrupting me with questions and it will give you a better understanding of what it is I'm trying to tell you."

"All right, I guess," Lienad had a complacent tone as he reached for one of the candies.

At this point, Lienad had given up trying to resist anything. He had realized there was nothing he could do to stop any of this from happening. Which was true. As I once heard an Earth traveler say, Lienad was stuck like a fly on a sticky trap. He ate the candy and began to taste the familiar flavor of buttered toast with strawberry preserves. Which is interesting because the candy, from what I understand, tastes however it is the person eating it wants it to taste. Why this was the flavor he had desired in that moment is a question I will always have.

As the flavor filled his mouth and the candy slid down his throat, his perception of reality began to change. At this point Lienad had grown so tired of this being a frequent occurrence throughout this venture thus far. Everything he saw morphed into a view that was best described as floating above all of time and space. A truly surreal experience that is difficult to accurately describe, but I will try.

Imagine, for just a moment, that you are floating inside of an object with a seemingly infinite number of planes. On each of these planes is a similar, yet different, galaxy looking texture that is in constant motion. It is an experience you won't forget. Yet at the same time, you'll never truly remember it either. If you ever have the opportunity to see this, I beg you to decline. It can drive someone completely insane. Luckily, the only known way to get here is through a visit with Neoshyt which is honestly not a likely position to find yourself in. Unless of course you are like Lienad.

"What is this?" Lienad asked—filled with a most confusing amazement.

"This is my room of everything," Neoshyt said, "Now, from here I will take over and you will be unable to speak until I am done."

Lienad went to ask what he meant by being unable to speak but found himself being, oddly enough, unable to speak. I am not sure what Neoshyt did exactly, but it was as if Lienad was present yet absent at the same time. He knew there was nothing he could do, and now nothing he could say. So, he just paid attention.

"In this room, we can look out at every dimension within every universe at the same time," Neoshyt began explaining, "Not only that, but we can view all of that has come to pass, what currently is, and the endless

possibilities of things that still yet may come."

He motioned his hands towards the various planes of view as he explained this. As you can imagine, this was all so overwhelming for Lienad. Which is a normal reaction, luckily it was not enough to mentally destroy him, yet.

"I tell you this because it is important. Every one of these dimensions and universes are connected to one another in some fashion," Neoshyt continued, "Let's go back to beginning, or at least as far back as I can go. Everything we know today started over a quadrillion years ago in what I call Universe 0.1."

As he said this, the room zoomed around the different planes of view until one became the singular view. This new view they had was intense, as it was nothing but darkness. No stars, no planets, not even any gaseous whisps.

"You see, everything came from absolutely nothing at all. This is where we will see the beginning of everything," Neoshyt had an increasingly serious tone, "From this endless nothingness, there was a flash and a boom."

It was as if he was controlling everything that happened in the past in real time, because right when he said it there was indeed a great flash and boom. As the flash faded, various stars and galaxies became visible. Above them all towered this imposing figure made of rainbow hues of light, stars, and gas. Somehow it was able to come together and make a seemingly physical person-like object. It was beautiful and terrifying at the same time.

"This large figure is the original celestial body," Neoshyt's story continued, "It stood alone, towering over the entire universe. This universe existed within a single dimension, what you see is all there was. Only stars, planets that had yet to flourish, rocks, gas, and dust. It was a lonely existence. The celestial decided to create a companion, these two became the celestial mother and father."

As he spoke Lienad could see the figure gather the stars. The stars came together producing another great flash. As the flash subsided, the celestial mother came into view. She looked almost identical to the celestial father, but somehow the features appeared slightly softer than his. Now, it is important to note that the celestial do not have any actual gender, but using these terms does make it easier to explain such a crazy concept.

"This action led to the creation of love, and it was pure," Neoshyt continued, "The love between the celestial mother and father was powerful. So powerful, in fact, that it managed to lead to the mother giving birth. Given that they were celestials, this was not a normal birth. There was no actual pregnancy as you would see in other species and there was no labor. The celestial mother just had an explosion of sorts. She, herself, did not explode. It was more of an explosion out of her. This was the creation of the seemingly infinite number of other universes, each with their own version of a celestial mother and father."

From here, Lienad watched the explosion, which

was magical. From the celestial mother's body came rays of colored light, shooting stars, colored gases, and more. Shooting out all around, consuming the entirety of what he could see. Slowly the visual from the explosion faded, and his view began to zoom out. As he zoomed out, he could see the other planes of view beginning to resurface. This continued until the room of everything was back to its original view.

"Each of the universes that were created from this was slightly different from the last. Especially when it came to the universe we live in, which is known as Universe 4.8.9," as Neoshyt explained this the view began to zoom into Lienad's universe, "Our celestials were nothing like the original mother and father, instead they were entirely opposing forces. One, Ganel, was the embodiment of purity. Good in every way there is. Loving, kind, caring, and more. The other, Velid, was pure evil. Filled with hate and a heart for destruction. They live together in a never-ending battle that started in the Ancient Dimension."

As the story progressed, Lienad could see it all happening. Ganel's celestial body was still colorful with blue, purple, and pink hues. It was pleasant to look at and brought a feeling of peace. Velid, on the other hand, was not. Their celestial body was made of nothing but varying shades of red. It was slightly distorted as well. Gazing upon it led to an uneasy feeling of discomfort.

"Most universes are built within a single dimension,

filled with various galaxies and star systems. Our universe is similar, but everything is divided into dimensions. This was a decision made by Ganel. Ganel is considered the 'mother' of our universe. She created every star, every planet, and every species in each of our dimensions. Each dimension was created in diverse ways to allow for distinct species. Basically, each creation was an experiment she performed to see how things would progress for each one."

"As you know this includes the Colored Dust dimension. This is the home of the Pixies, Snuln, and Fairies. Its space is filled with colorful clouds of dust and the planets are too small for anyone except for the species they were designed for. There is the Primary Dimension, where you will find the Earth and many other planets. Not every planet in every galaxy is inhabited by a species, but this dimension also has the greatest number of known species living in it natively. The Zenith, which is where you met me. Finally, there is the Gaseous Dimension. It is filled with stinky gasses, most of which are produced by the planet Sparebryr."

As Neoshyt went over the different dimensions Lienad's views were fixated on whichever he was being told about at that time.

"Ganel had tried her best to keep these dimensions completely separated from the Ancient Dimension where she and Velid exist. She had believed the only link was within her own telepathic field so she could communicate with inhabitants from time to time, which ended up leading to the religion based around her. This separation is important to know of for multiple reasons, the primary being the truth about the Gretualin. The Gaseous dimension was the very first one created by Ganel, the Gretualin was her first species. Her initial creation was pure, like her. They were created, if you will, in her image minus the celestial body."

Lienad witnessed as Ganel manipulated the stars into creating this dimension. It was a mystical thing to behold that is beyond the ability to describe. You simply would have to see it for yourself.

"Sparebryr used to be such a peaceful planet, and the Gretualin looked just like you. The gases it emitted had a pleasant smell, acting almost like an air freshener of sort for the dimension. You would have loved to have visited during this time."

The view zoomed to Sparebryr during this time. Human looking creatures were walking around, smiling. It was as if nothing bad had ever been known to anyone there. There was beautiful vegetation everywhere, dirt roads, simple houses. It looked like the perfect place to live, which it was at that time.

"After a while of the dimension existing, Velid discovered its existence and found a way to penetrate the dimension. Not just telepathically either, he physically went into the dimension. Which, as I am sure you can tell, was not a good thing," you could hear the concern in Neoshyt's voice, "Velid found a way to alter the genetics of Gretualin as they were conceived. This distorted them and made them what we know today."

Lienad saw a vision of Velid hovering over the planet of Sparebryr. Sending some odd-looking waves into the planet. As the waves went in, the beauty of the planet slowly began to rot away.

"By the time Ganel had discovered this atrocity, it was already too late. Fearing for her other dimensions, she found a way to completely lock out the Ancient Dimension from all her creations. This prevented not only Velid from visiting, but her as well. Velid was able to sense this was coming. Before he was cast out, he left a message hidden on Sparebryr."

Lienad saw what looked like lightning striking down into a mountain. His view zoomed into a cave entrance that had been newly created by the lightning strike. Inside the cave was a wall with strange hieroglyphs, like none he had ever seen before.

"The message was left there as the celestials were locked out. Over the ages, the twisted genetics of the Gretualin took over. The pure Gretualins were basically bred out. However, every so often there is still a pure one born. Sadly, these pure Gretualin are despised and killed at birth."

Lienad now started to see horrendous images of

babies being thrown into a pit. The sight and knowledge of this made his stomach churn. He became filled with so many emotions. Hate, anger, and sadness began to overwhelm him. Which is good, had he felt any other way I would not have been willing to tell his story. There is no room in any of the universes for beings that are fine with such atrocities.

"This was the ultimate demise of the Gaseous Dimension. The Gretualin slowly began to dominate the other planets and species within their dimension. After generations of the war and tyranny, they stumbled across the message left by Velid. Looking at it, they determined it was a message that their fate was to rule all the dimensions, which they then proceeded to start attempting to do."

Neoshyt paused to take a breath. "This led to the creation of organizations and factions like the D.I.C.K.S. to fight back against beings like Krind. Even some Gretualin were able to find it in themselves to fight back against their government. People such as your parents. When you were born, they didn't want you to be destroyed. Which is why they gave you away. Your brother, however, was born as the worst the species has ever known. His genetics are as close to pure evil as they could possibly get. So evil in fact, when he discovered your existence, he killed your parents."

Lienad was distraught as he sat through witnessing his real parents being murdered by his brother. Even though he never knew them, he felt the sorrow as if he had

been raised by them all this time. I won't go into the details of their murder as it is a bit too graphic, even for me. Shortly after this depressing vision, Lienad and Neoshyt were back in the chairs around the table.

"This is most of what I needed to tell you, but still not all," Neoshyt said, knowing how hard this could have impacted Lienad.

"Th-there is more than this?" Lienad asked. He was relieved he could speak again, but was having a tough time dealing with what he just experienced. "Please tell me I don't have to go through an experience like that to learn it again."

"No," Neoshyt said assuredly, "We don't have to go through that again, especially because you probably wouldn't be able to handle another round of that. But it is something especially important and I want you to brace yourself."

"Brace myself," Lienad questioned with a slightly aggressive tone, "I wasn't braced for any of this. You might as well just tell me."

"Fair enough," Neoshyt dryly stated, "The message left on Sparebryr is instructions on how to get to the Ancient Dimension. Velid left the instructions so someone could figure it out and open a path for him to return. Currently no one on their planet can decipher it, but there is a fear that your brother will be able to figure it out."

"Shit," Lienad said with despair.

"Yes, shit indeed. This is why you need to stop this from happening."

"How am I supposed to do that," Lienad questioned, filled with anxiety about all this.

"I can tell you how," Neoshyt said, sitting back in his chair, "But just know, it will not be easy. It can save every dimension, but it is at the expense of your own happiness."

"I can never be happy with the knowledge I have now," Lienad said in a shaky and sad tone, "I have to do what I can to stop this from happening."

"I'm glad you said that," Neoshyt said, smiling, "Because the truth is, your birth had been long awaited. It was always destined that you would be born. You are the only one that can put a stop to this. You have the spark of Ganel inside of your very DNA."

10

The Path

Lienad and Neoshyt sat in silence for what felt like an eternity. Each waited for the other to speak after the heavy information that had just been relayed. For Lienad, the silence made sense. I'm sure you would be in shock too if you had just discovered your brother killed your parents, you have a destiny to save the universe, and you have a piece of a celestial inside of you. As for Neoshyt, I'm not really sure why he waited. After all, one could say this was his fault. Not the impending doom of the universe, obviously—just for dropping all this on Lienad. Eventually, the uncomfortable silence was broken.

"So, why are you telling me this?" Lienad asked. "I thought you weren't on either side of them."

"You are correct, I do not pledge any sort of

allegiance," Neoshyt said, nodding, "However, I fear not stopping this would lead to the destruction of the entire universe. I really don't feel like having to hop to a different universe, or risk dying before I can."

"I see," he still wasn't sure about whether he fully believed Neoshyt or not.

"So, are you prepared to know what you need to do," Neoshyt had a hopeful tone to his voice.

"Well, hold on," Lienad said sternly, "I thought you said Ganel blocked all links to the Ancient Dimension. If that's the case, then how can your room of everything link there?"

"Well, okay, maybe not everything," Neoshyt said with an uncomfortable chuckle, "I can still link to the past events of the Ancient Dimension. But, no, I can't see what's currently happening there. Rest assured though; it used to be everything in a literal sense. Didn't want to change the name as one day I hope for it to be true again."

At this point, Lienad was convinced it was impossible to determine whether to trust Neoshyt or not. Everything seemed so bizarre. Which is true because it in fact was bizarre. As an old Earth song once said: "How bizarre".

"So," Lienad began, "Let's just say I believe you and I am willing to help. What will I need to do?"

"No," Neoshyt was very assertive with his tone, bordering on being aggressive, "There is no let's say. You must be fully committed to this. If you aren't, then there's no point in telling you anything."

"How can I just be expected to believe all this weird crap? I find it hard to be committed to something so outlandish seeming."

"You've seen what I had to show you. You've been given the truth. What you choose to do with it is up to you," Neoshyt's body language made it seem like he understood Lienad's position, but his tone did not.

"Do I have any time to think?" Lienad was anxious about the looming decision.

"No," Neoshyt grew even more serious, "You have already taken too long. This is being drug out far too long, I need a decision NOW."

"Alright," Lienad said in a solemn tone, "It seems like I don't really have many options here. I'll do it."

"Excellent," Neoshyt said with a sigh of relief, "I'm glad that's your decision. Now, we have a lot to go over about this. But first, hold out your non-dominant arm."

Neoshyt held out one of his hands and began forming a swirling light blue orb of energy in his palm. This began to make Lienad uncomfortable, and rightly so.

"Um," Lienad hesitated, "What are you about to do to my arm?"

"Oh, this," Neoshyt laughingly said, "I'm going to

implant a special device so that we will be able to communicate as needed. No need to worry, you won't feel a thing. It's completely undetectable."

Reluctantly, Lienad held out his left arm. He was unsure how to brace himself for this since he didn't really know what to expect. Neoshyt reach out and pressed the energy swirl into Lienad's arm. It absorbed swiftly and smoothly. He was right, Lienad didn't feel a thing. Which, in all honesty, is even more disconcerting. How many other times was something like this done to Lienad that he wasn't aware of? Luckily, the answer is none, but he didn't know that.

"There, that's done," Neoshyt said while nodding, "Now, do you remember what happened when you first stared into the orb? Not this time, but when you were physically in the cave?"

"Uh, yeah. I do," Lienad said, not really wanting to think about it, "It was a myriad of horrible scenes and images. Then a voice told me that this is a possibility for the future. That if I didn't follow the path, it would become a certainty."

"Yes," Neoshyt sat back and closed his eyes, "And then what happened?"

"The orb shattered. I felt hopeless," Lienad began to become filled with sorrow as he continued to speak, "I felt as if the future had already been decided, so I ran. I went to Remus, explained what happened, and went through the

PROTM."

"Before you did this, did Remus tell you anything?"

"Yes, Remus told me I didn't need to do this. That he knew it was not a certainty," Lienad said as a single teardrop fell from his left eye, "But he didn't see what I saw. How could he possibly know? I couldn't bear to live through that reality."

"I want you to know, Remus did know that this could be stopped," Neoshyt opened his eyes and leaned forward, "He knew this because I told him."

"You told him?"

"Yes, though he didn't know it was me. I sent a signal to his telepathic field. I watched as you were with him."

"Oh yeah, the room of everything. So, did I do the wrong thing?"

"Yes and no," Neoshyt said with a slightly higher pitched tone, "I do not think you should have run, but at that time Remus would not have known what to do. However, you also did not do the wrong thing. There was time that needed to pass before you could begin the path."

"So, now I'm ready?"

"Well, sort of," Neoshyt said with a slightly condescending tone, "It wasn't really about you being ready to start. There were just events that needed to happen before you could."

"Events like what?" Lienad asked, uncertain if he genuinely wanted to know the answer.

There was a long and uncomfortable pause before anything further was said. In all honesty, it probably would have been best if the topic had been changed. But as you have seen Lienad just loved to ask questions. It is one of his more irritating traits.

"Well," Neoshyt hesitated, "The ongoing battles continued. More civilizations fell victim to Krind's oppression. More groups of rebels began to pop-up across the dimensions. Krind learned about your existence and decided to set out looking for you specifically, most likely wanting to kill you like he did your parents; but you already knew that. Arura discovered a small taste of her powers. A whole lot of death and destruction. You know, the usual things to be expected."

"What," Lienad questioned with an extremely shocked tone, "Arura has powers? What are you talking about? Isn't she just a human?"

"Ah, yes, that," Neoshyt paused for a moment, "There are many things you don't know, even about your own lover. Things she doesn't even really know about herself."

"What kind of things?"

"To keep it short," Neoshyt sighed, "Arura parents experimented on her as a child by trying to infuse her DNA

with that of a fairy. They were successful but didn't know what all would come from it. Shortly after this they disappeared, never to return. To be more specific, they went into hiding after giving her away. They thought she would be safer that way. They have since died from parasites. It was a nasty business."

"That still doesn't tell me about her powers."

"Isn't that obvious? She has fairy powers."

"What does that mean?"

"Really? Have you never met a fairy?"

Lienad had, in fact, never met a fairy before. He had heard of them, but that was really the extent of it.

"So, like magic?"

"Yeah," Neoshyt was a bit frustrated, "But not like magic, it is magic. She recently discovered this on accident."

"I see," Lienad said, pondering on what he was just told.

"Now, are you ready to hear what you have to do now?" Neoshyt asked, exasperated.

"I'm confused," Lienad said, genuinely confused, "I thought this was all part of it."

"These are facts," Neoshyt said with a furled brow, "Facts and what you need to do are related but are not the

same thing."

"Alright, well, what do I need to do then?" Lienad asked—he was still confused.

"I don't know everything, but I will tell you what I do know," Neoshyt sat back, clasping his hands together in his lap, "The first thing you will need to do is to gather your team. The first two will be simple. You need to get Arura and Renka to join you on your mission. The three of you are to travel to Tesheraf, find Captain Aero, and convince him to be your pilot in this mission."

"So, you already have my team picked out for me," this annoyed Lienad a little, "What about a ship? If we have a pilot, we need a ship. You have that figured out too?"

"Yes," Neoshyt dryly said, "Captain Aero's ship is the exact one you need for this quest."

"Why is that?"

"He has certain amenities within it that will prove to be most useful."

"What else?" Lienad asked—hoping they could speed this along.

"Once you have your team you will need to seek out the fairy queen on the planet of Friyaldan in the Colored Dust Dimension. You need to convince her to unlock the full scope of Arura's powers. They will be needed, I'm sure."

"Okay, fairies and magic; got it," Lienad slightly felt

as though this was some sort of joke.

"Once that is done you will need to seek out the Crystal Cave on the planet of Pecoaphlyly. There you will find the crystal sword, which is imperative to the next step."

"I guess that's one of the reasons I need to bring Renka with me, since that's his planet of origin."

"Now you're catching on," Neoshyt said with a sarcastic tone, "After you get the sword, you will need to head to Atlantis. The Atlanteans guard the entrance into the inner Earth society."

"Atlantis? I thought that was a myth," Lienad was shocked at this.

"No, it is very real."

"How am I supposed to get there?"

"That's part of why you need Captain Aero. He knows how to reach it safely."

"Assuming he wants to join my crew."

"Don't worry he will," Neoshyt said with a noticeably confident tone, "Anyway, moving on. Once you get to the inner Earth society, you will need to seek out Swidom. He should be able to decipher the engravings left by Velid."

"What do we do after that?"

"Well, we won't know until you decipher the message that was left," Neoshyt closed his eyes, "I am sorry I

can't tell you more. I have not been able to get him to go to Sparebryr to look at it."

"What makes you think I will?" Lienad asked—concerned about the quest in front of him.

"Well, it is your destiny to stop this. But also, I just simply have hope."

"So, you're basically asking me to go out and do all of this based on nothing more than faith that I will succeed?" Lienad had a pit in his stomach as he asked this.

"Pretty much," Neoshyt understood Lienad's concern, "Remember, you can always reach me now should you need my help."

"How am I supposed to use this to communicate with you?" Lienad asked, holding up his arm.

"That's simple," Neoshyt said while grabbing his wrist, "You simply hold your wrist, clear your mind, and talk to me using thoughts with intent. I will hear you and will be able to respond."

"Okay, that does sound pretty simple."

"Now that we have gone over this, I will send you back to Remus," Neoshyt said while reaching out for Lienad's forehead, "Close your eyes and relax."

As Neoshyt's fingers made connection with his forehead Lienad felt a wave begin to overtake him. This feeling was as fast as it began. Lienad opened slowly opened his

eyes to look around, he was back in the green comfy chair in the room with Remus.

11

The Start

Lienad sat in silence, trying to process everything that had just happened. He wasn't sure if he believed anything he was told. I wish, for his sake, that he had dismissed it all and gone on living a normal life. Doing that would have been so much easier on him than this experience had already been. I can't say it would've been a happier life, though. He did, after all, seem quite happy around Arura. But at least he wouldn't believe the fate of the universe weighed upon his shoulders. Though, this does provide me something much more exciting to document. Anyways, the longer Lienad sat, the more it felt like his thoughts were driving him to the brink of insanity.

"Lienad," Remus' voice broke the silence, "Are you okay? What happened in there?"

"What?" Lienad blinked, clearly disoriented. "Oh, uh, yeah. I... I'm fine Remus; I think. I don't even know how to properly describe what all happened to me."

"I assume you met the one known as Neoshyt?" Remus asked, his tone concerned.

"Yeah, I did," Lienad felt a small pit in his stomach.

"Tell me, what were you told?" The concern in Remus' voice grew.

"Well, let me try and make it simple somehow. I'm not even sure I really know what I was told."

Lienad went on to tell Remus about how Ganel and Velid are real, they are locked out of the dimension, Velid has a plan to come back, and the path set before him to somehow stop this from happening. He went over the different steps he had to go through and that there would be more to come of which he wasn't already aware. I give you this brief break down of what all was said primarily because I didn't feel like writing all Lienad's uncomfortable pauses and the repetition of the word 'um'. I doubt you would have wanted to read that; it would have been quite boring and long winded. How Remus was able to take anything from the disaster that was Lienad's version of the story, I will never understand.

"I see," Remus had a dry tone, "I can see why you are having such a hard time dealing with what you were told."

"Yeah," Lienad retorted.

"Now, I don't know much about Neoshyt. Not enough to be considered an expert," Remus stated, the tone of concern returned to his voice, "What I do know is that I am not sure just how much I trust Neoshyt. You are the only one I know of that has been to the Zenith and returned well enough to continue even blinking. There is a lot of mystery surrounding that place. But what you are saying sounds at least a little reasonable."

"So, you think I shouldn't trust them?" Lienad asked—the pit in his stomach grew.

"Well, I don't know," Remus sighed, "I wish I could give you a better answer than this, Lienad. I don't know how the path you were given will truly put a stop to the previously foreseen horrid future, especially since it was not given to you in a complete sense."

"Just tell me what you think I should do," Lienad said, his tone filled with despair and desperation.

"That, sadly, is a decision you alone can make," Remus said in a solemn tone, "My only advice is to tread with caution, regardless of your decision. I think, perhaps, you should talk to Arura about this."

"Maybe you're right," Lienad was no less distraught than in the beginning of the conversation, "I guess I'll head back to her."

"Before you go," Remus grew a bit more serious in

his tone, "If it is something you wish for, I can selectively take the memory of what just happened away from you."

"While I know that would relieve this burden," Lienad said while getting out of the chair, "I fear this is simply a burden that I have to bear, no matter how great it is."

Lienad walked off and started his trek back to his room. When he got into the hallway, he glanced up at the clock; it read 0250.

"What," Lienad thought to himself, "How could it possibly be that so little time has passed?"

He was right to be curious about that, it is such an odd phenomenon. Did time here slow down while he was gone? That would have been a remarkably simple explanation, but that wasn't the case. Time runs differently when you are dealing with these types of experiences. You could be gone for what feels like an entire year, but only a few hours had passed back in reality. It is quite a bizarre concept that is tough to fully wrap one's head around. It was best that he had been left to just wonder along the remainder of his walk as opposed to being told how it was possible. It could have made his already damaged mental state break completely.

The walk back to his room with his current state of mind felt never-ending. Every step he took felt like the hallway was extending by a few additional steps. Every so often his depth perception would catch up. To give you an idea of what this was like, imagine your view was like a slingshot. Now imagine this sling shot kept getting pulled back and released repeatedly. This was happening repeatedly during his walk. Eventually he made his way through the constant push and pull. He stood there in front of his door, contemplating how to explain all of this to Arura.

He opened the door and watched as she laid there. She was everything to him, he loved her with every atom in his body. While looking at her, it became clear that he needed to do this; he had to try and save her. He gritted his teeth and forced out the feelings of stress and anxiety. This came as no surprise to me; love is an immensely powerful force.

He stood there for a while longer, just soaking in the moment of admiring her beauty before waking her up. While he was watching her, he noticed a faint pink glow around her that pulsated in sync with each breath she took. He was quick to figure out that this was related to her fairy powers, not that he truly knew what that fully entailed. He stood there, amazed by it all. She began to stir around a little bit, which seemed to cause the glow to change in hue ever so slightly. Her stirring turned to stretching as she began to slowly wake up, which caused the glow to slowly fade.

"Have you been watching me sleep?" Arura asked— followed by a sweet giggle. "Why are you so obsessed with me?"

"Because you are the epitome of perfection," Lienad was grinning ear to ear, in that moment he felt like he had no burdens at all.

"Come," Arura said, patting the bed next to her, "Snuggle me for a bit?"

"You don't have to ask twice," Lienad chuckled, "That's one of my favorite things to do."

Lienad crawled into the bed, sliding under the covers. He gently wrapped his hand around the back of her head and pulled their foreheads together. They sat like that for a while with their eyes closed. If you had been in the room, you would have been able to feel the energy being shared between them; it was intense. If you had looked close enough, you would have been able to see that 'spark' people always talk about. There are some, not me, that would say love is the most powerful magic there is. To each their own, of course. I have a firm belief that necromancy is far more powerful, but that is a discussion for another time.

As much as he wanted it to, Lienad knew this moment couldn't last forever. He had to tell her what was going on. He was struggling to do it; he didn't want to ruin such a beautiful moment. At least, that is how he thought about it. In truth, I never really found much beauty in these things. I'm more of a logic and reason type of person rather than the touchy-feely stuff. But this story isn't about me. Eventually he mustered up the courage to break away from the cheesy romance and speak up.

"Arura," Lienad's voice was shaky, "There-there's something we need to talk about."

"Is it good, or is it bad?" She asked, lifting her head to meet his gaze.

"Yes," Lienad nodded his head.

"I see," She glanced down, "Well I guess let's get this over with."

"Okay, so I guess let's start with something easy," Lienad shimmied to sit upright, "What's the deal with these fairy powers?"

"So, you found out about that," Arura also sat upright, "Well, I don't really know. One day we were out in the field, a projectile was coming close to hitting me. I raised my hands, fully believing I was about to get hit. Somehow, I was able to put up a force field that prevented me from getting hit. I spoke to the commander about it, and he said he suspected that I might have some kind of fairy powers caused by some experiments my parents were doing before they disappeared."

"Well, lucky for you then," Lienad awkwardly laughed, "Have you discovered anything else?"

"No," Arura had a sad tone, "I haven't been able to even replicate that field from before. I don't understand it at all."

"How do you feel about all of that?" Lienad asked— he was sincerely curious.

"I don't know," Arura hesitated in her response, "I feel like I'm a little closer to my parents, but I'm sad that I can't seem to do anything with it. I'm kind of confused; I don't know if I even want to explore it more. But I feel like I need to."

"Well," Lienad paused for an uncomfortable amount of time, "That sounds like a pretty heavy burden. I hate to add to it, but I have a lot to tell you and a huge favor to ask."

"What do you mean," Arura was visibly unsettled.

Lienad began to tell her the story of everything that he had been through and the things he learned. Throughout the story he could see her go through a variety of emotions. Scared, sad, uncomfortable, and angry. There is a good chance it was due to his poor storytelling, but it was probably because of the type of information she was hearing. She sat there, listening quietly, trying to soak in everything she was hearing; regardless of how it made her feel. When he finished telling his tale, they both sat there in silence for a moment. Arura needed to fully process what she had just heard, and Lienad was not going to try rushing her into a response.

"Okay," Arura slowly said, "So, let me make sure I understand. The end of the universe is coming and only you can stop it, but you only know a portion of what you need to do?"

"Basically, yeah," Lienad dryly said.

"Part of this has to do with me and my powers?"

"Also, yes."

"Well, I'm not sure I fully believe any of this," Arura was filled with uncertainty.

"I understand," Lienad slightly hung his head as he spoke, "I'm not sure I do either, but I feel like I must do this anyways. I get it if you don't want to help."

"Lienad," Arura paused for a moment, slowly growing a soft and sweet smile, "There isn't a thing at all that I wouldn't help you with."

"I love you," Lienad's eyes lit up as he spoke and he started to grin.

"I love you too," Arura said and leaned in for a kiss.

"So," Lienad chuckled, "I guess we're gonna do this then."

"Yeah," Arura smiled, "Guess so. At least this will give me a chance to learn more about these powers."

"That's one silver lining I suppose."

"It really is," Arura started to get up, "Well, are you ready?"

"Ready?"

"Yeah, shouldn't we go ahead and get started saving the universe?"

"Oh yeah," Lienad paused and started to pat the bed,

"Couldn't saving the universe wait a little longer?"

"As much as I would love to just lay here with you and watch the universe burn, we both know we can't because it's not the right thing to do," Arura leaned and kissed Lienad's forehead.

"I guess you're right," Lienad groaned while getting out of bed.

"Good boy," Arura joked. "So, I guess first we need to go get Renka?"

"Yeah, I'm not too worried about whether he will agree or not though," Lienad had a tone of absolute certainty in his voice, "I know he will."

Lienad was right of course. Renka was an interesting being. He was a breed between human and Serpisapion. As I'm sure you may already know, the Serpisapion species is remarkably similar to humans in terms of overall stature. They walk on two legs, have two arms, and a similar head shape to humans. Unlike humans, they have a face that is like that of a lizard, but with less scales, and no visible ears—yet they can hear like bats. They also have long tails with hard bone segments and moveable joints. Since Renka is also human, he's a bit different than that. He has short dark hair, ears, wears glasses, and a muted sage skin tone.

Aside from his different appearance, he is also quite different mentally speaking. Most Serpisapions are only known for being very tactical. They can camouflage into any environment. Renka, however, does not have that ability. He, instead, has a genius mind for science, which is uncommon for their species. Ever since being a child scientific concepts came naturally to him. Outside of science, the thing he loved most was reading novels about grand adventures. He has always wished he could go on one; that was why he joined the D.I.C.K.S. in the first place.

Alas, because of his brain they have kept him out of the field throughout his entire career. They have had him doing whatever it is the science team does. No one really knows what it is. I partially believe none of them do either. But, again, I digress. I will stop boring you with the details, I'm sure I have given enough on this topic. To remind you of where we were, Lienad and Arura were talking about going to get Renka.

"What time is it?" Lienad asked.

"It's 0813," Arura said, glancing at the clock that was right next to Lienad.

"Renka should already be in the MedBay by now then."

"Well, guess that's where we are going," Arura zipped up her black jacket, "If you ever finish getting ready that is."

Lienad had an embarrassed look on his face as he had basically done nothing to get ready. He rapidly got all his clothes thrown on and was ready to go. Lucky for him,

this was easy to accomplish. He always kept a set of clothes ready to go in his nightstand drawer. Lienad did an awkward collar pop with a slight nod, signaling he was ready to go. Arura placed her palm on her face, letting out an audible sigh.

"Well, let's get moving," Arura still had her face in her palm.

"Oh, don't act so ashamed, you like it," Lienad laughed and then gave her a little tickle.

"Stop," Arura laughed boisterously, "Stop."

"Alright, I'll stop," Lienad snickered, "Let's get going sweetie."

"Yes, let's," Arura was still trying to calm down from the laugh session.

Lienad and Arura left their room and began their trip to the MedBay. This was a long walk, the MedBay was in a separate building on the basement level. To give you a better idea, it was 1,289 feet from their room to the MedBay. Rather than go on and on about the long walk, I will give you some highlights. Passing by random workers, walls, windows, and bright lights. There was a lot of hand-holding and periodic glances into each other's eyes. All that strange romantic stuff people feel the need to do for some reason; I'll never understand that behavior. Eventually, their sweetheart walk came to an end as they reached the MedBay.

12

The Scientist

As they approached, the large steel-framed doors with frosted-glass windows slid open. They looked around through all the beds, each with their own medical contraptions next to it. They scanned the room, trying hard to find Renka. Looking to the right, in the far back corner, they were able to see him. He was working with what looked like an elaborate chemistry set, mixing test tubes filled with differently colored liquids by hand and jotting down notes after each step. They prepared themselves to interrupt his work and walked over to him.

"Hey Renka," Lienad gleefully shouted—though it didn't seem to faze Renka in the slightest.

"Re-e-enka," Lienad slowly said, leaving him unfazed yet again.

"RENKA," Arura shouted, slamming her hands on a nearby table. She had been so loud that everyone stopped to look for a moment.

Renka looked up and immediately had a look of disbelief.

"Am I dreaming?" Renka asked in shock. "Are you really back, Lienad?"

"I really am," Lienad chuckled.

"Six months," Renka said, his tone and expression grew solemn. "Six months with no contact from you. Not even so much as a call. I was so worried you were dead, and no one was willing to break the news to me."

"Don't you think I would've said something if he had died, idiot?" Arura asked in a huff.

"Who knows? It's not like you've been the nicest person since he went missing." Renka said.

"Well of course I wasn't," Arura said, "he was gone, and no one was helping me find him."

"I would have, if I could have," Renka said.

"Guys, no need to fight on my account," Lienad said, motioning his hands for them to calm down. "Listen, I had undergone the PROTM and was put into a whole new life on Earth. There was no way for me to make contact again. Then, Arura found me and brought me back."

"Hmm" Renka looked down at his feet.

"Anyways," Lienad said, letting out a long exhale. "What had you so sucked in that Arura had to yell to get your attention?"

"Oh, you know, science stuff," Renka shrugged, "I'd try explaining it to you, but you wouldn't really understand."

"Renka," Lienad paused for a moment, "Don't tell me you're working on a new 'perfume'."

"What, uh, no," Renka looked anxious, "Of course not."

"Uh huh," Lienad didn't believe Renka in the slightest, "Do I need to remind you what happened last time?"

"I, I would prefer that we didn't talk about that right now," Renka quickly put away his supplies.

"Renka," Arura said, with a disappointed tone, shaking her head. "You know what's going to happen if you get caught doing that again, don't be an idiot."

"I know..." Renka said, hanging his head.

For context, Renka does not actually develop perfume. This is just what he and Lienad call it to spare him the embarrassment of what it truly is. Renka believes that foul scent-based weaponry will be essential in winning battles in the future. For a lack of better words, and to make it simple to understand, he believes his fart weaponry is the future. Yes, go ahead and chuckle a bit. In his free time Renka is working on creating the perfect fart smelling liquid to be used in a variety of different weapon styles. He envisions a whole line of fart bombs, fart guns, fart canons, you name it. No one really knows why he thinks like this. I think it's merely a mixture of his scientific brain and a small part of him that never fully grew up.

The research and development Renka is doing is not sanctioned by D.I.C.K.S. in any way. In fact, he's not supposed to be doing it at all. Years ago, he was working on a serum that he thought was getting so close to perfect. However, someone accidentally knocked over his test tubes. Once they hit the ground and shattered, a horrendous smell was unleashed. It took three weeks to completely get rid of the smell, which was so powerful that it covered over half the entire military complex. Commander Scenkid decided his research needed to be stopped. To be fair, I do think it would have been an effective weapon due to its sheer strength. Now that you have this information, we can route back to the story.

"So, uh, what's going on?" Renka questioned, still a little nervous.

"We need to talk," Lienad quietly leaned in, "In private."

"I'm not getting in trouble, am I?" Renka was concerned that his continued research had been let slip and he was going to be reprimanded.

"No, this is way bigger than your research," Lienad quietly, but sternly, continued, "We need your help. Is there

somewhere we can go to talk about this?"

"I know a pretty good place we can go, follow me," Renka motioned his hand and started walking.

Lienad and Arura followed him, uncertain of where they were going. They just hoped it would be private enough to talk about what's going on. They walked through the MedBay, into a far back corner. Renka moved a box that had a keypad behind it. He typed in a combination and the wall next to it opened to a small room filled with supplies.

"Renka, this is a tiny supply closet," Lienad said, looking at Arura. She shared Lienad's confused expression. "I don't think we are all gonna fit comfortably enough in here to talk."

"Just wait," Renka held up his right index finger.

Renka walked into the closet and rummaged around in the far back corner. It was difficult to see what he was doing. Eventually, there was a click. Suddenly the back wall began to rise, revealing an entirely new room. Walking in, they saw a futon, some bean bag chairs, a television, a gaming system, a miniature refrigerator, and snacks galore. This looked like a teenager's paradise. This was only a testament to the fact that Renka was not a complete adult in the way he thought. Though, that really isn't the worst thing in the world. Arura, however, looked around as if she was ashamed to even be in there.

"Alright, pull up a chair," Renka said while

motioning his hand out.

"Renka," Lienad paused, "What is this?"

"This is my own personal space," Renka looked immensely proud of himself, "It is completely private in here. I created a special type of paint that blocks out sound and disrupts any signals to stop all attempts to listen in."

"Wow," Lienad looked around closely at everything, "That's actually pretty freaking cool."

"Yeah, I thought so too," Renka felt quite accomplished because of Lienad's compliment, "So, what's up?"

"Okay, brace yourself," Lienad placed his hands into the prayer position while touching his index fingers to his lips, "This is probably gonna sound bizarre—you might even think I'm crazy."

"Lienad," Renka had a joking look on his face, "I already know that you're crazy. Just tell me already!"

Lienad sighed, moved his hands from his face, and sat up straight. He chuckled ever so slightly at Renka's comment about him already being crazy. From here he went on to tell him the story about everything that happened and what all they were supposed to do next. Throughout Lienad's recounting of the tale, Renka looked like he was going to burst with excitement. Renka was completely enthralled by Lienad's story. So much in fact, that by the end of the story he didn't hesitate to speak out.

"Oh," Renka loudly exclaimed, "Please tell me you

want me to come with you, PLEASE!"

"Um, yeah," Lienad wondered how much attention Renka actually paid, "I already said we needed your help. Are you sure you heard everything?"

"Well," Renka laughed while rubbing the back of his head with his left hand, "I heard the important parts. Adventure, danger, save the universe, and so on. I am SO in. When do we leave?"

"It figures you didn't pay attention to everything," Arura said, rolling her eyes.

"I imagine we would need to leave pretty soon, but we still need to get ready," Lienad said.

Renka slapped a button on the wall behind him. Suddenly the tile in the floor began to retract and an overly filled backpack was risen on a platform.

"I'm ready," Renka quickly grabbing the backpack with excitement, "Let's go!"

"Woah," Lienad said, shocked, "Hold up bud, there are other things we have to do first."

"Well, yeah," Renka was a little embarrassed, "I know that. I'm just excited."

"I know you are," Lienad's voice was light-hearted, "We need to find a way to get to Tesheraf."

"Well, luckily we don't have to jump through any dimensions to get there," Renka replied, "Couldn't we just

take a ship there?"

"While that's true," Lienad said, "None of us have our own ship, and we certainly aren't the most skilled when it comes to flying."

"Yeah," Renka had a slight tone of disappointment in his voice, "That's true I guess."

At that moment, Lienad felt a presence enter to his thoughts.

"Lienad," he heard Remus' voice speak to him, "There is a secret room here on the base. That room contains access portals to every planet in our dimension. I can guide you there and get you into it."

"Perfect," Lienad thought back to Remus, "How do we get there?"

"Come to my door and turn to the wall opposite of it," Remus explained, "While you are there, the path forward will become clear."

"Cryptic," Lienad thought with a sigh, "Always cryptic."

"When you get here, you'll see I'm really not being that cryptic," Remus stated.

"Lienad." Renka grasped Lienad's shoulder, "Are you doin' alright over there?"

"Oh, yeah," Lienad shook his head to get his mind back to the real world, "I know what we need to do."

"Um," Renka paused, "So you sit there silent, with a serious look on your face, and decide you know what we need to do. Seems a bit weird, but with everything else you have told me it's not out of the realm of possibilities. What did your brain tell you."

"It wasn't my brain," Lienad said in an assured tone. "Remus entered my thoughts and told me how we get to Tesheraf."

"Well, that sounds uncomfortable," Renka joked.

"Renka," Arura interjected, "Now's not the time for silly jokes."

"Oh, Arura," Renka paused, "I almost forgot you were here. You've been so quiet."

"Well, it's kind of hard to say anything with how much you talk," she poked at him, "I'm just trying to make sure at least one of us actually pays attention to what we need to do."

"If you guys don't mind," Lienad said while clearing his throat, "We need to go to the PROTM room. There we will find where we need to go."

"I've never been in that room before," Renka started getting excited again.

"No, we aren't going in," Lienad stressed, "We are just going to the room."

"Well, that's far less exciting," Renka once again had

the sound of disappointment in his voice.

"Boo hoo," Arura playfully mocked Renka, "Lienad, based on what you said, we don't have time to waste; let's get going."

They all nodded in agreement and began to head off. The walk to the PROTM room was not a long one, there was a direct path from the MedBay. They stood in front of the doors, with Renka and Arura being very confused about what to do next. Which was expected, Remus couldn't speak into their thoughts through the telepathic field like he could with Lienad.

"We're here," Arura said while looking around, "What happens now?"

"Yeah," Renka nodded, "Where is this path you're talking about? All I see are walls and the door in front of us that you said we aren't going in."

"Well," Lienad turned his back to the door, "We look here."

He pointed to the wall. As he pointed, and the others turned around, a door began to morph from the previously barren wall. The door was plain looking. It was average-sized and looked like it was made of wood—the kind you'd expect to see on a medieval Earth castle.

"Well," Renka was surprised, "I guess that's where we go."

"Indeed," Lienad gave a confident nod, "Remus said

when we got here the path would become clear. Obviously, this is the path that has become clear."

"I guess onward we go," Arura started walking forward.

"Wait," Lienad said, putting his arm in front of her. "I'm the one getting the two of you into this. I should probably go in first—just in case."

"No arguments from me," Renka motioned towards the way forward.

"Where's all that excitement for the adventure now?" Arura mockingly asked Renka.

"Guys, stop," Lienad said, "We don't have time to squabble like children."

Renka turned and stuck his tongue out at Arura, and she rolled her eyes. Lienad walked toward the door, unsure of what he would see on the other side. This secret room was something he had never even heard a whisper of, how long had it been here? Well, he would have been surprised to know that it's been there for a long time. Access to it is completely controlled by Remus. In fact, the number of people who knew about this before Lienad could be counted on one hand—most of whom were now dead.

As Lienad opened the door, he did not know what to expect. However, he certainly wasn't expecting what he saw. Inside the room, all the walls looked to be made of pure sapphire. There was a single white light at the top of the room, shining brightly enough to illuminate the whole room. The refractions of light from the angles of the sapphire walls were an astonishingly beautiful sight to behold. In the center of the room was an emerald pillar, just tall enough to be the perfect height for an average sized human to place a book and read. The light was directly above the pillar, causing the most radiant green streams of light to mix with the sapphire floor around it.

Lienad and the others were speechless to the beauty in front of them. They slowly entered the room, soaking it all in. When the three of them were all in the room, the door closed behind them and disappeared. After a brief moment, a light began to shine on the top of the pillar. Lienad, walked closer to it and saw something that looked like a digital menu of sorts. There were buttons detailing different planets within their dimension. At this point they felt like they knew what they needed to do, but they weren't completely positive. They stood there, silent, thinking.

"Well," Renka broke the silence, "This is fun."

"Sarcasm, big surprise," Arura rolled her eyes at him again.

"Guys," Lienad let out a loud sigh, "Not again."

It's important to note here that—based on what I saw in Lienad's memories during the PROTM reversal—Renka and Arura often squabbled like siblings. However, she could be a bit more abrasive than she needed to be at times. There was no bad blood between them, from what I

could tell, just verbal friendly fire.

"I'm just saying," Renka continued, "It's pretty and all in here, but we are just standing around looking at this screen. Were you given any instructions, or should we just push a button?"

"I hate to say it," Arura had a slightly exasperated tone, "Renka's right, what are we doing?"

"I don't know," Lienad felt defeated, "I wasn't given any other information than just getting here."

"That means I know exactly what to do," Renka said while holding up a finger on his left hand.

Lienad and Arura looked at each other, completely confused. They had no idea what Renka meant. Before they knew it, Renka was standing next to the pillar with his finger hovering over the top. Their hearts sank, as they now knew what he was about to do. They quickly grabbed each other's hand and braced themselves.

"Ready or not," Renka exclaimed as he pressed his finger down, "That's odd, nothing happened."

The whole room instantly started spinning vigorously. Everyone was flung with their backs to the walls. It was like one of those Earth amusement park rides. I believe they were called a twirly-whirly, or something like that.

"Renka," Lienad screamed, "What did you do?"

"I just pushed the button for Tesheraf," he yelled

back.

"You had no idea what was going to happen," Arura screamed in frustration.

"It's not like you had any better ideas," Renka loudly retorted, "We had to try something."

"Well," Lienad continued, "Now what do we do?"

"Ask Renka," Arura yelled, "He seems to be the one full of great ideas today."

"Hope for the best, I guess," Renka would have shrugged if he could, but the spinning had him pressed too tightly against the wall.

"Wow," Arura sarcastically yelled, "Such a brilliant idea, did you think of that on your own?"

"Arura," Lienad exclaimed, "The sarcasm isn't help-ing. All we can really do right now is, like he said, hope for the best."

"I know," Arura said, still very frustrated, "But can we at least all agree that this was not a very well thought out plan of action."

"Agreed," Lienad and Renka yelled in unison.

Suddenly, the spinning stopped, and they fell to the floor. It was a far from graceful landing for any of them. They stood up, regaining their balance. They had no idea what had just happened—all they knew was that they were still in the room. Unsure of what to do next, they stood there looking at one another. There was a deafeningly awkward silence. Then, a slight sound—almost like someone playing with slime—broke the silence. They looked over and saw the wooden door re-appear. No one knew what was going to be on the other side of it this time, and they were uncertain whether they wanted to know.

"I mean," Renka started, "I guess we should go through the door."

"I'm not so sure we should listen to your ideas," Arura snapped.

"Remember what happened last time there was a door," Renka retorted, "It disappeared."

"Obviously I remember that," Arura crossed her arms tightly and aggressively, "It was just before you decided to push a button."

"I don't think we have many other options," Lienad's voice conveyed his feelings of uncertainty, "I think we have to see what's on the other side. Who knows, it might just take us back to headquarters."

"I guess we could always push another button," Renka joked sarcastically.

"NO," Lienad and Arura shouted out.

13

The Captain

The group slowly walked towards the door. Hearts were racing, uncertain of what they would find. This is another situation where they could have turned back. Renka was absolutely right; they could have pushed another button. They could have gone back to headquarters and given up on this whole mission. But they didn't. Lienad reached his hand out and grasped the doorknob, pausing for a moment to gather his thoughts. Slowly, he opened the door.

"Woah," all three of them said in unison, looking out to what was on the other side of the door.

None of them have ever visited Tesheraf before, so they had no clue what to prepare themselves for. As the door opened, they were greeted with a glorious presence. They were atop a mountain, looking out at a majestic

scenery. There were mountains and treetops as far as the eye could see. None of them had ever seen anything quite like it.

"This is beautiful," Renka said, "But how are we supposed to get down from here and where the heck do we go?"

"I have to agree on both points," Arura said reluctantly, turning her gaze to Lienad, "What's the plan, babe?"

"Well," Lienad paused, "All I know is who we are supposed to find here. I wasn't really told what to expect once we got here."

"Awesome," Renka sarcastically said, "We are extremely high up, on a mountain, with no plan."

"Now is not the time for your sarcasm," Arura said sharply. Though, she did agree with the way he felt. But, of course, she didn't want him to know that she agreed with him.

As they stood there wondering what to do next, they started to hear an odd sound approaching them. They were looking around and didn't see anything but did start to feel a strange change in the wind around them. They started getting worried that there was a storm of some sort coming. As the wind got stronger, they could feel it coming from above them. They looked up and, much to their surprise, there was a large birdlike creature descending upon them.

"Well, now we are about to get eaten," Renka nervously chuckled, "I hope we taste good at least."

"You idiot," Arura lightly smacked the back of his head with her hand, "We aren't going to get eaten. That's a Heagowl, don't you know anything? They don't eat humans."

"Oh, that's a relief," Renka said with a sigh.

"I mean, if they think we are a threat we will probably be imprisoned," Arura had a very dry tone.

"Oh," Renka paused, "Guess that's better at least."

"Guys," Lienad interjected, "I think it's probably best if you just let me do the talking here."

"Fine by me," Renka said with a smile. He was relieved that he didn't have to take charge in this at all.

"Be my guest," Arura said while waving her hand out as the giant creature gracefully landed just above them, looking down at them.

Lienad and Renka both looked up in the direction that Arura was holding her hand. There was a large Heagowl towering above them. It had to be at least 7 feet tall. Which they thought was huge, but it is a rather average size for them. They would have known this if, like Arura, they took the time to learn more about the varied species that inhabit the universe. The feathers on its body, of which there were many, had a vast mix of white and brown hues. The face was like a blown-up version of what people on Earth know as a barn owl.

The Heagowl was just as, if not more so, curious

about them as they were of it. After all, it wasn't every day three random beings show up on the top of a mountain. There was a long pause filled with intense staring before someone finally spoke.

"Who... who... who," the Heagowl repeated before clearing its throat, "Apologies, I had something stuck in my windpipe. Who are you and why are you up here?"

"Um," Lienad paused, "I am Lienad, this is Arura, and this is Renka. We came through a strange portal in search of Captain Aero."

The Heagowl paused for a moment, peering a little closer at them.

"The portal you say, hmm," the Heagowl said while leering at them, "I do not know the last time this portal had been used. I thought it was broken or something. Are you sure this is what happened?"

"Either it really happened, or someone had slipped us a nasty dose of Wizard's Tongue," Renka chimed in with a laughing tone.

As you may, or may not, be aware, Wizard's Tongue is an immensely powerful hallucinogenic. It is very widespread throughout the universe and is quite a problem in certain areas. On Earth it may be compared to something like the drug known as Acid. However, Wizard's Tongue is significantly stronger. Some people say that you can see through to the parallels to this universe and beyond while using it. I cannot tell you for certain, though, as I have yet to partake in its use. Enough about that, as I am sure you are eager to get back on with the tale.

"Wizard's Tongue?" the Heagowl questioned in a serious tone, "So you are some drug junkers or something?"

"No," Lienad said with an audible sigh of frustration, "You have to forgive Renka, he is an idiot. We are from the Dimensional Intervention Containment and Kill Squads. Remus sent us through this portal on our search for Captain Aero."

"Oh yes, the D.I.C.K.S," the Heagowl chuckled, "Such a stupid name. Why hasn't anyone decided to change that?"

"Um, I'm not sure," Lienad uncomfortably said.

He, too, knew it was a ridiculous name and often wished they would change it. Looking at Arura and Renka, he could see they shared similar feelings. But all three of them knew there was no time to sit around wasting time on the name of the organization.

"So," the Heagowl continued, "What do you need Captain Aero for?"

"Well," Lienad hesitated, "I really should only tell him directly what is going on. To keep it simple, I need to enlist his help to save the universe as we know it."

"Ba-HA," the Heagowl boisterously laughed, "Save the universe, that's a good one. Your organization does take things so seriously all the time. Let me guess, someone got stuck in a tall tree and now it's the end of the universe as we know it?"

"No," Lienad retorted with an offended tone. "What we are here for is not officially through the organization."

"To make sure I got this straight," the Heagowl said, calming down from his laughter, "You're with a poorly named organization, you aren't here on their behalf, and you claim this will save the universe. Does that sound about right?"

"I mean, that is an extremely simplified version of it, but yes," Lienad said, feeling like this conversation was progressing excruciatingly slowly.

"Well, if it's really that important then why are you still up here," the Heagowl jeered, "If I had to save the universe, I don't think I'd be hanging around on top of a mountain."

"That's pretty obvious, isn't it," Lienad aggressively questioned, "It must be clear to you by now that we can't just flap our wings and fly."

"Obviously, you are a lesser species after all," the Heagowl had a very condescending tone, "But I guess you must also be of *significantly* lesser intelligence since you didn't just use the elevator."

"The... elevator?" Lienad felt like he was being lied to just to make him seem stupid.

"Where do you see an elevator," Renka rudely responded.

"Right there," the Heagowl said in a demeaning tone while pointing at some stones.

"All I see are stones," Lienad said, feeling defeated.

"So," Renka got loud as he pointed to the stones, "You mean to tell me that these stones are somehow a magical elevator."

He walked over to the large stones and examined them. He didn't easily see any sign that this could be anything more than what is looked like, a bunch of rocks. Everyone in the group was beginning to get a bit irritated by this exchange. Though, the Heagowl did have some good points. They were, after all, considered a lesser species by the Heagowl. It doesn't mean they are right, but still, it is what they believe.

"Did you try touching the stones," the Heagowl questioned.

"What could have possibly driven us to touch the stones?" Renka was beginning to get slightly aggressive with his tone. "Who just goes around touching stones hoping for an elevator?"

As Renka said this, he slammed his hand on to one of the stones. Much to everyone's surprise, aside from the Heagowl, a veil dissipated, revealing a door. At this point, the group felt defeated. All this time spent arguing with a

Heagowl and staring off the side of a mountain when tall they had to do was touch the stone wall. Though, who would have thought to do that in reality? I'm willing to bet you probably wouldn't have. I know I wouldn't. Renka was right, who just goes around touching stones? But I digress, yet again. Enough of my rambling about stone touching, back to what you care about.

"You know, it was a real rude to try and make us feel stupid about a hidden elevator," Arura sharply said to the Heagowl.

"I didn't try," the Heagowl retorted, "I succeeded, BAHA!"

"Look, can you at least do one cordial thing and tell us how we can find Captain Aero?" Lienad asked with an exasperated tone.

"I could, but I won't," the Heagowl said, flying off before anyone from the group could respond.

They stood there for a moment, stunned. They were all thinking the same thing in that moment, that Heagowl was one of the rudest beings they had ever met. Which, I'm sure they were right; but there are many others out there that would make this exchange feel like it was a positive experience.

"Well," Lienad said, breaking the silence. "I guess we should use this damn elevator."

"Yeah," Arura and Renka said in unison with the

same melancholy tone.

They were upset, understandably, but they really needed to get over it. As they still had quite an adventure head of them. They entered the elevator and were surprised at its simplicity. There was nothing more than two arrows, one for up and one for down. They took the obvious choice of pressing the down arrow, which was luckily the right one. They all had a moment of fear that this too was possibly another trick, it wasn't.

As they rode the down the mountain, they were greeted with some of the most pleasant music they have ever heard in an elevator. It was a myriad of woodwinds playing a soft and warm tune. Back at headquarters, the sounds of choice were nothing but the sounds mechanical whirring. Because of this, they had a peaceful trip down. So peaceful, in fact, that it seemed to go by so fast.

At the end of the trip the opened the door on its own and they were greeted with an inside view of beautiful dense forests they had previously viewed from above. It was amazing, until they looked to the right of them. There he was, the same Heagowl from the top of the mountain, leaned back against the stone. This irritated everyone in the group.

"Well," the Heagowl said, "It's about time. Did you have a tough time figuring out how to push the down arrow?"

"Why are you here?" Lienad asked through gritted

teeth. "Haven't you bothered us enough?"

"No," the Heagowl said with a chuckle, "I don't believe I have."

"Look," Arura stepped in with an irate tone, "Unless you're going to help us find Captain Aero, please just leave us alone."

"Fine, you know what," the Heagowl said, followed by a long pause. "I'll help you find him."

"What?" Lienad asked as his jaw relaxed, "What, uh, what made you change your mind?"

"I dunno," the Heagowl said while stretching his wings, "I just kinda feel like it. Should I change my mind back?"

"No, no, definitely not," Lienad quickly said.

"Alright, then I'll need all of you to close your eyes," the Heagowl assertively said.

They didn't know if they could trust him, but they listened. All three of them closed their eyes tight. During this, all of them had a similar thought that when they opened their eyes again that the Heagowl would be gone. Patiently they waited, unsure of how long they would be willing to wait before just opening their eyes; prepared for disappointment.

"Alright, go ahead and open your eyes," the Heagowl said with an oddly confident tone.

"Okay," the group managed to say completely in sync as they opened their eyes.

"Ta-Da," the Heagowl said in a sing-song tone.

"Ta-da what," Lienad said, completely confused.

You see, when they opened their eyes, nothing had changed, it was still the same Heagowl they had been dealing with. The only difference was that he was now wearing a jacket. The jacket was like what the people of Earth know as a bomber jacket.

"Are we supposed to be impressed with the jacket," Arura said, just as confused as Lienad.

"It's a nice jacket," Renka joined, "But it's not something spectacular."

"Wow," the Heagowl said with a chuckle, "You guys really aren't the brightest."

"Again, with the insults," Lienad went from being confused to irritated, "Look either help us or leave us alone."

"I am helping you," the Heagowl had a hint of irritation in his voice, "It should be obvious. I am the one—the only—Captain Aero."

"How was that supposed to be obvious? All you did was put a jacket on," Arura said, placing her hand on her forehead.

Lienad, while thinking Captain Aero an ass, was

relieved that they were able to find him.

"Well, now that we have that out of the way," Captain Aero said with a nonchalant tone, "Tell me why you are looking for me."

Lienad took a deep breath and began to tell Captain Aero about everything he learned and what they were supposed to do. During this Captain Aero was visibly paying close attention to everything Lienad was saying. It looked as if he wanted to make sure he didn't miss a single word. Which was odd, given their first impression of him. One would not have assumed he would take this as seriously as it looked like he was.

There was a long pause after Lienad finished telling the tale thus far. Captain Aero was processing all that he had heard. Lienad, Arura, and Renka sat there anxiously waiting for a response from him. The three of them knew that the story sounded crazy, so they really hoped he would believe them.

"Okay, so some weird creature who lives alone in a place no one can travel to told you all of this?" Captain Aero had a serious tone, "Then he specifically told you I was the perfect pilot for this?"

"Basically, yeah," Lienad said, uncertain if this meant that Captain Aero doesn't believe him.

"Well then," Captain Aero adjusted his jacket, "Sounds like this guy really is smart then. After all, I am the

best pilot there is."

Lienad could see that Captain Aero was very sure of himself, which was a benefit. Now Lienad knew that all he had to do was stroke his ego. Which was true, Captain Aero loved to have his ego boosted as frequently as possible. It was, after all, the easiest way to get along with him.

"That is so true," Lienad said, attempting to sound as genuine as possible, "He was very specific about just how amazing you were."

"Like I said," Captain Aero gleefully said, "The guy knows his stuff."

"So, does that mean you'll help us?" Lienad asked—filled with anticipation.

"Hmm," Captain Aero paused, "I suppose I will. I mean, no other pilots can successfully save the universe like I can."

"I am glad to hear that," Lienad said with a sigh of relief, "So, I guess we should get going. Let's head to your ship now."

"Just so you know, my ship is very unique," Captain Aero said with a low chuckle. "There are some things you're gonna need to know."

14

The Ship

The crew followed Captain Aero through the vast forest. It was a good thing they had a guide, as it was easy to get lost within the woods of Tesheraf—it had happened many times before. This forest is what has kept this planet safe from most attacks. There are traps riddled throughout that make it nearly impossible to safely navigate them without knowing the land inside and out. Aerial strikes are out of the question as the forest is so dense you would have no idea what you are striking. For all you know, you would just be hitting an empty area. This leaves destroying the entire planet as the only option, which isn't practical if your goal is to conquer the civilization. No one has taken the time to try making a map of the world here and the planet's inhabitants would like to keep it that way.

"Well, I guess I should get to know you a bit,"

Captain Aero said, "How did you two love birds meet?"

"Well, we've basically always known each other," Lienad said, looking over and smiling at Arura. "I was raised at the D.I.C.K.S. orphanage since I was born. When she was young, she lost her parents and came to the orphanage too. I still remember the day she arrived; I was captivated by her even then."

"He sure had a funny way of showing it though," Arura giggled. "Always making little jokes at my expense. Nothing mean, of course, but they did get tiring. Though, eventually, I guess you could say he grew on me, haha."

"What do you mean, you guess?" Lienad asked in a playful manner, giving Arura's side a tickle.

"Hehehe, stop it," Arura laughed wildly. "You know I love you, butthole."

"I know," Lienad smiled. "But I've loved you longer. From the moment I saw you I knew I loved you. You were so nervous being there, but you tried your best not to let it show."

"You were the first person to talk to me there," Arura said, "Do you remember what you told me?"

"Of course I do," Lienad looked at her intently. "This place kinda sucks, but you learn how to deal with it. If you need anything, I'm yours; I've got it all figured out by now."

"Since that moment, even with all your teasing, I knew I never wanted to be anywhere you weren't," Arura

smiled and Lienad leaned in to kiss her.

"How is this my first time ever hearing about this?" Renka asked.

"Because you never cared to ask," Arura snapped. "All you wanted to do was make fart jokes and do your science experiments."

"BAHA," Aero laughed, "guess that tells me everything I need to know about that one then."

"Yeah," Arura said, sticking her tongue out at Renka. "That's Renka in a nutshell."

"Duly noted. Well, it was a cute story," Aero said before stopping and pointing ahead. "Anyway, we are here."

The group looked in the direction he was pointing and found themselves at the foot of an entire civilization. There were beautiful homes built within the trees all around them, connected by a vast network of rope bridges. None of them had ever seen anything quite like it. On Earth, there is an ancient tradition of fathers building a house within a tree for their children. This is like that, but far more extravagant. One might say that this looked more like an expensive resort rather than a regular community.

"Wow," Lienad was amazed, "I don't know what I was expecting, but this wasn't it."

"What, never thought a bunch of birds could have nice things, huh?" Captain Aero asked in jest.

"I just didn't expect everything to be as lavish as this," Lienad hoped that Captain Aero wasn't taking offense, "This is higher quality than what I have seen on so many planets."

"Well, when you aren't spending so much time fighting stupid wars and actually work together you can achieve great things," Captain Aero was filled with a sense of pride.

"I can see that," Lienad was still just so amazed by what he was seeing.

"I've read about your cities here," Arura said while looking around, "Seeing it in person puts the descriptions to shame."

"You know, babe," Lienad said while grabbing Arura's hand, "This could be a romantic spot for a vacation when this is all over."

"I think you're right," Arura said, smiling and giving him a kiss.

"Well," Renka clicked his tongue. Arura gave him a side-eye for breaking up the moment.

"Oh, right," Lienad said, breaking away from the kiss, "Sorry, got lost in the moment. About that ship you had mentioned?"

"Yeah, it's over this way," Captain Aero motioned to his left, "Follow me."

The group followed Captain Aero through the town until they stopped at the base of a gargantuan tree. In front of them was a very rustic looking door built into the tree's trunk. Just by looking at it, the door appeared to be at least 10 feet high and 5 feet wide.

"Your ship is inside of a tree?" Renka asked, unsure of what to expect in response.

"Yes and no," Captain Aero chuckled, clearly amused by their lack of knowledge. "Just wait and see."

Captain Aero reached forward and inserted a small iron key into the door. He paused, glancing back at the group for a moment. As he turned it, the frame began to glow dimly with a warm, pale-yellow light. As the light grew, a mechanical whirring and grinding began. Slowly the door rose up, unleashing a thick cloud of fog that smelled of metal and oil from underneath it.

"Woah," Renka exclaimed, "Is this room super cold or something?"

"What?" Captain Aero was initially confused. "Oh, you mean because of the smoke coming out? No, I just thought it would be pretty awesome to have a fog machine installed. That way every time I open this door; I could feel like an action star."

"Mission accomplished," Renka said with excitement, "It does feel like we're in an action movie or something."

Captain Aero had a sly grin as his ego was stroked. The door continued to rise, and fog continued to billow out. Once it reached the very top a chain of white lights began to click on. I do mean that literally, there was a loud click sound as each one turned on. The lights led down a long stairwell, which Captain Aero led them down. They continued down the stairs until they stopped in front of a metal door secured with what looked like a biometric lock of some sort. However, it didn't have a microphone or optical scanner. Instead, it had a hole with a green ring around it.

"You know," Lienad said, "I never knew your species was so advanced. I don't mean that in a bad way, I just never knew that much about this planet before now."

"We have always been underestimated," Captain Aero responded, "Which largely works out well as we get left alone for the most part."

"The Heagowl have been around for an extremely long time," Arura chimed in, "Those who have studied Tesheraf all agree that this planet was one of the first to have any sort of technological advancements. Some argue that the Heagowl are responsible for some of the advancements that took place on the planet Earth."

"And now those humans don't even know we exist," Captain Aero said with a sigh, "We have many descendants there now that have suffered reverse evolution. It's sad to see. Well, anyways, let me get this door open."

Captain Aero reached into his side pouch and pulled

out what I was convinced were worms. He placed them into his beak and started to chew. Lienad and company were confused—they weren't sure what stopping for a snack had to do with unlocking the door. They soon found out.

After a while of chewing, Captain aero leaned forward and placed his beak into the hole. While he was leaned over, he began to make retching sounds. This made everyone else extremely uncomfortable—Arura looked less squeamish about it than the others. No one really knew what to think about this. After a moment, the lock chimed, and the door opened.

"Um," Renka hesitantly said, "Are you doing alright over there?"

"Yeah," Captain Aero wiped the residue off his beak, "I was just unlocking the door."

"With your vomit," Renka had a clear tone of disgust in his voice.

"You do realize we are birds, right," Captain Aero sounded as if Renka should already have been aware of this practice, "The locks use our genetic makeup for validation to unlock."

"Couldn't you just spit into it," at this point Renka felt nauseous himself.

"Have you ever seen a bird spit," Captain Aero was beginning to question Renka's intelligence.

"I don't really know a lot of birds," Renka loudly

sighed, "So, no I haven't."

"It's pretty obvious what's going on here Renka," Arura had a condescending tone to her voice, "The lock responds to the DNA found in their saliva. Birds don't spit, but they do regurgitate their food for the young."

"Yeah, I get it now," Renka didn't have the most convincing tone in his voice.

"It's pretty amazing if you ask me," Arura said while crossing her arms, "It is a difficult biometric lock to break into. Vocal patterns and eyes can easily be mimicked, but DNA can't without an existing sample."

"Okay," Lienad said, "So, we have a really cool biometric lock system. But could we please get to the ship? We have stuff to do after all."

Normally, Lienad would have been more interested in this instead of trying to rush it. However—ever since he had been given the mission from Neoshyt—Lienad had an internal struggle going on. He tried not to let it affect his normal fun demeanor, but the universe resting on his shoulders constantly gnawed at him. I assume the group understood this, as no one gave him any flack about it. Instead, they continued forward in good spirits.

The door they were in front of opened to a large air hangar with various ships. Many of them were all very sleek looking. Primarily they were all chrome, with seating enough for two people, a sharply pointed nose, two wings on each side, and the tail went to a thin point. Looking at them you would think they were modeled after a bird of some sort, which they were. They walked through the corridor, every aircraft looking just like the last. After passing by what felt like 100 ships on repeat, they reached the end of the line where there was an empty space. Captain Aero stopped in front of it and waved his wing out towards it.

"Well, here she is," Captain Aero said with gusto, "My amazing vessel."

"Um," Renka paused, looking at the others.

"Are you sure," Arura seemed just as confused as Renka.

"There's nothing here," Lienad felt more frustrated than he did confused by this.

"What do you mean, it's right here," Captain Aero said while reaching down.

As Captain Aero came back up, it looked like he was holding a small toy space craft. The toy looked slightly different from the other ships here, so it couldn't have been a model of them. It had orange, white, and green paint on it. It was a sort of oblong sphere with a fin on top and a heavily arched wing on each side. This caused even greater confusion and frustration among the group.

"It's..." Lienad tried his best to remain calm, "A toy."

"So, you have a tiny toy ship," Renka was beyond confused.

"How is this supposed to help us?" Arura questioned in frustration.

"Toy," Captain Aero scoffed, he was taken back with offense, "How dare you, this is no toy. This is the greatest ship you will ever find."

"If that's the case, then how are we supposed to get in it," Lienad was beginning to get angry, thinking that this was a huge waste of time, "If you haven't noticed, all of us are normal-sized, not fun-sized."

"How are you supposed to fit in?" Captain Aero asked with a grin. "Like this."

He tossed the toy into the air above the empty spot. As it started to come down, he pushed everyone back with his wide wingspan. Everyone, other than him, was ready to get on with this and go find someone with a real ship. But then, just before it hit the ground Captain Aero made a very specific sounding whistle melody. Suddenly the toy popped into being a large space craft, bigger than the others in the hangar. Everyone was amazed by this, which made Captain Aero feel successful.

"That... was unexpected," Renka said with great surprise, the others nodding in agreement.

"Well, what do you think?" Captain Aero asked while slapping the ship with his wing. "This is the one and only HS-24-A-50, but I call her Sussu."

"Well," Lienad paused, "It's certainly no toy, that's

for sure."

"At least it's bigger than the rest of these," Renka was relieved, "Even before the toy incident I was worried how we would all fit in a two-seater."

"I wouldn't be caught dead in one of those boring things," Captain Aero scoffed.

"What makes this ship so special," Lienad wondered out loud, though he had meant to internalize that thought.

"You mean other than the fact that it has me as a pilot? Baha," Captain Aero jested. "Rather than some long-winded list of details, how about we go ahead and do the grand tour?"

"Sounds good," Lienad was slightly embarrassed for letting his thoughts come out. The others nodded in silent agreement.

They followed Captain Aero to the rear of the ship where a ramp was automatically lowered for them to walk up. It was as if Captain Aero and his ship were completely in attuned to one another. As they walked in, they were blasted with a slightly dense white mist, which was surprisingly forceful.

"Ah, yeah, should have warned you about that," Captain Aero chuckled, "That's a debugging spray. Don't want any bugs coming along all nestled in your feathers."

"Yeah, sure don't want my feathers getting bugs," Renka joked.

"That wasn't a very good joke," Captain Aero had a disappointed tone, "Let's keep going. Up here are the sleeping quarters."

He motioned to his left where there was a room with three sets of bunk beds fastened to the walls.

"As you can see, we all bunk together. So, no weird stuff," Captain Aero let out a quick and boisterous laugh.

"With so many beds, do you have more people in your crew?" Lienad asked, taken aback, he wasn't prepared for there to be more joining in the team.

"Well, the ship was built for a crew," Captain Aero started to flex his wings, "But I'm so amazing I don't need a whole crew."

"If it's built for a crew, does this mean we need to learn how to help fly it," Renka was concern because he wasn't much of a pilot, and didn't want to have to try.

"Not at all," Captain Aero laughed, "I already told you I'm all that's needed. Besides, even though it's made for many it can still only be flown by one at a time."

"Oh, okay," Renka let out a sigh of relief.

Renka was relieved because he knew his attempt to fly this craft, or really any ship for that matter, would ultimately end in a crash. Continuing the tour of the ship, most things needed no description from Captain Aero; things like the table with seating, which was clearly a place to eat meals or just hang out. Near that was a bathroom, which

Captain Aero stopped in front of.

"This is the waste room, you can relieve yourself here," he pointed toward the bathroom.

"I feel like that kind of goes without saying," Lienad said with a little bit of confusion, "Is there something specific you need to tell us about it?"

"Only that it's an amazing facility," Captain Aero sounded as though he was proud of the bathroom, "It doesn't matter what type of waste you put into the receptacle, it will be converted into fuel for the ship."

"Oh, I've heard of this," Renka got excited, "You mean to tell me you have refining bots here?"

"What are refining bots," Lienad hadn't the slightest idea what Renka was talking about.

"It's a newer type of nanobot technology that is able to take any type of organic matter and refine it into fuel based on the type of craft they are programed for," Renka's excitement grew as he spoke, "I have only heard of them but never seen them in action before."

"That's right." Captain Aero was now swelling with pride after hearing Renka rave about the technology. "Why wouldn't we have it? We invented it, after all."

"No way," Renka was completely shocked, "I had no idea they were invented here. The article I was reading about them made no mention of it. In fact, come to think of it, there wasn't any mention of a planet of origin at all."

"Of course it didn't," Captain Aero nodded, "We do like to fly under the radar after all. If it got out that we had all these crazy advancements, there would be a huge target on us."

"Hmm," Renka nodded in agreement, "Yeah, that makes a lot of sense."

"Sorry to interrupt," Lienad was anxiously scratching the back of his head, "As cool as this toilet is, we really need to get a move on. There is a universe to save after all."

Arura let out a quiet giggle, she found the whole conversation to be a bit amusing. Which, I suppose it was kind of humorous that so much time was being spent talking about a toilet. But to be fair, it was intricate and useful technology. Advancements like this are the precise reason why Tesheraf has remained beautiful and pollution free while still being one of the most high-tech societies out there.

"Right," Renka had a more serious tone and a nod, "Sorry Lienad, you know I get carried away when I start nerding out."

"Nerding out is an interesting statement," Captain Aero held the tip of his wing to the base of his beak, "Is that what your people call talking about awesome technology?"

"In a sense," Renka chuckled.

"Yes, can we please move on now," Lienad said with a slight frustration, he was ready to get on with the plan to

save all of existence—but his fuse was a bit too short about it in moments like this.

"Apologies, come," Captain Aero waved and walked forward, "Most of the other stuff is not essential to explain and labelled to easily comprehend. Electric panels, armory, and so on."

They continued to walk forward until they reached the cockpit—or command center if you prefer. It was quite a remarkable sight. There was a large control board in the very front, with a bunch of buttons and knobs. There was one large, extremely comfortable looking, chair in the front-center of the board. Against the wall on both sides of the doorway were long bench seats that seemed to have ample cushioning. In the center of the room was a high-tech pedestal of some sort.

"This is the main event," Captain Aero said while opening his wings to the room.

"Neat," Renka exclaimed, once again excited.

"What all do we need to know about in here?" Lienad asked.

"Well first, and most importantly," Captain Aero had a profoundly serious tone. "This chair in front is my chair. Never sit in my chair."

"What about this pedestal in the middle here," Arura said while reaching out to touch it.

"Don't touch that," Captain Aero shouted abruptly,

"That is a holographic navigation device. It is extremely sensitive. We use it to get a view of the stars for the dimension we are in the help chart our course. Without knowing how to use it properly, I advise against even trying."

"So far it seems that basically we can't touch or use anything in this room," Lienad was annoyed at Captain Aero snapping at Arura.

"Well, that's not completely true," Captain Aero let out a nervous chuckle, "You're free to sit on those benches. There is also a machine on the left wall you are allowed to use to get refreshments."

"So, basically, this is just a lounge for us while you taxi us around?" Arura asked.

"Hey now," Captain Aero snapped back, "I'm not just some driver. I will be manning all the defense mechanisms while we fly, managing the navigation, and I'm quite sure I will more than come in handy when we land too."

"Hey, I have a glaring question," Renka raised his right hand, "Shouldn't someone else know how to work this thing just in case something was to happen to you?"

"Well just hope nothing happens to me BAHA," Captain Aero laughingly said, "On a more serious note, should something happen to me... Press the home button on the control panel. It will immediately transport the ship, and anyone who is in it, back to Tesheraf. Once that button is used the ship will become completely inoperable. It is a

single use—emergency only—fail safe.”

As he was saying this, he had walked over to the control panel and motioned everyone over. He was pointing to a small yellow button with the image of a bird's nest on it. This button couldn't have been any larger than about an inch in diameter, using Earth measurements.

“I see,” Lienad had a solemn tone as he understood that should they ever need to use this button, it will most likely mean that their mission was a failure.

“But what if you need a nap or something,” Renka was still stuck on the belief that someone else needed to know how to operate the craft.

“This ship is so fast I wouldn't have time to sleep,” Captain Aero had a vainglorious tone, “Besides, if I need rest while flying, I can just use a Z-Capsule.”

“Oh yeah, I didn't even think about those,” Renka stopped pressing about someone else learning how to operate the ship.

For any readers who may not already be aware, a Z-Capsule is a special pill used by military units. One Capsule can revitalize all the cells in your body. It's like having a deep sleep for multiple hours without the need for actual sleep. Side effects of its use may include, and are not limited to, nausea, vomiting, diarrhea, loss of sight, loss of smell, fatigue, insomnia, depression, split personality, indigestion, constipation, dry mouth, skin rash, heart palpitations, liver damage, kidney failure, general discomfort, lock jaw, tremors, brain damage, schizophrenia, memory loss, and in rare cases even death. It is not advised to use it on a regular basis as it is not a sustainable solution for continued sleep replacement.

"What about medical supplies?" Arura asked.

"There is a button in the bathroom that will turn it into a med-pod," Captain Aero was getting a bit tired of the questions.

"Great, we know everything we need to know," Lienad was trying to rush everything along, "Now let's let Captain Aero do what he does best and get us on with the mission."

"Sounds great to me," Captain Aero happily responded, you could easily see that he felt his ego stroked by Lienad's comment.

"So, how are we supposed to get to see the Fairy Queen?" Renka asked—it was something he had been pondering for a while.

"I hate to say it, but he has a good question," Arura was sick at the thought of agreeing with Renka yet again, "The Fairies are in the Colored Dust Dimension. Which, from everything I have read, is extremely small."

"You're absolutely right, it's so tiny," Captain Aero had a sly grin, "That's why we have this."

As soon as he said that he slapped a button on the

control panel. Suddenly everyone started to feel their bodies warp and compress. They felt like they were being squished and pulled at the same time. This only lasted for a split second but felt like much longer. When everything stopped, they were unsure of exactly what happened. They all felt sick to their stomachs and had horrible headaches. Renka ran to the bathroom and vomited.

15

The Missing Planet

"Thank you for fueling the ship!" Captain Aero shouted through uncontrollable laughter.

"What just happened?" Lienad queasily asked as he held his stomach and head.

"Oh," Captain Aero paused his laughter, realizing he was the only one who knew what was going on, "That button shrinks us and the ship down to a size small enough to get to and navigate through the Colored Dust Dimension. There's no other way we could get to the Fairy Queen. Guess I probably should have warned you about the effects of it."

"You get used to it after a while," he added with a shrug.

"Are you okay, babe?" Lienad asked Arura while

rubbing her back.

"Yeah," she said with a slight dry heave, "Better than Renka, at least."

"Yeah, a warning would have been nice," Lienad was holding back a potential vomit of his own.

"How long are we going to feel like this?" Arura asked, covering her mouth.

"Usually only a few minutes," Captain Aero tried to sound reassuring, "Though vomiting like he just did usually helps speed it up."

This was a true statement. In fact, when Renka left the bathroom, he didn't feel bad at all anymore. He felt completely normal again.

"Guys," Renka was visibly relieved, "If you feel as bad as I did, go blow chunks. I feel loads better."

"RENKA," Arura loudly exclaimed, "That's so gross! No one wants to hear about your trip to the bathroom."

"Hey," Renka let out an immature chuckle, "Just thought you should know."

"Well, we didn't want to hear it," Arura scoffed as she turned around and crossed her arms.

"Guys," Lienad yelled out, louder than the moment warranted, "We don't have time to act like a brother and sister picking on each other. We have a mission to accomplish. Can we focus on that instead of Renka's time with the

toilet?"

There was an awkward silence for a while. The air was so thick with tension, you could cut it with a rubber spoon. At least, I believe that's the phrase I heard while Lienad was on Earth. No one really felt comfortable speaking. It was like younglings that had just been scorned by their father.

"So, we are tiny now," Lienad broke the silence, "Aero, how do we get to the Colored Dust Dimension now?"

"That's easy," Captain Aero sounded as though he had the utmost confidence, "One of the best things about Sussu here is that I can instantaneously hop to most dimensions with a single button. No need to fly out to one of those Hop Stops."

A Hop Stop is a place where you can go to hop to another dimension. It's not really a very pleasant place. It's often a hub for pirates and smugglers. The facilities are usually very run down as well.

"No more waiting around then," Lienad said in a rushed tone, "Let's get to it."

"We are already there," Captain Aero said while laughing.

"What," Renka looked around in disbelief.

"How would that have even been possible?" Arura asked—she was shaken.

"While all of you were busy talking about expelling fluids I went ahead and pushed the button," Captain Aero let out yet another boisterous laugh, "It happens in such and instant that you can't even tell."

"Excellent," Lienad sighed with relief, "Thanks for being a step ahead during all of that nonsense."

"It's just what I do."

"If I'm not mistaken, the Fairies are on the planet Friyaldan," Arura said with confidence, "But how do we find it in all of this dust?"

At this point it is important for me to tell you a little about this dimension, since you most likely have not been yourself. The Colored Dust Dimension is very appropriately named. The entire space of this dimension is filled with clouds of dust in varying colors. The only explanation for this is that it radiates from each planet due to the prominent levels of magical activity. There are only three known planets in this dimension. They are Friyaldan, Cerulyt, and Spnark. However, the dust makes it hard to find them.

"We have the navigation device," Captain Aero pointed his right wing at the pedestal, "It can't be completely accurate while we are here, but it will at least give us a general idea."

"Not a very good nav system if it can't be accurate," Renka was concerned at the thought that they didn't have a reliable navigation system.

"Hey, everything about Sussu is perfect," Captain Aero gently rubbed the control panel, as if he was consoling the ship after it had been offended, "That weird dust in this dimension just throws everything off. I thought you were a smarty pants. You didn't know that?"

"I'm an engineer, not an explorer," Renka was cut deeply by the remark at his intelligence.

"Okay, so," Lienad interjected, "That still doesn't explain how we find it if the nav system will only be slightly functional?"

"That's easy," Captain Aero said while walking over to the pedestal, "I have all three planets that I know of logged in the map. It will detail how to get from one planet to another. If we find one, we can get to them all."

"None of us have ever been here before," Arura softly said, "Do you know how to identify the planets when you see them?"

"Oh, BAHA," Captain Aero let out a deep belly laugh, "I can identify these planets. Let's just say you've never been to a party until you've been to a Pixie party."

Lienad, Arura, and Renka looked confused by Aero's remark about the pixie parties. They weren't aware that the Pixies are known far and wide as the ultimate party animals, as well as the creators of Wizard's Tongue. Though, I always wonder if it would be dangerous to go to one—they are greatest pranksters in the universe after all. Should you

ever go to one of these parties, please try to be careful.

"So, how do we identify them, then?" Arura asked.

"Don't worry about that," Captain Aero put on an interesting looking pair of glasses, "You just leave that to me."

Captain Aero's glasses were very odd looking, to say the least. Large circular lenses over each eye, forming a single piece like goggles, and there were mechanical looking parts around the edge. The easiest comparison I can make is that they were like the Earth style known as Steampunk. However, they were a pastel blue color.

"Those are...interesting," Renka hesitated. He was not a fan of them and honestly thought they looked ridiculous.

"I know they aren't stylish," Captain Aero had a lighthearted tone, "But they help me easily see through the dust."

"Well, glad they have a purpose then," Lienad laughed, "Otherwise we would have to call the fashion police."

"Who are the fashion police?" Captain Aero's tone suddenly grew serious.

"Oh, no one," Lienad grew uncomfortable, "It's just an Earth saying I picked up. It's something you say when someone's style is less than ideal."

"Hmm," Captain Aero paused, "Then did someone

call the fashion police on you guys? BAHA!"

"Heh," Lienad forcibly chuckled, "Yeah, you got it."

"I know I do," Captain Aero confidently stated, "I'm so glad I have me to entertain me."

"Woah," Arura interrupted, "Am I crazy or am I seeing a bunch of forks floating around?"

"No," Renka said in surprise, "I'm seeing them too."

"We must be near Cerulyt," Captain assured, "Pixies must have done another prank on the Snuln."

"With forks," Renka questioned, he was very confused.

"Renka, you really need to study more about other species," Arura was disappointed in him for not already knowing, "Everyone knows the Pixies prank the Snuln with forks. I just didn't know they did it to this degree."

"Oh yeah, it can get pretty intense," Captain Aero said with a grin, "One time they covered the entire planet with forks and Snuln couldn't find any of their spoons."

"I'm not even gonna ask about the spoons," Renka shook his head.

"Good, please don't," Lienad got stern with his voice, "We don't have time for you to catch up on the nuances of other species. Where is Friyaldan from here?"

"Once we reach Cerulyt, we follow the white

stream—it will lead us straight to it," Captain Aero said with confidence.

Everyone sat back and waited as Captain Aero continued to fly in search of Cerulyt. As they searched for the planet, Captain Aero was seen somewhat frantically looking around. This made everyone else in the group quite uneasy.

"Everything alright there, Captain?" Lienad asked—he hoped this was nothing more than another quirk of his.

"Unfortunately," Captain Aero shuddered, "No, it's not."

"What do you mean?" Lienad's heart sank as he asked.

"You're about to see," Captain Aero said with a very solemn tone, "We are almost at an empty spot in the dust."

"Empty spot?" Lienad asked in shock. "I thought this whole dimension was completely covered."

"Normally it is, but not anymore."

"Not any—," Lienad stopped speaking as his jaw dropped open.

They flew into the empty space Captain Aero had warned them about. In the dust void there were forks, broken and whole, along with other debris lifelessly floating. This was the spot where Cerulyt should have been. Now, there were only the remnants of destruction. This was not

something anyone had expected to see.

16

The Garden Castle

They silently stared at the lifeless remnants of destruction. So many questions and theories raced through their heads. Was this a Pixie prank gone severely wrong? Had they accumulated so much silverware that the planet could no longer contain it, causing an implosion? While these options would have been far more whimsical and humorous, they knew the truth had to be something far more sinister than that.

"I assume this was Cerulyt," Lienad shuddered.

"Yeah," Captain Aero's tone grew very solemn, "It sure was."

"What could have happened here," Arura had a lump in her throat.

"I wish I knew," Captain Aero closed his eyes and

bowed his head, "Hopefully we can find some answers. Let's hope this is the only planet like this in this dimension as well."

"Well, is your guiding line to Friyaldan still here," Lienad was hopeful that this was the only unwelcome news they had to deal with right now.

"Yeah," Captain Aero adjusted his hideous goggles, "I still see it."

No one said another word for the rest of the trip to Friyaldan. An air of sadness and discomfort settled over them. Everyone feared this might not be the only planet to suffer this fate. What would they do if Friyaldan had suffered the same fate? Their whole mission would be ruined if they couldn't meet with the Fairy Queen.

As they continued to follow the white line, they heard Captain Aero let out what sounded like a sigh of relief. Everyone immediately perked up and looked ahead. Within the dense fog of dust, a large radiant ball of glowing pink and purple hues began to materialize. They were in luck, for this was Friyaldan. At this moment, everyone felt an almost unbearable weight being lifted from their shoulders.

"I assume that is Friyaldan," Lienad stated with hope.

"You assume right," Captain Aero said with a nod. "Hopefully we can get some answers about what

happened."

"Yes, that would be nice," Lienad softly said, "Of course my primary concern is the mission though."

Captain Aero gave a nod to show he understood. Though, his mind was more focused on getting answers rather than the mission. He was, after all, the only member of the group that had an actual relationship with the Snuln. Because of that, it's easy to understand why this affected him more than any of the others.

"Everyone get ready," Captain Aero started flipping various switches, "We are about to descend, and it might be a bit bumpy."

"Why would it be bump—" Renka began but was cut off by a violent jolt.

As they descended the ship began to violently rock and shake. Renka, who was the only one not already seated at the time, was thrown back. After seeing this, Lienad and Arura buckled themselves in. Which was a smart move, as they continued to descend Renka was thrown about in multiple directions. It looked like a scene straight out of a slapstick comedy.

"Alright," Captain Aero pulled back the steering controls as they landed, "The queen's throne isn't far from here. But it'll be best if we walk."

"Great," Renka struggled to speak while laying with his chest on the ground.

"Are you okay, Renka?" Arura asked.

"Oh yeah," Renka sarcastically responded, "What a fun time that was."

"Go use the MedBay. Maybe next time you will brace yourself when told," Arura said, sighing with disappointment.

"Not like I actually had a chance to," Renka muttered under his breath as he stumbled to the bathroom.

It was only a few moments before Renka was finished using the MedBay in the bathroom. When he walked out, he looked completely revitalized. This was one of the benefits to a MedBay, it can heal any ailment you may be dealing with; even ones you may not even be aware of. If it is an issue with a known remedy, it will be fixed.

"Ah," Renka sounded renewed, "Much better now, should we get going?"

He looked around and realized they had already left. Frantically, he ran out of ship searching for them. When he got outside, they were all at the bottom of the ramp waiting for him.

"Oh," Renka was trying to catch his breath, "I thought you guys left me."

"We thought about it," Arura said, her tone a blend of light mockery and teasing.

"Nope," Lienad chuckled, "We were just waiting for

you to finish getting dolled up."

"Well, thanks," Renka was once again embarrassed. He intentionally avoided acknowledging the comment about getting dolled up.

"So, which way do we go now?" Lienad asked Captain Aero.

"Hmm," Captain Aero was tapping his beak as he looked around, "Let's see, which way do we go."

This made Lienad start to panic a little bit. He was starting to think that Captain Aero may not have been entirely honest about how familiar he was with the planets in this dimension. He was also wondering if this delay meant that something bad had happened here as well. Since this was Lienad's first time on this planet, he had no idea what to expect. Luckily, he was worried or no reason.

"I'm just playing around, BAHA," Captain Aero cackled, "It's this way, follow me."

They followed Captain Aero, quietly admiring the scenery. There were no moons or stars to light their path. Instead, the planet was bathed in the glow of luminous mushrooms. That's what made the landscape so breathtaking. The forest around them was a sea of multicolored mushrooms—towering, clustered, and glowing in all sizes. It was unlike anything they had ever seen in person. Except for Captain Aero—though that didn't mean he loved it any less. If they weren't seeing it with their own eyes, they wouldn't believe it was a real place; just something out of a fantasy novel.

"Wow," Arura couldn't contain the sound of her amazement, "I have never been somewhere this beautiful."

"Me either," Lienad had a similar tone to his voice, "It's so serene here."

"If you like this," Captain Aero said, remembering how he felt his first time here, "Wait until we get to the city. It's just around this bend."

They entered the clearing beyond the forest, jaws dropping at the sight of the city. Captain Aero was right, it was incredible. The pathways through the city were lined with small luminous mushrooms on each side. The houses and buildings were all made from large mushrooms with very wide stalks. It was a fantastic, breathtaking, and radiant mushroom village. In the not so far distance, they could see what could only be described as a glorious and glowing mushroom castle.

"That big castle at the end of the road is where we are going," Captain Aero pointed his right wing ahead.

"You know, I didn't know what to expect when coming here," Lienad's eyes were so wide, it looked like a gentle nudge might make them pop out. "But at no point was I ever expecting this."

"Pretty wild, isn't it?" Captain Aero asked.

"You can say that again," Renka's voice was filled

with enthusiasm.

They walked along the path through the city, admiring every sight they passed by. Enthralled in the beauty, Lienad reached down to hold Arura's hand as they walked. He looked over at her and it was as if the glow from the mushrooms enhanced how beautiful she was. The further into the city they got, the more there was to behold. In the center quad, there was an enormous fountain. The water droplets in the air surrounding it were like shimmering sparkles floating around, the sound of the splashing water lulled listeners into a state of pure zen, and there were insects that looked like a small glowing orbs with wings hovering around it. Unbeknownst to them, they were not insects but were, instead, baby Fairies.

As they got further down the path, the castle grew larger in sight. It was, in a single word, stupendous. If you need more words than that feel free to use astonishing, remarkable, phenomenal, or simply just spectacular. The castle was built entirely from massive luminous mushrooms, larger than any they had seen so far. It was surrounded in a rainbow glow. The roof had a fountain that was spewing colored dust straight above, covering the sky and spreading to the stars.

"Wow," Renka was astonished, "So this is where all that dust comes from."

"Well, some of it," Captain Aero let out a small chuckle, "Each planet has their own castle that spews this dust from it. Cerulyt had one as well, when it was still around that is."

The air around them grew awkward with a tense silence. Again, it didn't really affect the others as much as it did Captain Aero. But they still felt sadness about it. A whole planet had been destroyed, which was certainly no joyous matter. Unless, of course, you were a villain of some sort. At which point I do imagine it would give you the warm and fuzzies. If this is the case, please stop reading this story and go crawl in a hole. The deepest and darkest one you can find. One you preferably would not be able to get out of on your own. The universe already has enough villains, it could stand to lose some. I don't know which planet you are reading this from, but I imagine they probably plague your planet in some way as well.

They were nearing the front doors to the castle. The doors were a bright pink, with masterfully etched designs on them. The designs were floral in nature, flowers and leaves on intertwining vines. There were Fairies standing on each side of the door, as if they were the guards. Yet their posture was very relaxed. The closer they got, the more beautiful they could see the Fairies were. They had long bodies, perfectly radiant skin, flowing hair that was vibrant with colors, and stunning unique wings.

"Hey, Aero," a Fairy on the left, with purple wing and green hair, said while waving.

"Ladies," Captain Aero had an oddly suggestive tone

when he spoke to them, "How we doin' tonight?"

"Well, that depends," a Fairy on the right, with red hair and pink wings, said in a bubbly tone, "What brings you here?"

"Unfortunately, it's not a social call," Captain Aero sounded genuinely apologetic, "I'm here for something important that I need to meet with the queen about."

"Aw, no fun," another Fairy on the right, with blue hair and yellow wings, said in a pouting tone.

"I'm not sure she'll want to see you with such a large entourage," the red-haired Fairy said.

"I'm afraid we don't have any other options right now," Captain Aero had gotten more serious with his tone, "It's essential she meets with us, I can't take no for an answer."

"Ooo, I've never heard you get so serious before," A Fairy on the left, with pink hair and light blue wings, said with a giggle, "You should use that tone more often, it's so... masculine."

During this whole exchange, Arura watched closely to see if they were looking at Lienad—and vice-versa.

"Well," Captain Aero grew a sly tone in his voice, "We can talk about that later. Right now, we need to keep moving forward."

"Alright Aero, see you soon," the Fairies all said in

unison while blowing him a kiss.

After this exchange the doors began to slowly swing out towards them, revealing their new path forward. They entered the castle and were greeted by a large garden filled with every sort of flower you could think of, and even more that you don't even realize exist. It was a gorgeous floral rainbow. There were various fountains throughout the garden that all connected to a stream that flowed around the entire perimeter. This was a place that showed you the meaning of serenity in its purest form. Everyone felt completely at peace within the garden. At least, they were until Renka opened his mouth.

"So," Renka broke the peaceful silence, "You seem know those girls pretty well, huh, Aero?"

"Yeah, you could say that," Captain Aero let out a cocky chuckle, "That's all I'll say on that one though."

"Well, think I could get an introduction?" Renka asked—which made things awkward.

"Renka," Arura shouted while slapping his arm, "This is not the time for things like that you pervert."

"Come on man," Lienad shook his head in disappointment.

"BAHA," Captain Aero guffawed, "Unfortunately, I have a reputation to uphold—and introducing you might knock it down more than a few pegs."

"Hmph," Renka quietly pouted in disappointment.

"Now, come on," Captain Aero rushed the group, "The queen's room is at the back of this garden. Let's go get some answers."

They rapidly walked through the pristine garden to the back where there was a pair of giant pastel blue doors. Though they all wished they could have taken a slower pace to really enjoy their scenery. The doors were just solid, no design at all. There was no knob, handle, or button in sight. They were just plain solid doors. As they stood in front of the doors, they heard a feminine and echoing voice fill the room.

"Hello, Aero, and friends," the voice sounded friendly.

"Fyr, my lady," Captain Aero had a cheery tone, "Are you going to let us in? I like looking at you when I talk to you."

After he said that, the doors quickly flew open. Though the way they opened was a bit odd. It happened at a speed that you would expect it to seem forceful, but it wasn't. Instead, it was still very calm. A light smoke cloud and a ton of sparkles billowed out of the dark room. Then the room slowly illuminated from the light of the luminous mushrooms, as if a dimmer switch was being gradually turned on. There had to have been well over two hundred small mushrooms in there.

In the center of the room there was an exceptionally large flower with its petal closed tight. It was remarkably

similar to the Earth flower they call the Curious Lotus. However, it was also quite different as well. The petals had pink and white hues to them, there were multiple twirling strands of golden light surrounding it, and the leaves around the base were each a different shade of blue.

As beautiful as this was, most of the group was confused. Was this flower the Fairy Queen? No, it wasn't, and they were stupid for even thinking that it might have been.

"To see the queen, we have to get the flower to open," Captain Aero had an oddly serious yet ominous tone.

"How do we do that," Renka suddenly grew very uneasy.

"I'm glad you asked?" Captain Aero placed his left wing on Renka's shoulder. "It's really quite easy. Would you like to help?"

"Um," Renka nervously gulped, loud enough for everyone to hear, "I guess so."

"Excellent," Captain Aero slowly pulled out a knife from the interior of his jacket, "Opening the flower requires a blood sacrifice!"

Captain Aero quickly geared the knife back, pointing it at Renka. Trepidation filled the air. Before anyone could react, he forcefully swung the knife down. Stopping just before touching Renka. Everyone else was so unsure of what was going on, or what they should do.

Suddenly, the flower twirled open with a massive and dazzling spray of sparkles all around. When the sparkles faded, a beautiful Fairy was revealed. The most beautiful to have ever existed in fact. Her skin was a pale purple, her wings were pink with golden trim, her hair was a glistening sapphire blue, she had a perfectly curved figure, and her eyes were a bright red. Everyone, including Arura, blushed at the sight of her.

17

The Fairy Queen

"There she is—the Fairy Queen," Captain Aero said, slapping Renka's arm in jest. "I had you totally fooled, BAHA!"

"Yeah, so funny," Renka was still extremely uncomfortable.

"Wow, she is so beautiful," Arura was in awe. She quickly realized she said the out loud and her face grew dark red in embarrassment.

"She really is, isn't she?" Captain Aero was staring intently at the queen, "Fyrnip, it's been a while. It's good to see you're still as gorgeous as ever."

"Oh Aero, you are so kind," Fyrnip sweetly giggled; her voice was like a melody, "What brings you and your generous flattery out this way?"

"Well, there is—," Lienad started, before being cut off by Captain Aero.

"What happened on Cerulyt," Captain Aero had slight aggression in his tone.

"Oh, it was so sad," Fyrnip's tone grew sorrowful, and the pink of her wings turned blue, almost as if the color was reacting to her mood, "The Snuln were doing as they always did, exchanging forks for spoons in the other dimensions. It seems one of the spoons they brought back was armed with an explosive. It seemed almost planned. Whoever planted the explosive knew that eventually the spoon would get brought back to their planet."

Fyrnip paused for a moment out of grief.

"We have no idea who or why. The only Snuln left are the ones that weren't on the planet at the time of the big boom. I have given them a place to stay here, in the castle, until we can fashion them new homes. If the explosion had been any bigger, there is a chance it could have gotten our planet or Spnark as well. We are incredibly lucky that it wasn't."

"I wish there was something I could do," Captain Aero gritted his beak in anger, "If I ever find out who did this, I will make them pay. The Snuln never hurt a single species, not even an insect. They didn't deserve this."

There was a long and uncomfortable silence. No one said a word until the tension started to dissipate. It was one of those moments where the silence only lasted a few minutes but felt as though it was an eternity.

"Queen Fyrnip," Lienad spoke softly, breaking the silence, "There is another reason we are here, if I may."

"Oh please, you don't have to be so formal when addressing me," Fyrnip had a soft and sweet tone again, her wings returning to a pink color, "Please, speak your piece dear child."

"I was given a mission by Neoshyt to assemble this team and come see you," Lienad started, shortening his lengthy tale, "To keep it simple, our overall objective it to take out Krind and thwart his evil plans. To do that, we need your help with Arura and her powers."

"Well, I am not sure who this Neoshyt is. But I would love to help stop the evil cloud from spreading any further in this universe. We have already had enough here in our dimension from just a single event," Fyrnip nodded with her eyes closed, "How can I help and who is Arura?"

"I am Arura," she said while stepping forward.

"Oh," Fyrnip gracefully glided over to look Arura in the eyes, "Yes, I knew you would eventually come here. You want to awaken your powers, don't you?"

"Um, yes," Arura slowly spoke, "How did you know that?"

"How could I not know that?" Fyrnip asked, gleefully laughing. "After all the work I did with your parents, I

was always expecting this visit! Though it is quite a bit later than I would have imagined. How are your parents?"

"Missing, actually," Arura's tone fell into a depression, "They have been missing since I was little. They vanished without a trace, and no one has any clues as to what might have happened. I only recently discovered that I even have any powers. What do you mean the work you did with my parents?"

"Oh, I am so sorry to hear about them. They were always such lovely people," Fyrnip grew a glum tone, her wings once again turned to a blue shade, "I worked with them to combine my blood with other species to create hybrids. Our species is not as bountiful as it used to be. I wanted to find a way for us to live on in some way, but it is hard to find suitable mates for proper reproduction. A hybrid species might have made it easier for us to do so. When all our testing was completed, we had performed the final experiment on you, and it was a success. So, naturally, I knew one day you would come finish the transformation. I just thought that your parents would still be around, and you would have been much younger."

"So that means you will be able to help?" Lienad asked, speaking up so Arura could have a moment to process what she was just told.

"Well, it means I can try," Fyrnip paused in thought. "This is something we had not tested yet. I cannot promise you that it will work."

"Trying is still better than nothing," Lienad assured, "What do we need to do?"

"Wait," Arura interjected, "Do you have any way to be able to help find my parents?"

"Oh... My sweet, sweet girl," Fyrnip hesitated, "I truly wish that I did. I would love to see them again myself. But, without knowing where they might be, I'm afraid I cannot."

"Oh," Arura now had a large pit in her stomach.

There was yet another uncomfortable pause with uneasy tension, which seemed to be a trend in this journey so far. This one was slightly different from the last. You could see that Arura was trying her best to hold back tears, as if her heart was slowly breaking. No one knew what to do or say. This wasn't just a moment that felt longer than it was—it truly lasted a while and felt even longer.

"Do not be so troubled dear," Fyrnip now had a loving tone, "I am confident they are still alive and that you will see them again. Have faith in this, your parents were so intelligent and resourceful. I believe in them."

"Thank you," Arura pressed her hand onto her eyes, presumably to forcefully stop any tears from flowing, "I like to believe that too."

"Now, sweetie," Fyrnip turned back towards the flower, "Are you ready for your transformation?"

"Yes," Arura sniffled and wiped away the small tears

that had begun to form in her eyes, despite her best effort to prevent them.

"Then let's get started," Fyrnip waved her hand down at the flower in the floor.

As she waved her hand, glitter spewed out and smothered the flower. Once it was completely covered, it snapped closed. They could feel the ground begin to rumble and grumble beneath them. Suddenly, the flower exploded open with a quickness, spewing the glitter all around. It was so rapid that the glitter rushed by like a sandstorm. In the center of the flower was now something that looked like a pod of some sort. It was a dull silver and looked very plain compared to everything else they had seen in this room and on this planet.

"I cannot promise this will work," Fyrnip cautioned, "This was the next step your parents and I were discussing, but we were never able to test it."

"We have to try," Arura was ready to see her parent's plan fulfilled, "What do I need to do?"

"Please go into the silver device and I will handle the rest," Fyrnip motioned towards the pod.

Arura began walking towards the pod and the suspense in the air grew thick. Everyone was anxious to see what was to come next. Lienad was plagued with thoughts of the potential ways this could go wrong and the guilt he would feel if it did. As she got within inches of the pod, it opened automatically. There was just enough room for a single human of average stature to stand. She stepped inside, and the door closed behind her.

"Alright," Fyrnip hesitated, "Now comes the tricky part."

This being referred to as "the tricky part" increased the overall level of anxiety among the group. They stood there, watching intently. Fyrnip geared her hands back and thrust them toward the pod with vigor. Rays of blue-violet light shot from her hands, engulfing the pod. Sparks of an electric green wildly flew around as the rays made contact. There was loud whirring, whooshing, zipping, and zapping filling the area as a swirling wind began to pick up. It was as if there was a small storm within the room. With every passing moment the perturbation increased among the group.

After a while, I can't really say exactly how long, Fyrnip lifted her hands to stop the rays. The pod pulsed with a bright periwinkle light. Fyrnip snapped her fingers. Suddenly the pod was engulfed by the flower, closing so fast that if you blinked you would have missed it happening. Smoke quickly began to rise from the tip of the closed petals. The anticipation of it all was almost completely unbearable. After about a minute or two, the petals slowly opened. Once the flower was completely open the room became deafeningly quiet.

"The process is finished," Fyrnip sounded

exhausted.

"Did it work?" Lienad hoped for the best but still had lingering fear that things had gone awry.

"We are about to find out," Fyrnip had a hopeful tone. Though her not already knowing the answer didn't help for softening anyone's fears.

The smoke around the center of the flower began to dissipate. They could see the pod, still pulsing with light, come into view. Slowly, the pod began to open. As it did, a pink fog rolled out of it. They could see Arura standing there, completely still with her eyes closed. When she opened her eyes, they were a glowing lime green color. Her eyes were electrifying to say the least. Whether this whole experience was a success or not, it was clear that something happened.

"Arura?" Lienad timorously asked. "Are you okay, my love?"

There was a long moment of silence. No one said a thing. No one moved a muscle. The longer this went on, the less positive and hopeful everyone felt. This went on until eventually every ounce of hope had all but dissolved. Then finally, it was stopped.

"I'm fine dear," Arura spoke softly and slowly, "I'm fine."

"Wonderful," Lienad cheered as his heavy heart had just been lightened ten-fold.

"I don't know," Renka joked, "If I know anything about women it's when they say that they are fine it means something is actually wrong."

"Renka," Arura yelled, "The only thing wrong here is you."

"Well, guess you are still you," he laughingly retorted.

As Arura looked at Renka, gritting her teeth, you could see her eyes start to turn a vibrant orange. It was almost as if her eyes, like the Fairy wings, changed color in reaction to her mood. Which, at this current time, was irritated.

"So, how do we know if this was a complete success," Arura relaxed her jaw and looked up at Fyrnip.

"Well, the only way to really know is to have you do something that only a Fairy can do," Fyrnip said, softly biting on her left index finger. "Let me think. What would be a good entry level thing to test, hmm."

She sat there pondering for a moment, gliding around in a pacing motion. Everyone was curious what she was going to have Arura do as a test, as there had to be plenty of things that only a fairy could do. That train of thought was absolutely correct. There is a plethora of things that only a Fairy can do, and it falls within a very wide range of difficulty.

"AH," Fyrnip shouted, "I know what to do!"

"What is it," Arura was filled with a mix of excitement and panic.

"This," Fyrnip snapped her fingers.

After she snapped, a small book materialized in her hand. The cover had a soft green glow to it and the pages had a pale-yellow glow. From here everyone assumed that this book was in some way the answer, which they were correct about.

"This is the Fypendiumedia," Fyrnip said with a smile, "This is a book that only Fairies can read. It contains all our magic spells."

"Really," Arura was very confused, "But it's so small. Are the words inside really that tiny?"

"Oh no dear," Fyrnip said with a laugh, "That's just part of the magic behind it."

She handed the book over to Arura. Which, much to Arura's surprise, revealed so much. The title of the book came into clear view. Arura opened the cover, revealing a lengthy table of contents. This book was like an electronic tablet-sized computer of some sort. She scrolled through the contents, and it stopped on a specific spell: Sparkotusalis. She decided to press it, which immediately took her to the spell page. It was a pretty awesome artifact. Here it had information about what the spells does, and how to do it. Unfortunately, I don't know enough to tell you how to do the spell. I am, after all, not a fairy.

"I think I'll give this one a try," Arura decidedly said.

The group watched, wondering what was going to happen next. Arura closed her eyes, held her right hand out, and focused. Suddenly, in her palm a beautiful blue lotus flower bloomed. She opened her eyes, proud of herself for getting that far. Then she snapped with her left hand. The lotus petals swung closed, and from their tip burst a fountain of pure white sparkles.

"Oh, the Sparkotusalis spell," Fyrnip said, clearly impressed, "To be able to do that so quickly, after just reading about it is quite a feat. It seems not only was the transition successful, but you have more power than your parent's and I could have hoped for."

"Really?" Arura was a little choked up, holding back tears of a bittersweet feeling of accomplishment. "I'm so happy to hear that. Fulfilling their dreams..."

Lienad wrapped his arms around her and pulled her in close. He tightly embraced her as she laid her head on his right shoulder. It was a very emotional moment. No one ever really thinks about how emotional moments make everyone else around them feel. But it really is a little awkward, Captain Aero and Renka weren't sure what to do or say; so, they stayed quite until it was over.

"So," Renka started, "Now that the whole Fairy stuff is over, what are we supposed to do next?"

"Don't you ever pay attention?" Arura snapped at

him, rolling her eyes.

"BAHA," Captain Aero laughed, "You have heard this explained so many times and still you ask? I've heard it less times than you, I'm sure, and even I know what we do next!"

"Renka," Lienad shook his head and placed his hand to his forehead, once again disappointed in him, "From here we need to travel to Pecoaphlyly to get the crystal sword. Was it really that hard to remember?"

"Listen a lot has happened, it can be easy to forget," Renka hung his head a little. He felt a bit abashed, and rightfully so—considering he had heard this explained more than once already.

"Did you say the crystal sword?" Fyrnip asked, her tone slightly concerned. "I just realized you never told me more about this mission past what you needed from me. So, your next stop is to retrieve the crystal sword?"

"Yeah, that's our next step," Lienad had a calm tone.

"My dear child," Fyrnip said, turning her gaze to Arura, "Take that copy of the Fypendiumedia with you. I believe you're going to need it. Place your hand on the book with intent of what you're wanting, and the spell will be revealed to you, always remember that."

"Thank you," Arura gave a gracious curtsy.

"I can see why you needed me to try all of this," Fyrnip said, "Long ago it was we Fairies who crafted the crystal

sword. We imbued it with our magic and only a Fairy can release its bind. I don't know what your mission entails after the sword, nor do I think I want to. But should you ever need my help again, please do not hesitate to come see me."

"Thank you, your majesty," Lienad gave a slight bow. "We should get going."

"My queen," Captain Aero said, giving a far more lavish bow; almost as if he was trying to outdo Lienad's. He then turned to the rest of the group. "Let's start our walk back to the ship."

"Oh," Fyrnip said with a giggle, "There's no need for that."

She reached her hands above her head and clapped. In an instant the group was smothered in a colorful cloud. As the cloud dispersed, they could see they were now inside Captain Aero's ship. They quickly shook off the change and got ready to leave. Arura took herself to the sleeping quarters to ensure she had peace and quiet, she planned on reading the Fypendiumedia on their flight to Pecoaphlyly. Captain Aero got settled in his captain's chair, Renka went to the dining area for food, and Lienad sat down closing his eyes to process everything that had happened thus far.

18

The Stink

Captain Aero made some adjustments on his dash and walked over to the navigation system. He flipped through the holographic options. While he was doing this, Renka walked over to observe what he was doing. Captain Aero stopped and looked over at him.

"What's going on? Do you need something?" Captain Aero asked, his tone abrasive.

"No," Renka backed up a little, "Just watching what you're doing."

"I mean, it's pretty obvious what I'm doing," Captain Aero clearly wanted Renka to leave him alone.

"Yeah, it is," Renka was oblivious to Captain Aero's cues.

"Can you go bother someone else," Captain Aero grew frustrated, which was easy to see from his tone and body language.

"Woah, what's with the harshness," Renka was still confused why Captain Aero was getting so frustrated with him.

"Just getting a bit tired," Captain Aero said while pressing his wing to his forehead, "I just need a Z-Capsule."

Captain Aero walked over to his pilot's chair and pressed a series of buttons on the left arm. A hatch opened on the right arm and a Z-capsule levitated out. He took it and rapidly started to feel better. Though he would have been better off just getting some actual sleep. The moodiness he was dealing with was just a symptom of the prolonged use of Z-capsules. It makes emotional regulation exceedingly difficult and requires a full detoxification to return to normal.

"See, all better," Captain Aero gleefully said.

"Yeah, sure," Renka was a bit uncomfortable by this interaction, as it was obvious Captain Aero had too much of a reliance on those pills, "I'm gonna go over there."

"We should be at our destination before you know it," Captain Aero assured.

Renka walked away to use the bathroom and Captain Aero finished up at the navigation station. Captain Aero sat down and pressed the dimensional hopper. Before

anyone realized it, they were in the Gaseous Dimension. Which was, as you could guess, very gassy.

"Oh, ugh, it smells absolutely rancid," Arura dry heaved and pinched her nose, "How is that scent getting into the ship?"

"It's not," Captain Aero said, confused, "There's no way for it to penetrate inside. I have never had this happen before."

"I see," Lienad grew a very irritated look.

Frantically, Lienad looked around the room. He was trying to see if he could find the source of the smell. Maybe there was a leak that Aero wasn't aware of, at least that's what he had hoped. As he rummaged around, he picked up a small bag. Once he held it, his face turned green.

"RENKA," Lienad screamed louder than anyone had ever heard him shout—hurting everyone's ears. "ARE YOU KIDDING ME?"

"What is it?" Renka asked, wiping his hands as he left the bathroom. "Oh—What is that smell?"

"I don't know," Lienad angrily held up the small bag, glaring at Renka, "Why don't you tell me?"

"Oh..." Renka grew quiet. "That."

"What do you mean that?" Arura's face flushed with anger. "You mean to tell me that you know what's causing this smell? Which means it's probably your fault!"

"Yeah..." Renka hesitated, "I brought some research along with me. I didn't know what we might find out here that may help me along with it."

"Research," Arura shouted, "So you mean to tell me that you brought—"

"Yes, some of his special weapons," Lienad interrupted her, trying not to state the exact nature of Renka's research in front of Aero.

"What's that supposed to mean?" Captain Aero was starting to get a bit irate. "What did you bring on my ship, kid?"

"Yeah Renka," Arura had a mix of anger and sass in her voice, "Why don't you go ahead and tell him?"

"Well, you see, I am leading the charge in developing a very special type of weaponry," Renka had a tentative confidence, "For a lack of better words, they are flatulence-based weapons that disarm enemies through the use of smells."

"Um," Captain Aero paused, "Did you really just try to make a fart blaster sound fancy and scientific?"

"It's not a fart blaster," Renka retorted, embarrassed and upset.

"I mean, it kind of is bud," Lienad softly placed his right hand on Renka's left shoulder. "It kind of is."

"Whatever," Renka had a melancholy tone, "One

day you guys will understand their importance.”

“So, you just brought a whole bunch of stink juices into my ship,” Captain Aero snapped to a more serious tone, “That is something that should have been mentioned to me in advance so I could have told you to get rid of them. I don’t want that crap inside of Sussu.”

“Sorry,” Renka stared down, rotating his left foot on the floor.

“You need to get a new hobby kid,” Captain Aero gave out the slightest of chuckles, “Please tell me you at least know how to get rid of this smell.”

“Well,” Renka said, followed by a variety of nervous sounds, “Here’s the deal. With this formula, I have only been able to get the smell away with time.”

“I’m going to kill you!” Arura lunged out towards Renka—her fist clenched and geared back—but was restrained by Lienad.

“How much time,” Lienad was hoping it wasn’t exceedingly long.

“Well, sometimes it goes away within just a couple of hours,” Renka responded.

“A couple of hours,” Lienad dropped his head, “That’s not great, but it could be worse.”

“What do you mean by sometimes,” Captain Aero was now giving Renka a death glare.

"Well, in rare cases, and I do mean very rare," Renka hesitated, debating whether or not to be honest, "It can last a full week."

"A WEEK?" the remainder of the group yelled out in unison.

"Wow did you all practice that or something," Renka attempted to make the situation lighter with a joke. He was not successful.

"STOP IT," the group yelled out.

The group looked at each other, shocked by being in perfect unison once again. Then they turned a piercing gaze toward Renka. During all of this, I was incredibly surprised that no one cared to figure out how vial of filth broke. It was, in fact, Renka's fault. When he was going to the bathroom, he accidentally kicked his bag, breaking the vial. If they had known this, the situation would have probably been worse for him.

"I'm going to go see if there is anywhere that doesn't stink," Lienad walked off while covering his nose inside his shirt.

The others nodded in agreement and left the area. Renka, however, stayed behind in a shitty pity party. Captain Aero stayed up front in his chair. The smell was still there, but not as strong. Because of his genetics, his sense of smell was the least developed among the group; this made it easier for him to deal with. Lienad and Arura went back to the sleeping quarters. It was still malodorous, but it wasn't nearly as bad.

Arura has started reading the Fypendiumedia again, hoping to learn as much as she could in her available time. Lienad had decided he was going to try and take a quick nap, even if it were only long enough to be a power nap. He laid his head upon the pillow and closed his eyes. As soon as he started to drift off Arura yelled out in excitement, startling him awake.

"Huh," Lienad exclaimed, flustered, "What's wrong?"

"Nothing's wrong babe," Arura gave a cute giggle, "In fact, it's the opposite. I have the solution to our problem!"

"And which problem exactly?" Lienad asked while rubbing the sleep out of his eyes. "We have a number of them to choose from."

"The one actively plaguing us," Arura had a serious yet playful tone, "The scent problem."

"Oh, that problem," Lienad said, laying his head back down and closing his eyes. "What's your solution to that one then sweetie?"

"I found a spell in here called Florascentmyst," Arura said, extremely excited, "It fills the area with a floral scent and eliminates any odors."

"Well, that sounds promising," Lienad said as he let

out a yawn. "You go try that and I'm going to get some sleep."

"What?" Arura exclaimed in irritation. "You're not gonna come watch me do something amazing?"

"Oh, no," Lienad let out a timid chuckle, "Of course I'm gonna come watch. I was only kidding."

"Mhm, that's what I thought," She responded with sass, "Come on then, let's go."

They walked out of the sleeping quarters and into the main area of the ship, which was still extremely rancid. Renka was still sitting within his self-pity, and Captain Aero was continuing to man the front. Arura clasped her hands together and focused. She raised her hands to her face, placing her mouth onto a hole she made between her thumbs. She then took a deep breath in through her nose and slowly blew into her hands. After a few seconds of blowing she opened her hands, revealing a light green, mist-like, orb floating there. She took another deep breath and blew the orb with a moderate amount of force. This caused the mist to rapidly spread and dissipate, leaving the room smelling like a flower garden.

"Oh," Lienad said, taking a deep sniff. "That is so much better."

"Yay!" Arura said as she clapped her hands together, beaming with pride and excitement. "I'm so happy that it actually worked!"

"Me too," Renka sadly chimed, "Sorry I caused it in the first place."

"You know," Arura said with a soft smile, "I'm honestly not even that mad anymore."

"Wow," Renka's demeanor brightened up a little, "I thought for sure you were angry. I mean let's be honest it was so bad."

"Yeah, it was. No need to remind me, unless you're wanting me to get angry again," Arura said with a tone that was upbeat, yet a tad aggressive as well, "The only reason I'm not still mad is because it gave me a chance to test out something from this book."

"You know, I love you so much," Lienad said, pulling her close for a passionate kiss.

'Oh," Arura said while caressing his face with her right hand, blushing, "Not that I'm mad at it, but what got into you there."

"Nothing, just how smart and beautiful you are," Lienad stared deeply into her eyes, "Plus the smell of flowers helped set the mood."

"Well, don't let me stop you now," Arura pulled his face back in for another romantic kiss.

"Um," Renka uncomfortably chimed, "You know me and bird man are still here, right?"

"Bird man?" Captain Aero abruptly shouted. "Please

give me more respect than that. Besides, who cares? If you don't like watching it, go do something else."

"Sorry guys," Lienad chuckled, "I guess I got so lost in the moment and forgot that the universe was anything more than just her and I."

19

The Guide

"Yeah," Renka slowly said, "That's really sweet and all, but there's other rooms in the ship for a reason."

"Renka!" Arura shouted, punching him in the left arm. "Do you really have to ruin every moment?"

"Ouch," he winced. "There's the anger."

"There's more where that comes from if you don't shut your trap," she retorted.

"Sorry to interrupt your little tiff," Captain Aero waved his right wing, "We are approaching Pecoaphlyly".

"Wow," Arura said with awe, "I've never seen so many beautiful crystals in one place."

"How long has it been since you have been here?" Lienad placed his left hand on Renka's right shoulder.

"Not since my parent's died so long ago," Renka started feeling a little sad, "It's nice to see it again."

Lienad gave Renka's shoulder a little pat and moved over toward Arura. He wrapped his left arm around her waist as they looked out on the planet. It was, after all, quite beautiful. Because of the high crystal content on the planet, it was a shimmering and sparkling sight to behold for sure. As they descended, everything became so clear. It was as if the crystals somehow deflected the gasses that filled the space of this dimension. Under better circumstances, it would be a romantic destination. Sadly, they only had limited time to take it all in since they were on a mission.

"You know," Lienad whispered into Arura's ear, "When this is all over, we should come have a picnic here."

"Oh," she softly responded, "I would love that. We'll add it to the list of places we will go."

"Then it's a date," he winked and leaned in for a kiss.

"Ahem," Renka interrupted, "Sorry to break up the love session here. But we are in the dimensions where they bad guys are, on a mission to stop them. We probably don't have any time to waste."

"Fine," Arura angrily looked at Renka. She was contemplating on whether or not to hurt him for ruining yet another moment.

"So, romance killer," Lienad joked, "Since you're so pressed to get on with the mission, care to tell us where the crystal cave is? We're on your planet after all."

"Oh, um... that," Renka stuttered, his voice anxious, "Here's the thing, I don't actually know."

"What?" Lienad said, starting to feel a little irritated, "Why are you just now telling me that you don't know where it is?"

"Well, I didn't really want to put a damper on things," he responded while hanging his head, "Sorry about that."

"If I may," Captain Aero joined, "I'm not really one to stick up for this kid, but let's be fair about this. There are crystals literally everywhere and I'm fairly sure there is more than one cave on this entire planet."

"You're right," Lienad sighed, "I'm sorry for getting irritated there. Do you remember anything about any legends from here that may help?"

"Actually, I do," Renka responded, lifting his head with a hopeful look, "I'm not sure how much it will help, but I do remember one."

He proceeded to tell them the one legend he remembered. Rather than hear his wretched version of recounting the legend, I think we would all enjoy simply reading my version of it. Not to seem too full of myself, but I am a far superior storyteller than Renka. If you knew how bad his rendition was, you would be very thankful to me for shielding you from it.

Long ago, before memories were reliably kept, the planet was visited by a creature of starlight. It knelt before the king, warning of a power too great to be destroyed. One that threatened the very fabric of time. The creature pleaded for the king's aid, that this power was hidden until the very last star fizzled from the sky.

The king's lands were barren, his people were suffering. He offered a bargain: save his people and he would pledge his kingdom's protection, a promise that will bind all future generations. The creature readily agreed and produced a single seed. Plant and water it for four days and on the fifth day his lands would flourish, it instructed.

Skeptical but desperate, the king obeyed. He planted the seed and watered it daily. On the fifth day, he awoke to a surprise. His whole kingdom shimmered with crystals of all shapes and size. The creature revealed that the crystals were eternal, and their uses were endless.

True to his word, the king sealed the covenant with a handshake. The power was hidden in a village far off, its location shrouded in secrecy. No maps would be made, nor paths to be marked, ensuring its protection until the end of time.

I hope you enjoyed my version of the tale. It was a drastic improvement upon the inane dribble Renka thought would pass as a decent story. I cannot stress enough how lucky you are to read mine instead of his. Unfortunately, that was not the case for the group, they all had to endure his.

"Okay," Arura said as she placed her right hand on her chin, "So, to summarize your story, there was a thing that brought some kind of item to a king here, for the king to hide it the thing helped create all these crystals, and now the item is hidden somewhere that no one knows. Is that the gist of the story you told?"

"Yeah, basically," Renka said with a nod. "But it's just an old children's tale. So, I'm sorry if it didn't help."

"Well, let's just assume that the legend is true. I think the item from the story was most likely the crystal sword," Lienad pondered, "Or at least something to do with the crystal sword."

"You know what, when you put it like that..." Renka gasped. "I think you're right! I never would have guessed that."

"Clearly," Captain Aero laughed, "Since you didn't even think that tale would help, BAHA!"

"Guys, there's still one big problem," Arura said, moving her hand to her forehead. "The way the story goes no one has any idea where it is or how to find it."

"Oh yeah," Lienad now had a stressed tone and began rubbing his temples. "This is such a headache."

From there, none of them really knew what to do. Captain Aero went back to his seat in the front. Arura went to the back to keep reading. Renka went to the bathroom.

Lienad decided the best thing he could do was to try and reach out to Neoshyt. Unfortunately, no matter how hard he tried, he was unable to make any contact. This was very disheartening, as it made him feel even more hopeless than he already did. Neoshyt was always supposed to be available for this mission that had been thrust upon Lienad. Yet here he was, with radio silence. Now he really had no idea what they were going to do.

"YES," Arura shouted so loud that it reverberated through the entire ship, "I know what to do!"

"What is it?" Lienad loudly asked—now feeling a glimmer of hope.

"There is a spell for this exact situation," Arura said while running into the main room of the ship.

"There's a spell that was designed for finding the crystal cave?" Renka asked in surprise.

"No, you idiot," She sarcastically responded, "There is a spell for finding things that you want in general. It's called Rewayvelus Luminpathis."

"Oh, babe," Lienad said with glee, "Leave it to you to once again be the solution to our problems. You're so amazing."

"Thank you," she giddily responded, blushing a dark red.

"Well," Renka asserted, "Do it then, what are you waiting for?"

"Can you not be such an ass," She said, lightly punching him in the arm. "Give me some space and silence."

She closed her eyes, focused intensely, placing two fingers from each hand on her temples. She then slid them to her eyes. Everyone kept their distance and remained so quiet you could've heard a blade of grass hit the floor. After a few moments, she put her hands down and opened her eyes.

"Wow," she exclaimed, "Can you guys see that?"

"Um," Lienad slowly said as he looked around, "See what exactly, sweetie?"

"The colorful stream," she was initially surprised no one else could see it, "It's so bright!"

"It must just be a fairy thing," Lienad said, trying hard to look around for this stream. "I can't see anything, what about you guys?"

Captain Aero and Renka both looked around, also unable to see what Arura was talking about. They shook their heads, almost in unison. With this being the case, Lienad knew what needed to happen next.

"Arura," Lienad said with a lightly serious tone, while grabbing her hand. "You're going to have to be our guide and tell Aero which way to go. Seems only you can see the path."

"Oh," Arura grew a bit nervous. She started thinking

about the different things that could go wrong if it was just a hallucination. "I'll do my best."

Captain Aero got ready in his chair, Renka anxiously sat back down, and Lienad held Arura's hand as she got ready to give directions. It may not see like a big deal, simply telling someone which direction to fly. But they were in an unfamiliar place and Arura had to trust that what she saw was real. She led them along various twists and turns, Captain Aero flying as cautiously as he could. This went on for a while, until they got stopped in front of a huge crystal structure with no openings. It looked like a dead end.

"Well, what now," Captain Aero said, looking to see if there was a visible way around this blockage.

"The stream looks like it keeps going straight into the crystal," Arura was beginning to feel even more worried that what she saw really was just an illusion.

"So, this thing you see just wants us to crash," Renka exclaimed with an alarmed tone.

"I doubt that's the case," Lienad moved his hand onto Arura's shoulder for comfort, "Maybe there just isn't something we see."

"I can't see any other way around this thing," Captain Aero Continued looking from side to side, "Who knows what will happen if we try veering off. What's the next great idea?"

Arura felt so bad, she led them into a whole lot of nothing. Lienad could easily see how bad she felt, which hurt his heart. Everyone sat there, pondering what to do next. But Lienad had an idea.

"I trust Arura," he said, giving her shoulder a slight squeeze, "We should just move forward."

"You want me to fly straight into this thing," Captain Aero questioned in complete disbelief.

"Are you insane?" Renka asked, filled with panic. "We will crash!"

"Even I'm not so sure about that," Arura said in a solemn tone.

"I am," Lienad declared with confidence, "There's no way you could be wrong, Arura; I believe in you. Aero, we don't have time to waste—and we're out of other options."

"Alright, here we go then," Captain Aero said, filled with uncertainty.

Captain Aero braced his controls, hesitating to start. Renka put his head between his knees, hoping for the best. Lienad held Arura tight and stared deeply into her eyes. Captain Aero pushed forward, slowly, bracing himself for impact.

"I love you, more than I could ever describe," Lienad said while still staring into Arura's eyes. He wanted to make sure that just in case something happened, those would be

the last words he said to her.

The whole team got ready for a potential impact, closing their eyes at the last second. But as they finally reached the crystal, they simply passed straight through. They opened their eyes and saw they were now inside of it. Revealing a small village down on the floor. All of them were just as amazed as they were relieved.

"I see the path again!" Arura exclaimed—her voice full of excitement.

"Well, my dear, then please lead the way," Lienad said with a wide grin.

Arura continued to guide them along the path she saw, which wasn't much longer of a trip. Soon they approached a high up plateau that had a cave entrance on top. They had arrived at the Crystal Cave, assuming that wasn't already obvious.

20

The Crystal Cave

Captain Aero landed the ship near the cave's entrance, and they all went outside. As they exited the ship, they noticed a Smeglin with teal skin standing in front of the cave's entrance. I realize that some of the less explored readers may be unfamiliar with what exactly a Smeglin is, so I will give you a brief breakdown. The Smeglin are a unique species in that they have two heads atop individual necks, each with their own mind. Their skin is usually of a blue or green hue. It is common that at least one head will have one or more horns on it, sometimes this is seen on both heads. However, rarely, there are occurrences of neither head having any horns. They are known for having average, or slightly above average, intellectual capacities. Outside of their crystal farming abilities, there isn't much that stands out about them.

Naturally, they were all on guard when approaching the Smeglin. After all, the Smeglin were supposed to be under the control of Krind and his thugs. When they got closer, they could see that both heads had leather-like helmets on, they were wearing a protective chest plate, and they had a spear in hand. While the gear was not very advanced, the group was still prepared for potential hostility. They paused about 20 feet away from the Smeglin, and Lienad stepped forward.

"Hello, my name is Lienad," he raised his right hand, "We do not come to you as a threat."

"You say you're not a threat," the left head said, "And that we shouldn't fret."

"But this place is well hidden," the right head spoke, "And visitors are forbidden."

"Um, is the rhyming thing on purpose, or just how you naturally talk?" Lienad asked, scratching the back of his head.

"You ask of our rhyme," the left head started, "I ask if it's a crime?"

"Can our words not flow?" the right head asked. "Like a poem?"

"You idiot," the left head shouted, "That doesn't rhyme. We have been waiting forever to have a visitor to be able to do this to. We finally have one and you try to rhyme flow with poem! How stupid can you be?"

"Sorry," the right head said while drooping a bit.

"You got that right," the left head said while glaring at the right, "Anyways, I am Cri, and this is Stol. We are the guardians of this cave. How and why are you here?"

"We have come for the Crystal Sword," Lienad expressed, "We got here by following a magic trail."

"How could you possibly know about the crystal sword?" Cri frantically asked.

"What do you mean a magic trail," Stol added, "There are no maps or marked paths that can lead anyone here. Plus, we are hidden inside of a giant crystal."

"Okay," Lienad sighed, "Let me explain, and brace yourselves because it's a long story."

Lienad then went on to explain their story once again. At this point he was getting tired of telling the tale and would streamline some most of it. During the recounting Cri looked genuinely interested in what Lienad was saying. Stol, however, did not. By the time he was finished, their expressions did not change.

"So, what do you say," Lienad was slightly exasperated from the long story, "Can we go in and get what we need?"

"Oh, yeah, sure thing," Cri excitedly answered.

"NO," Stol yelled out, "Why would we let them in, just because they told us some boring story? For all we

know they are lying about all of it!"

"Why do you always have to think the worst?" Cri asked.

"For starters, this guy said that our people are under control of this Krind thing. If that's the case, why wouldn't we already be aware of that?"

"Because we are hidden away from everything and everyone, obviously," Cri snickered.

"Okay fine, that's a fair point," Stol was still frustrated, "But how do we know that this person isn't really Krind?"

"Well, I guess we don't," Cri paused for a moment, "But he seems like a nice guy, I think we should trust him."

"Well, I don't," Stol argued back.

"Yes," Cri shouted.

"No," Stol tried to shout louder.

This went on for a while. A non-stop back and forth between the two heads. Lienad had contemplated whether he could just sneak in while they were busy arguing but ultimately decided not to. Eventually, this argument came to an end.

"We have come to a decision," Cri looked at the group.

"Indeed," Stol joined, "We don't know if we can fully

trust you."

"So here is what we will do."

"Two of you may go in."

"The other two have to stay with us."

"Um, yeah, I think that sounds fair," Lienad nodded in agreement, looking at the rest of the group.

"So, who is going?" Renka asked with a quiet gulp.

"Well, since we are here because of me I will obviously take the risk," Lienad said with certainty, "The real question is who is coming with me?"

"I'll go," Arura quickly answered, "It needs to be me, who else is going to protect you?"

"How funny my love," Lienad smiled, pulling her in tight.

"Well, I won't argue that," Renka was relieved that he didn't have to go in, "Guess you should get going. You know, time crunch and all."

"You sure you don't want to come instead?" Lienad asked in jest.

"Oh, heh, no, I think you two got this," Renka slowly backed up a bit as he said this.

"Don't worry, I'll keep him out of trouble and the ship ready," Captain Aero assured.

Lienad and Arura turned and walked towards the

cave. They stopped at the entrance, looked at each other, smiled, and clasped hands. Then they walked into the cave, hand in hand. It was a surprisingly short walk until they found themselves in an alcove where the crystal sword was floating in the center. Lienad reached out to grab it but was unsuccessful.

"Argh, uh, humph," Lienad grunted while trying to get the sword, "This, sword, just, won't, BUDGE."

"Don't waste your strength," she placed her hand on his shoulder.

"You're right," he sighed, "Maybe there is a clue or something around here on how to get this damn thing."

The two of them looked around, until Lienad saw an engraving of sorts on the wall. It was not exceptionally large. But, if he focused well enough, he could make it out. It looked like winged figures standing around a sword. One of the figures looked as though it was blowing a kiss toward the sword, with swirling lines coming from their hand. He immediately stopped to show Arura.

"Looks at this," he said, pointing at the pictures, "Maybe I'm wrong here, but I feel like these figures around the sword are supposed to be fairies."

"You could be right," she squinted a bit while giving her answer, "I wonder if the creature of starlight from the legend was a fairy."

"That's what it looks like at least," he moved his

finger, "What about this one? What do you think they could be blowing from their hand?"

"I'm not sure. I didn't bring my bag, so I don't have my book," she had a disappointed look on her face.

"There's no way you could have known we would need it," he pulled her in for a hug, "We will think of something here."

Lienad held Arura tightly, she laid her head upon his chest. Neither of them really knew what to do next. Lienad tried to think, but deep down, he knew he would probably be useless in this situation. Which was true, he was. Suddenly, Arura lifted her head up and rapidly patted his chest twice.

"I just remembered something," she gasped, "There was some spell I had glossed over in the book that mentioned breaking a crystal binding. I don't really remember too clearly, but I think it was called Crysbrea Brisunaish."

"Oh, that's amazing," he said with excitement, wincing a little because she didn't realize how hard her pats were, "Do you remember how to do it? It would probably be worth a try."

"Not really," she was slightly disappointed in herself, "But, I mean, I can try to remember."

"I believe in you," he hugged her tighter, "Just try your best to remember."

She stepped back and closed her eyes, completely

focused on trying to remember. As the seconds passed, the anticipation grew. After a while, she opened her eyes and gave a nod. She then cupped her hands in front of her, twisting them as if she was forming a snowball. Slowly light began to shine through the gaps of her hands. When she opened her hands, there was a bright pink orb in the palm of her right hand. It was so radiant that it illuminated the entire alcove as if the sun was in there with them. She leaned forward and blew the orb towards the sword. Once the orb touched the sword, it exploded into a million shimmering sparkles. When the light dimmed back down, nothing looked any different.

"Everything still looks the same," she was completely defeated, "I thought for sure that would work."

"Hey," Lienad tried to sound comforting, "We still don't know if it failed."

Lienad reached forward and grabbed the handle of the sword. He sat there for a moment, bracing himself. He pulled the sword with all his force, which sent him backwards falling to the ground. He stood up, sword in hand, smiling.

"See," he said, pulling Arura back to him, "I knew you were amazing. Let's get back out there now."

Arura hesitated to leave his embrace, just as he hesitated to let her go. But they knew they had to get on with their mission. They walked back through the cave, hand in hand once again. Upon exiting the cave, Cri and Stol were sitting right next to the entrance. In the distance, Renka and Captain Aero were right next to the ship; it looked like they were having a bit of an argument.

"You're back," Cri turned his head towards Arura and Lienad.

"I see you have the sword," Stol sounded disgruntled.

"Hey," Captain Aero shouted while waving as he walked over, "So this part of the mission is complete now, yeah?"

"Yeah, that's all we needed here," Lienad looked at the sword and twisted it in his hand, "Now we can move on."

"I still don't trust you," Stol huffed.

"But I do," Cri reminded them, "I hope you can succeed in saving everything like you talked about."

"We will try our best," Lienad paused, "I'll do whatever it takes to succeed."

"Well, good luck, guess you should get going," Cri gave them a little wave.

"I still think this was a bad idea," Stol looked away from the group.

"Well, hopefully you never have to realize how right we are, and this gets fixed before it ever reaches you," Lienad placed his hand on the shoulder on Cri's side of the

body, "Thank you, for letting us do this. I hope to see you again one day, under better circumstances."

"See you then," Cri waved as the group started walking back to the ship.

When the group returned to the ship, there was a general feeling of relief among them. This was yet another major milestone completed towards saving the universe. They all grabbed a drink, sat around the table, and settled in for a moment. The air around them was light as they relaxed.

"So," Lienad broke the peaceful silence, "I guess we should game plan the next move."

"Yeah, Atlantis is next, right," Captain Aero nodded with his eyes closed and head leaned back.

"That's right," Lienad took a sip of his drink.

"Where is that at," Renka assumed he wasn't the only one with this question.

"Big surprise," Arura sarcastically retorted, "Renka doesn't know something."

"Ease up babe, it's completely fair that he doesn't know an old Earth legend," Lienad rubbed her shoulder, "Not everyone takes the time to learn everything they can when they can like you."

"Fine, you're right," She softly said, leaning her head onto his hand, "Atlantis is an old Earth legend about a lost

civilization. There are plenty of theories about it, but no one really knows for sure.”

“Wait, we have to find something that no one knows where it is?” Renka let out a disgruntled sigh as he dropped his head.

“BAHA,” Captain Aero chuckled, “Once again, that’s part of why I am so amazing. I know where it is and how to get there.”

“That’s part of why Neoshyt had us get Captain Aero as part of our crew,” Lienad raised his glass towards him, “It seems most of our mission has had a heavy reliance on him. We should all be grateful.”

They all raised their glasses and clinked them together before slamming them back in one swig. It was true, Captain Aero was one of the most integral members of the team. Which boosted his ego tremendously. He clearly appreciated all the praise. Following the drink, they all started to get up from the table.

“I’ll go start getting the ship ready for travel to Earth,” Captain Aero started walking towards his control panel, “Things will get a little bumpy on this trip, I suggest using the facilities now, BAHA!”

They did not hesitate to do just that. After the issues they have had on other moments of the trip, they wanted to avoid a potential mess they had to clean up. Once each of them finished they joined Captain Aero in the front of the ship. They all sat down as he finished doing whatever he was doing to get things ready.

"We all ready?" Captain Aero called out. "Doesn't matter—we're off anyway!"

"Oh crap," Lienad exclaimed, "I just realized we haven't said anything to Commander Scenkid since before we even left Anigav! We should probably call him."

Lienad, Arura, and Renka gathered around as Arura pulled out her Trans Dimensional Communication Device. It was a small, round, silver circle that provided holographic communications. They dialed in to call the commander as Captain Aero started their trek off the planet.

"Agent Arura, Spleen, and Brelain," Commander Scenkid had an incredibly stressed tone, "Where have the three of you been? Leaving the quarters without notice is unforgivable."

"To keep it short sir," Lienad had a dry tone, "We left in a hurry on a mission to save this universe from being destroyed by Krind. We are leaving Pecoaphlyly right now to continue our mission."

"Well, good thing you aren't here Agents," Commander Scenkid's tone grew solemn, "We are currently under attack by Krind's forces. You say this mission of your will stop him?"

"UNDER ATTACK," All three of them yelled out.

"Yes sir, this is supposed to stop him," Lienad felt

very panicked.

"Good, then keep on and get it done. We will hold it down here," Commander Scenkid asserted, "Signing off."

Everyone sat there for a moment, taken back by what they had just heard. An attack on Anigav was something they had never expected. No one knew what to say. The air was thick with a mix of panic and fear.

"We have to keep moving," Lienad slammed his fist onto his leg, "We have to stop him!"

"Well, no time like the present then," Captain Aero held up his right wing, "We are off the planet and are about to hop dimensions."

As Captain Aero lowered his wing to press the button, and it was like time slowed down. As they looked at Pecoaphlyly, ten large ships surrounded it. In perfect unison they shot orange beams directly at the planet. Just before they hopped dimensions, they saw the entire planet obliterated.

21

The Hidden Societies

There was depressing silence among the group. None of them wanted to believe what they had just seen. So many questions raced through their heads. Did Krind somehow know they were there? Was this just a random attack he was already planning? If he did know they were there, then how? Would this have happened if they didn't go there? No one had any answers, nor did they want to make any assumptions. All they could do was continue moving forward.

For the rest of the trip to the planet Earth, no one said a word. It made the trip feel like an eternity. I can safely say that nails on a chalkboard would have been more pleasing than this deafening silence. Renka sat by himself, twiddling his thumbs. Captain Aero stayed in his chair, still as a stone. Lienad and Arura sat together, wrapped within

each other's arms for comfort.

"We've reached Earth," Captain Aero dryly stated, "Not much longer on our trip now."

"With Atlantis being considered a myth," Lienad attempted to bring some life to his voice, "Where are we heading to get there?"

"That's easy," Captain Aero chippered up a bit since he was the most knowledgeable on the topic, "There is a spot on Earth that is largely avoided by humans because of strange things that happen there. It's called the Bermuda Triangle. The strange things that happen are because it's a portal to Atlantis."

"I see, so how does it work?" Lienad stood up as he asked.

"Well, for starters, you're gonna want to sit back down and buckle up," Captain Aero smiled, "That's where things get a little bumpy. Once we fly in, we will be faced with turbulence and a lot of electromagnetic interference. We only have one shot. Either we navigate perfectly into the portal, or we become another broken down ship that sinks into the depths."

"Well, that's comforting," Renka panicked to make sure his safety belt was properly secured.

"BAHA," Captain Aero guffawed, "That's why you've got me! Get comfortable and get ready."

No one hesitated to listen. Lienad and Arura rapidly

sat down and got secured. Each of them checked one another belts to make sure it was perfect. Lienad wrapped his arm around her and held her tight. Renka checked his belt three more times, until he tightened it to an uncomfortable level. They quietly sat, preparing themselves.

As the crew flew closer to the Bermuda Triangle, they could feel the turbulence begin to kick in. Initially, it was just small bumps. But it gradually increased to harsh hits that violently shook the entire ship. Once they were fully within the boundaries of the triangle, the different instruments on the control panel began rapidly beeping as if something was wrong. The crew held on tight, hopeful that Captain Aero would be able to get them through this.

The further in they flew, the worse things seemed. The control panel was screaming with non-stop beeps. The ship was in a constant state of being knocked around. Then, the ship started to spin out of control. Fear and anxiety were at a level that felt as though they were in physical pain. Suddenly, a loud whooshing sound erupted. Then everything was still, quiet, and completely dark. Was this it, were they set to become a forgotten item in the bottom of the ocean?

"Well, the worst part is over," Captain Aero calmly stated, "We are in the portal."

"Why is it so dark," Renka rapidly questioned, still in a state of panic, "Are you sure? Are we dying? Oh no, what happened?"

"Calm down Renka, trust Captain Aero here," Lienad tried to calm him down. But truth be told, he also was still panicking inside.

"Look ahead," Captain Aero pointed his right wing forward.

Ahead of them was a small light that grew as they kept moving forward. Once they were fully immersed in light, they saw the beautiful city of Atlantis. Earth legends believe this city to be underwater and filled with mer-people. This is nothing more than a fallacy. The city was technologically advanced and very well hidden. Everything was shiny and made from what looked like silver. There were no roads or cars, everyone travelled by hovering crafts. The citizens looked like humans, though their attire was quite interesting. Everyone wore royal blue one-piece suits and had these pale blue visor style glasses. Sky high walls of ice surrounded the city, and in the center was a giant castle-like structure.

They started flying towards the castle when four black and white crafts surrounded the ship. They transmitted some sort of energy field that prevented the ship from moving. The crew looked at each other, worried about what was going to happen next. As they tried to figure out their next move, they heard a beeping from the control panel. After ten beeps, a voice came through the speakers.

"You have been halted by Atlantis Law Enforcement," the voice said in a very professional tone, "You will be escorted to our correctional facility, where you may plead your case. Please do not attempt to fly off, as you are unable to move while you are within this energy bubble."

They didn't bother trying to resist. They had a mission to complete here, and breaking rules intentionally would not help them. They sat back and patiently waited to arrive at their destination. Along the trip, they admired seeing more of the city. They noticed many pointed structures in the architecture. I suppose you could say it was a very sharp society. Bad jokes aside, it was a beautiful city. They arrived at the correctional facility, where the entire ship was lowered into a cell through a rooftop hatch. Once the ship was landed, the hatch above closed.

"Please exit the craft with your hands in the air," the same voice came through the control panel.

They did as they were instructed. It was all a bit surprising, how polite the law enforcement was being. Because of this, they weren't afraid. Once they exited the ship, everything was pitch black aside from an illuminated circle that was barely larger than the ship that they were standing on. They stood there, with their hands in the air, waiting. They were unsure of what was to happen next, or if they should be the first to say something.

"Will the leader of your crew please state their name and your intentions for being here," the voice from the ship said over an intercom.

"Where are you," Lienad shouted, "We would like to

see who we are talking to."

"It is a best practice not to get personally involved with prisoners," the voice retorted, "Do you identify yourself as the leader of this group?"

"Wait," Captain Aero whispered to Lienad, "Let me handle this."

"If you're sure," Lienad whispered with a nod.

"My name is Captain Aero," he said loudly, "We are here to see Peetnum. Tell him that the bird boy has returned, as your people so graciously coined me. I won't say anything more unless it is to him directly."

"Bird boy," Renka snickered before getting a dirty look from Captain Aero.

"If you refuse to say anything else, you may return to your ship," the voice responded, "Your ship is in a gravity lock and cannot be moved until the lock is released. Please wait patiently while your we verify your claims."

They all went back inside the ship. They waited there, in complete silence for over an hour. None of them really knew what to do with themselves, or how much longer this would take. During this time, they all decided to retire to the sleeping quarters for a rest. The least they could do is get well rested in the hope that they would get to move forward. They slept for a while, until they were awoken by a blaring siren coming through the control panel. This caused them to jump and rush to see what was

going on.

"What's happening," Captain Aero frantically looked around.

"My sincere apologies," the voice said, stopping the siren, "We had tried verbal communication many times with no response."

"Well, we are here now," Lienad was frustrated, "We were just sleeping. What is it?"

"Bird boy and company, Peetnum has agreed to meet with you," the voice seemed unphased by Lienad's frustration, "Your ship will be escorted to the palace."

The hatch above them opened. As Captain Aero sat in his chair to fly, the ship was once again being lifted by an energy field. It seems that being escorted merely meant being transported. When they arrived in front of the palace, they were struck with surprise. It was a lot larger up close than it seemed from afar. The ship was gently landed right in front of the doors.

"You may now go meet with Peetnum," the voice said, "He is waiting for you just inside, in the throne room, have a pleasant rest of your day."

Everyone left the ship and started walking towards the palace. The air was exceptionally light and clean around them, refreshingly so. When they got close to the palace, the giant silver doors opened on their own. There was a long path, with seating on both sides, which led straight to two thrones. The left throne was empty and sitting on the right was an exceptionally large man wearing a sapphire crown. In his left hand was a silver trident taller than he was. He looked like a human, but I cannot stress enough how giant he was. This was clearly Peetnum, the king of Atlantis.

"Aero, my good bird fellow. How grand it is to see you once more," Peetnum's deep voice bellowed, "To what do I owe this honor of meeting with you and friends after such a long time?"

"We are in need of some assistance my lord," Captain Aero kneeled, "I believe only you may be able to provide it to us."

"Oh, come now. After our history you have no need to kneel," Peetnum let out a boisterous belly laugh, "Whatever you need, it is yours."

"We need to get to the Inner Earth Society," Captain Aero paused for a moment, "The fate of everything depends on it. We were led to believe the entrance is somewhere in Atlantis."

"The fate of everything, hmm," Peetnum had a curious tone, "That sounds a bit extreme. It is true, the entrance is here. However, it is sealed. The key was mysteriously destroyed many years ago. No one has been able to come in, or out. I do not believe that I can help you on this."

"Can you at least tell us how to get to the entrance,"

Lienad blurted, pausing for a moment before kneeling, "My lord."

"Who are you to address me so abruptly," Peetnum sounded irritated, "I have a friendship with Aero, but you I do not know."

"I am Lienad, I assembled this team as part of my mission to save the universe," he remained knelt, "If you could just tell us how to get there, you would help more than you know."

"I am tempted," Peetnum pondered silently for a moment, "Because of Aero I will tell you. Behind the palace there is a path that leads into the ice. Follow it all the way down to find the entrance."

"Thank you, King Peetnum," Lienad bowed his head.

"Aero, is there anything else I can help you with while you are here," Peetnum turned his gaze back to Captain Aero.

"No sire, that is everything we need," Captain Aero bowed his head.

"Well then," Peetnum stood up, towering above them, "I suppose you should be off. Try not to be gone for too long next time. Perhaps even come for a solo social call soon."

"Nothing would please me more," Captain Aero raised his head.

"Until then," Peetnum gave a short bow of his head towards Captain Aero.

Everyone gave a bow to the king and went back to the ship. Once inside, Captain Aero went straight to his chair and got the ship off the ground. He flew behind the palace, found the path, and followed it into the ice. The end of the path seemed like a dead end, nothing more than a stone wall. The team got out of the ship to look around.

"Was I the only expecting some kind of door," Renka chimed.

"Maybe not a door," Lienad replied, "But I certainly expected more than just stones."

"So, Aero," Renka giggled, "You want to tell us about your history with these people? The king seemed fond of you."

"To keep it short," Captain Aero said dryly, "I've been here many times before starting when I was a kid. The first time was an accident, and I got lucky. From then I would visit with them and share some of the advancements we had on Tesheraf. There more to it than that, but that's all I feel like divulging."

"Come on," Renka dragged out his words in a teasing way, "A king wants to help you out with such ease. Tell us mo—."

"HEY," Arura shouted, interrupting Renka, pointing at the floor, "Look what I found."

Everyone came over and saw there was a rectangular hole in the ground. Not very large, but not extremely small either. Bordering the hole were engravings that looked like a language of sorts, though no one here could read it. All of them agreed this hole had to have something to do with getting into the Inner Earth Society.

"You know what," Lienad placed his right hand on his chin, "We had to get the sword because we needed it for getting into the Inner Earth Society. Let me try something."

Lienad walked back into the ship. He went to the sleeping quarters and grabbed the sword, which he had securely stored under the bed that he and Arura would sleep on. He walked back out to the group, who were still standing around the hole. He held the sword over the hole, took a deep breath, everyone watched with anticipation, then he forced the sword into the hole. However, nothing happened. It was disappointing for the group, but I honestly found it humorous; all that build up for nothing.

"Huh," Lienad looked confused, "I was sure that would have worked."

"Did you stick in in far enough?" Renka asked light-heartedly.

"Yeah, I mean, it didn't feel like it would go in any more than it did," Lienad tried pushing the sword in more.

This, of course, still did nothing. Everyone stood around, each taking turns examining the sword and trying to make something happen. Captain Aero tried jiggling it, but there was no change. Renka tried pushing it in, even though Lienad already did that; this obviously didn't change anything either. Arura tried channeling some fairy magic into it, still no changes. Everyone was beginning to grow frustrated with the situation. Lienad gasped, as if he had a revelation, and walked up to the sword. He placed his hands on each side of the cross-guard, holding them tightly. Then, with all his might, he turned the sword like a key in a lock. Suddenly the engravings around the hole lit up with a red glow. The sword slowly descended into the ground. When only the hilt was still above ground, the sword stopped. The stones in the back faded like a disappearing mirage, revealing a large stone circle. Around the circle there were engravings like the ones on the ground. They also began to glow red. Then, in the center of the circle, a swirling red and white light appeared.

"This must be the entrance," Lienad had excitement in his voice.

"How did you know that would work though," Renka looked as though he was having a tough time figuring it out.

"Renka," Arura placed her right palm on her forehead and sighed, "It's so simple. If you think of the hole as a lock, and the sword as the key, it makes complete sense. I'm just kind of upset I didn't think of it myself."

"Oh... right," Renka appeared to feel stupid having

such a simple concept explained to him.

"Well, let's stop wasting time and get in there," Captain Aero was beaming with excitement, "I have never been here before, I can't wait to add it to my checklist."

They rushed back to the ship and got ready. Given that this was territory none of them were familiar with, they were cautious. Everyone, even Captain Aero, buckled their safety belts tight. The ship powered up and engaged as everyone took a deep breath in unison. Then, Captain Aero propelled the ship forward through the portal. As they passed through it felt like lunging into a large body of water. But there was also an odd sensation everyone could feel on their skins, almost like being pleasantly shocked. Once they were fully through the portal, everyone's eyes widened in utter amazement.

They were hovering above a courtyard in front of a large building. It was a castle made in Earth's style known as Gothic Architecture. The area around was molten lava. It was like being inside a volcano without burning to a crisp. They could see more buildings around them, all built in a similar style. They landed and got out of the ship. As soon as they exited, they were greeted by an ambush of creatures that looked terribly similar to Serpisapions. However, these creatures looked far more like lizards and were scalier than Serpisapions. They were all pointing large spears are the group. They all raised their hands in surrender.

"We come in peace," Lienad said, looking around at

them all. "We are looking for someone named Swidom."

"What do you want with him," an orange one on the right said, followed by a flick of his tongue.

"That is something I would rather only discuss with him," Lienad tensed a little as his said this.

"Not a good answer," a dark green one on the left shouted, moving his spear closer.

"You are all our prisoners. We are going to take you to Zidral," the orange one on the right lunged his spear forward and tilted his head towards the castle.

The crew, with their hand still in the air, walked toward the castle. Though, it's not like they really had much of a choice. As they walked, they were all incredibly surprised at how mild the temperature was. I believe the stone architecture somehow acted as a heat barrier. When they entered the castle, it was very dark. There were pews on either side made of stone. Black metal chandeliers hung from the ceiling, each filled with burning candles. Walking through this corridor felt like something you would expect to see in a scary film or a horror style video game. They approached a giant black throne; it looked like it was made from the Earth mineral Obsidian. From the left entered a giant version of these lizard people, his scaly skin was covered in varying red hues. He had a black tail and sharp looking claws.

"So," he had a raspy and guttural voice, "Whoever

you are somehow managed to enter our society."

"Yes," Lienad gulped, "We came here through the portal in Atlantis."

"LIES," he yelled, "I can't remember the last time that portal worked. We have been trapped here for so long because of it."

"No, I swear it is the truth," Lienad began to sweat, "We found the key and unlocked it."

"Let's just assume I believe you," he hissed, "Why are you here?"

"We are on a mission to save the universe and need to find Swidom to do that," Lienad started getting filled with anxiety.

"This seems all quite farfetched," he began to pace, "Why would I trust any of this?"

"I... I don't really know what to say here," Lienad began to shake, "We have no reason to wish your people harm. Until this moment we didn't even know what you looked like. We don't want to bother you for any longer than we have to. If we could just meet with Swidom, we could be out of here in no time. We would never return if that is your wish."

"Hmm, you seem nervous and scared with how you ramble on," He stopped and looked at the ceiling, "I guess that means you aren't brave enough to wish us harm. My name is Zidral, I am the Emperor here."

"Zidral," Lienad kneeled, the rest of the crew followed his lead, "Can you please help us?"

There was a long moment of silence that would make you feel queasy. Zidral looked at them as they kneeled before him. He seemed to relish in that fact. I firmly believe he kept them waiting for so long simply because he could.

"Tell me about this mission to save the universe," Zidral commanded.

"Well, I'll keep it short," Lienad took a deep breath, "There is a bad guy named Krind who is hell bent on taking over the universe. For some reason it is our destiny to stop him. So far we have met with the Fairies, gotten a crystal sword, met with the Atlanteans, and now arrived here in search of the Swidom. Our mission hangs on whether he will accept coming with us to read a language that only he can read."

"I am inclined to believe you, tiny human," Zidral paced a bit more, "Only because the Atlanteans allowed you to come to the portal. I will choose to put my faith there, as opposed to believing they are turning on us and sent you here to annihilate us."

"Oh, hehe," Lienad nervously chuckled, "Certainly no annihilation here. So, you will take us to Swidom?"

"No, I will not take you. I am an Emperor, not a chauffeur," Zidral scoffed, "Swidom is not here. He has returned to a time of magic before we were forced to seclude

ourselves down here."

"We don't have the means to time travel," Lienad grew disappointed.

"You may not, but we do," Zidral said, letting out a shrieking laugh, "You may use our portal. It will transport you directly to our old Citadel."

"Is this portal big enough for our ship," Lienad perked up.

"Unless your ship is bigger than this castle it will," Zidral paced a little more, "The portal is to the west of the castle. You will see a stone path that leads directly into a lavafall. Fly your ship into the lavafall and you will be whisked away."

"Thank you, Emperor Zidral," Lienad bowed his head, "With your permission we will be on our leave."

"You are dismissed," Zidral motioned his hand, "But know this, tiny human and company. If we discover any part of what you said to be a lie, we will follow through the portal after you. You will not enjoy the outcome of that."

Lienad nodded in understanding. The crew walked back through the corridor and into the ship. They gathered around as Captain Aero got into his chair. He got the ship off the ground and flew up until he could see the path to the west. He flew along, following the path as instructed. As they approached the lava fall at the end, the stopped and hovered for a moment. Everyone had the same thought:

what if this was a lie and Zidral was sending them to a fiery death? After a few moments, Captain Aero pressed forward.

They made their way into the lavafall, and everything got strange. Everything they could see began to twist and twirl. Movements felt like they were slower and faster at the same time. It was hard to discern what was going on. Suddenly, everything started blending and swirling at a rapid rate. After a while, it started reversing even faster than it was moving before. When everything settled, and sight became normal again, they were in a completely different area.

They were now in the center of the citadel. A giant stone wall surrounded the area. The houses were made from stone, stick, and straw. In the far back there was a large building that looked like a combination of a castle and a coliseum. The crew got their bearings and went outside. As soon as the hatch shut behind them, they were ambushed. They were all bashed on the head and blacked out. What a warm welcome.

22

The Citadel

When they finally came to, they were in a prison cell. Stone walls, dirt floor, and iron bars for a door. At least they were all kept together, though it would have been better without shackles on their arms and ankles. In the distance they could hear stomping footsteps approaching them. As the sound grew louder, they could see two figures approaching them. They looked just like the beings from the Inner Earth Society, but with more medieval looking attire. They both had metal helmets, chain mail shirts, a large brass shield, and a short sword. When they got in front of the cell door they abruptly stopped and turned toward Lienad and company.

"What business hast thou, appearing thus unbidden within our walls?" the lime one on the left aggressively questioned, he had a very shrill voice.

"Um," Lienad hesitated, unsure if he needed to try and speak in the same manner or not, "We come in search of the one known as Swidom."

"Why dost foul beings, in such strange attire, seek him," the yellow one on the right gripped the handle of his sword, he also had a shrill voice.

"We just need his help reading something," Lienad raised his hands to try and come off as non-threatening, "That's all we need, and then we will leave."

"Thou shall leave once the Emperor giveth his command and not sooner," the lime one got more aggressive with his tone.

"On your feet, wretches! We shall take you to the Emperor's audience," the yellow one yelled in a hissing tone as he motioned his rusted sword in an upward motion, "Hold thy tongues, save that which is bid, lest ye wish to be parted by steel."

The iron gate was opened, and the group was led out. They were forced to walk in a single file, led by the yellow one and followed by the green one. The scenery of the walk was very bland. Stone walls, dirt floor, torches fastened to the walls, and empty cells. They approached large wooden doors and were brought to a halt.

"Beyond these gates, thine fate shall be decided," the green one said as he placed his hand on the right door.

"Thou shall bend thy knee before the nighty

Emperor and offer reverence of the highest degree," the yellow one said as he placed his hand on the left door.

In unison, the two of them pushed the doors open. They motioned for the group to enter and closed the doors behind them. They were now in the base of some type of pit in the center of a stone circle. Ahead of them, atop the wall, was a throne. In it sat a rather large one of these lizard people, with a mixture of red and yellow scales. They walked to the center of the pit and knelt, as this had to be the Emperor.

"Thou hath intruded upon my Citadel," the Emperor's voice boomed, "What purpose could there be for such a transgression?"

"We come from a different time, allowed through a portal by your people in the future," Lienad yelled to make sure he could be heard, "We are searching for Swidom. We need his help with a translation. We bring no ill will with us."

"Hear my decree," the Emperor yelled after a moment of thought, "If thou canst pass a trial, I provide aid in what thee desires."

"What is this trial?" Lienad was worried about what it could be.

"By my order, let the trial commence," the Emperor slammed his foot down three times.

A section of the stone wall beneath the Emperor's

thrown began to rise. They began to hear a rhythmic boom, each making the ground vibrate, that seemed to match the pattern of something walking. The booms grew louder and the vibrations more violent. As this continued, anxieties rose among the crew. Suddenly, a behemoth burst through the opening where the stones had been. It was a gargantuan lizard with spikes running down its spine, large sharp teeth, black eyes, and smoke coming from its nostrils.

"Well," Lienad began to panic, "I guess this is the trial!"

None of them knew what to do. They were all still in shackles and had to think of a way to fight off this beast. The lizard ran towards Lienad with its mouth open, its razor-sharp teeth prepared to chomp. He just barely lunged out of the way. He felt the heat of its breath as he flew to the side, had he been a second later it would have been all over. The force from its bite sent sand flying everywhere.

"What do we do," Renka was trembling with fear, "I don't want to die."

"We'll find a way out of this," Lienad wasn't very sure about that, but he wanted to try and calm Renka down, "Babe, you got any ideas?"

"Kind of hard to think right now with a giant monster trying to eat us," Arura shouted in a panicked state.

"We need to separate and keep moving, I have an idea. Sort of," Captain Aero started running in a zig zag

motion away from the group.

Everyone else followed his lead, spreading out across the arena. After all, the monster could only chase one at a time. Luckily, the chain for the shackles on their legs was just long enough to allow them to run. As it ran, its massive tail stirred up enough sand into the air that it was like a sandstorm. Renka had to stop to rub the dirt out of his eyes. When he opened them, the beast was heading straight for him. Visibility was limited because of the sand. Renka took off running, as fast as he could. Screaming a very high-pitched scream with every step. When the monster was right behind him, he did the only thing he could think of: he immediately dropped into the fetal position. The beast couldn't react quickly enough and bashed its head into the stone wall. While it was laid on the ground, everyone ran back together.

"So, what's your plan Aero," Lienad was gasping for air.

"That was basically it, run around," Captain Aero was having a little more difficulty breathing with sand getting clumped in his beak. He took a second to forcefully blow it out.

"That's a terrible plan, I almost died," Renka was uncontrollably shaking at this point.

"How much time do you think we have?" Arura asked, looking around to see if she detected any movement.

Before anyone could answer, they heard the booming steps and felt the ground tremble once again. The beast was up. The group ran apart from each other once again, their views still limited. The change in pattern of the lizard's steps showed that it was still disoriented from the hit to the head. Lienad saw the beast emerge from the sand shroud and begin running towards him. But he noticed it was not running in a straight line, shaking its head as if it was seeing double. Lienad ran to the side, still watching as the beast stutter stepped attempting to follow him. Because he wasn't paying attention to where he was going, he inadvertently collided with Renka, causing them both to fall.

"Are you okay," Lienad stood up, dusting himself off.

"No, I'm not," Renka sat up, "We are probably going to die from this giant thing. Nothing about this is okay!"

"Well, we don't have time to pout," Lienad looked behind him, "That gargantuan lizard is coming. Come on, get up, we gotta go!"

Lienad started running, and Renka was slow to get up. He wasn't sure if he cared anymore at this point. He could feel the monster getting close and started trying to run. But he was too slow. He was knocked back to the ground, landing on his face. The beast, still disoriented, lunged its head forward with its mouth open. Fortunately for Renka, it missed him. Its open mouth slammed into the ground, and it let out a roaring scream of pain. As it lifted its head from the pain, Renka had an idea. He had just re-membered that behind his belt buckle there was a special weapon he had been working on.

He rustled behind his buckle and pulled out a silver disk with a bright green button in the center of it. He set it on the ground and pushed the button. It made a sound like it was charging up before shooting a short, bright green, beam overhead. It exploded like a green firework, causing a green rain that smelled of death to come pouring down. Many droplets entered the beast's mouth, causing it to violently shake and heave in disgust. The monster stomped and flailed around. Then, it got some of the liquid in its eyes.

It became completely frantic, now that its eyes were burning and its mouth was filled with such a disgusting liquid. The behemoth started running around in all directions, causing more sand to fill the air. No one could see what was happening, but they heard a non-stop banging that felt like an earthquake. It then became mysteriously quiet. Everyone stood still. After a while, the sand settled, and things became clear. The beast was laid on the ground, head completely smashed. There was a large pool of blood around it, with bone and tissue inside of it. It slammed its head into the ground so many times that it killed itself. In the distance there was a slow clapping.

"Thou hast proven thyself in the trial," the Emperor declared, "I shall join you and impart unto thee the

knowledge thou dost desire."

The group came together by the lifeless body of the beast. They were all relieved that this was over. More than that though, they were all surprised at how it ended. None of them, aside from Renka, every thought one of his inventions would prove to be useful; much less be something that saved their lives.

"Wow," Lienad was coughing and gaging from the stench, "You did it Renka."

"I wish it didn't smell so bad, but thank you Renka," Arura placed her shirt over her nose to try and guard herself from the scent.

"I'm just glad that didn't happen inside the ship, BAHA," Captain Aero was not as affected by the scent as it was less concentrated than it was when the vial broke inside the ship.

"I told you guys my weapons would be useful," Renka was panting and still trying to stop trembling, "Everyone doubted me, but look who the hero is today."

The crew laughed as the doors they came through before were opened. The Emperor was walking toward them. He was significantly larger than they thought when he was still sat atop the wall. As he got close, he stopped and started smacking his lips. His face grew a look of utter disgust. He started heaving as some of the particles had entered his mouth.

"By the ancients, that is abhorrent," the Emperor gagged, "Come, with haste, join me outside. Let us be away from this vile miasma."

The Emperor quickly turned and left the pit as fast as he could. The rest of the group laughed and followed him. When they got outside, the doors were closed behind them. The guard from before unlocked their shackles. Lienad rubbed his wrists, happy to be free from them. They looked up as the Emperor towered over them. I estimate he was in the realm of eleven feet tall.

"Thy combat style was unusual, but admirable still," the Emperor was still trying to spit out the stench, "I am Emperor Ladnarmesa. What names doth thy warriors claim?"

"I am Lienad, this is my team. Arura, Renka, and Captain Aero," he pointed to each of them as he gave their names, "You said you will help us now that we defeated your beast?"

"Curious names, for equally curious warriors," Emperor Ladnarmesa looked intrigued, "I shall impart unto thee the knowledge requested. Whether this aids thee or not is of no consequence to me."

"That is all I ask Emperor Ladnarmesa," Lienad bowed his head, "Please, where can we find Swidom?"

"To the west of my Citadel thou shall find the ancient Red Forest," Emperor Ladnarmesa pointed west,

"Deep within its heart, at its densest part, a fungus door awaits. Behind that door, next to the fairy lake, thou shall find the man thee seeks."

"Thank you, Emperor Ladnarmesa," Lienad knelt, and the others followed his lead.

"Come, feast with me," Emperor Ladnarmesa chuckled, "We shall celebrate thy glorious victory in the pit."

"If we had the time to, I would love nothing more," Lienad looked at Emperor Ladnarmesa with sincerity, "Unfortunately, time is of the essence, and we must be off."

"I understand," Emperor Ladnarmesa looked as though he took no offense, "Be off then, and shouldst thou return to my Citadel, we shall hold a grand feast in thy honor."

The guard showed the crew back to their ship. Once inside, they took turns getting cleaned up. After which, Captain Aero went straight to his control panel to get ready for the next stop. Lienad, Arura, and Renka sat down to try and relax after the day's events. Everyone was completely exhausted, but knew they had to keep moving forward.

"You know," Renka sat up, looking at Lienad, "I've never been to a feast in my honor before. You sure we can't spare some time?"

"Renka," Lienad sighed, "We have already wasted enough time. Maybe, when this is all over, we can come

back. Until then, if you're hungry go get something to eat here."

"Fine," Renka gave a slight pout and leaned his head back.

Captain Aero got the ship off the ground and flew west, until they reached the Red Forest. It was aptly named due to all the tress having crimson red leaves. He flew high above the forest, searching for the densest point. They approached a point that was so dense it looked like the ship could land on top of it and be supported. Just a little further left there was a clearing just big enough that he could land the ship without damaging any of the trees.

Once they landed, they got out and started walking in. The deeper they got, the darker it got. The treetops were so tightly packed that even though it was broad daylight it looked like night in the forest. Once they got into the darkest part, the tree trunks made a thick wall. They were grown together, almost fused, with thick vines tangled around them.

The group walked around the wall, staying close to it. They were certain that that would be the best way to find the door they were looking for. Eventually, the forest grew so dark that it was difficult to see anything. Then, in the distance they began to see a faint glow. They continued walking toward it, keeping their hands on the wooded wall to ensure they didn't get lost. The more they walked, the more intense the glow became; until they had a tall glowing

line of mushrooms right in front of them.

They walked around the line to get a better view, it was the fungus door. Around the door were shelf like growths, bulbous shapes, and tendrils of glowing fungi. The door itself was a tapestry of brown, grey, and green mushrooms of varying sizes. They were all clumped together in one large mass. Lienad placed his right hand on the door and pushed it open, revealing the fairy lake.

Much like the scenery on Friyaldan, there were bioluminescent mushrooms everywhere. The diverse colors reflected off the lake, creating a beautiful neon rainbow look. There were what looked like fireflies drifting around. To the left of the lake was a house that looked like a large mushroom with smoke billowing out of its chimney. They walked up it and Lienad knocked on the door. They waited for a few minutes, but no one answered. Lienad knocked again, this time noticeably louder. The door swung open, revealing a very thing looking lizard person. He wore glasses, leaned on a brown cane, smoked from a long pipe, and looked quite old.

"What do you want," he had a gruff voice, "Can't an old man go anywhere to be left alone?"

"Are you Swidom," Lienad looked him over intently.

"Maybe I am, maybe I'm not," he looked at Lienad just as intently, "What does it matter to you?"

"We are looking for Swidom," Lienad was sure this

was him, "We are trying to save the universe and need his help with something. We were told he would be the only one who would help."

"So," he blew out a large cloud of smoke, "The war has gotten worse. I am in fact Swidom. Come inside for some tea, I hope you like mushrooms."

They walked inside and took a seat around his table. The cottage was quaint. There wasn't much in the way of decorations. It was just one large room that contained the living, sleeping, dining, and kitchen areas. All the furniture was simplistic in nature. Swidom poured them all some mushroom tea. Captain Aero and Renka drank it without an issue. But Lienad and Arura merely sipped on it to be nice, neither of them enjoyed mushrooms. Swidom stood beside them, placing both hands atop his cane.

"I came here to escape all of that," Swidom sounded frustrated, "Now tell me, what is it that you need from me that you have to disturb my retirement?"

Lienad went on to tell him about the mission, focusing on the engraving they needed him for. As he talked, Swidom lightly paced around. He did not look happy about what he was hearing. When Lienad finished telling the tale, Swidom stood with his back turned to the group. He looked at the ceiling and let out an audible disgruntled sigh.

"It's true, I can read the script of the ancients," Swidom looked at the floor, "I may be one of the only ones who can. I don't know why, but I am able to translate any

language there is. It's something that just sparked in me while I was in my youth."

"Does that mean you will help us," Lienad looked at Swidom hopefully.

"I don't really want to," Swidom paused, "But, if everything you say is true, I don't know that I have much of a choice."

"I'm sorry that we are having to ask this of you," Lienad stood up and slightly bowed his head out of respect, "If the situation weren't dire, I wouldn't be here now. Thank you for being willing to help us."

"Yeah, yeah," he grumbled, "Listen, things in the universe aren't bad right now. We should visit Sparebryr now instead of returning to the future. We will have a greater rate of success."

"Understood, we should head out then," Lienad threw back the rest of the mushroom tea, his face twisting into a grimace.

Everyone left Swidom's house and navigated back through the Red Forest to the ship. None of them had realized how much time had passed, it was already night out. Overhead, just before they got to the ship, they saw a large dragon fly past. This was the first time any of them had ever seen one, it was a wonderous sight. One that, over time, would slowly disappear from Earth.

23

<u>The Engraving</u>

Once they got on the ship, they gave Swidom a very brief tour; in which he didn't really seem interested. If you had seen him, you could tell that he was just ready to get this over with. Which is fair—all he had wanted was a quite retirement as a recluse. The group got settled in at the front of the ship, and Captain Aero adjusted some configurations in the navigation panel. He then sat down in front of the control panel.

"Well, I don't know how well this will go," Captain Aero took a deep breath, "I've never travelled back in time so I don't know how the dimensional hopper will react."

This instantly made everyone nervous, so they got tightly buckled in. Once Captain Aero confirmed everyone was secure, he held his hand over the button. They braced themselves. Renka grabbed his armrests tightly and closed his eyes. Lienad and Arura clasped hands and looked deeply into each other's eyes. Swidom just sort of sat back as if he didn't genuinely care what happened. Captain Aero slammed his hand down.

They opened their eyes and let out a sigh of relief. Everyone was still in one piece and things seemed perfectly normal. They looked out the window and were clearly in space. Captain Aero confirmed on the navigation device that they were, in fact, in the Gaseous Dimension. Which surprised everyone, it was nowhere near as gassy, or stench ridden, as it is in their time. From here, they started their course for Sparebryr.

Once they descended into the planet's atmosphere, they were even more surprised. The terrain was mostly beautiful. With what they knew Sparebryr to be, they never would have believed it could have looked like this. There were blue-violet fields of grass, tall trees, rainbows of blooming flowers, and a clear blue sky. It was beautiful and tranquil. It's a shame this all became twisted and grotesque in the future.

"He was right," Lienad looked around in awe, "This planet really did use to be pristine. I wish we could save it from what is to come."

"You can't," Swidom said, his eyes closed—he looked as though he was deep in thought. "What is to come for this place must come. We cannot change anything in the past as it will create an irreparable paradox."

"Yeah," Lienad let out a saddened groan, "I figured as much. Do you know where we go from here?"

"You mean to tell me," Swidom opened his eyes and looked at Lienad with frustration, "You dragged me into all of this, and you don't know where we are going? No, idiot boy, I don't know where we need to go. This is your mission, not mine. I am only reluctantly providing you limited assistance."

Lienad felt stupid, as he knew Swidom was right. He lightly kicked the ground for a moment and got an idea. He was going to try and contact Neoshyt. He intently focused, trying to reach him. Unfortunately, it was once again a failed attempt. Lienad figured it must have been due to them being in a different time. But that didn't really make sense to me. Neoshyt was supposed to exist outside of time, so you would think he could still contact Lienad. I was a bit more suspicious about this than Lienad was. So, he sat there thinking about what else he could possibly do.

"Hey," Arura stood up and shouted, "Why don't I just do the same thing I did on Pecoaphlyly?"

"Duh," Lienad smacked his forehead, "How could I have forgotten about that! Yes, my love, please go right ahead."

Arura nodded and focused on performing Rewayvelus Luminpathis. Once the spell was complete, she guided them along the path. They could tell they were getting closer to the engraving because the landscape began to change. It seemed that everything slowly started to become decrepit as they got closer. Eventually they were flying over a wasteland. No grass, dead trees, pools of black sludge, and a most foul odor all around them. In the center of this was an island that had a large stone sitting on it.

They landed on the island near the stone. When they got out, they were hit with what smelled like boiling sulfur. It was hard to maintain composure, but they knew they had to. When they got up to the stone, they could see the engravings. To almost all the group, it looked like random scribble. But not Swidom, he walked over and began to analyze them. As he looked at them, and touched them, he was making different humming sounds. I'm not sure if this was part of his thought process or the translation process, but it was interesting to see.

After a few moments, he stepped back and stared at them. He placed his hand on his chin and stood still. You could tell he was deep in thought. He began to pace, hand still resting on his chin. Every so often he would stop and glance back at the stone. I wasn't watching a clock, so I couldn't tell you exactly how long this went on for. Though, I can say it felt like quite a while. Then he abruptly stopped, walked back over to the stone, and motioned for everyone else to come over.

"I believe I have this all figured out. There is a key

made of stars," Swidom moved his hand along as he translated for them, "This key opens a door. I can't say what happens when it opens, that part is scratched and eroded. It looks like there are instructions on finding this key in the form of a riddle. Are you with me so far?"

"Yeah, I'm following," Lienad nodded his head, "So, what's the riddle?"

"Meet three to find the key, false idols you must see. Search more for the door, and find the land of lore," Swidom dropped his hand and looked back at the group, "The only part of this riddle I have figured out is that you need to visit the planet of the Gods. I am not sure what it means to meet three, nor do I know anything of this land of lore that is mentioned."

"What is the planet of the Gods?" Lienad looked at both Swidom and Arura.

"Don't look at me," Arura shrugged, "Believe it or not, that's one I've never heard of."

"Every species has a variety of religions they follow," Swidom looked at the sky, "All of these idols that each religion follows is real, granted they are not the true supreme being of the universe. They all come from the planet of the Gods."

"Well, how do we get there," Lienad was surprised by this.

"That is something I do not know," Swidom looked

back at Lienad, "I don't even know how they got there. I merely know of its existence to be a fact, having met some of these false idols myself."

"So, we are back to not knowing what to do," Lienad hung his head.

"I am sorry," Swidom sounded sincere, "Now, it seems I have outlived my usefulness in this situation. Might you be able to take me back to my retirement?"

Lienad nodded and they went back to the ship. It was quiet trip back to the red forest. Arura mostly just kept reading the Fypendiumedia. Renka laid in bed, trying to get a short nap. Captain Aero focused on the flight. Swidom just sort of sat there, still as stone. Lienad sat with his head leaned back. He looked up at the ceiling, trying to figure out what they should do next. None of them knew about this planet of the Gods before this, much less how to get there. It was a tough position to be in.

When they landed, back by the red forest, the whole group left the ship and walked back to Swidom's hut. Not that they had been invited. In fact, there had been no discussion prior to this about them coming back with him. They just assumed they were welcome. Swidom didn't say anything to them along the trip, so they assumed he was agreeable to it. However, once they reached the hut, he quickly closed the door before they could come in. They looked at each other in confusion and Lienad leaned to knock on the door.

"WHAT," Swidom swung the door open before Lienad could land the first knock, "Why are you following me home now? I have served my purpose, let me retire in peace."

"We don't know how to get back to our time," Lienad had a stern look on his face.

"Ah, yes," Swidom murmured and looked around, "Well, the portal you originally came through is one way only. This leaves you with two options. You can go back to the citadel and beg to use the other portal. If you are lucky, one of you will be allowed to."

Swidom stood there with a silent stare for a while.

"And?" Renka loudly questioned.

"And what," Swidom aggressively retorted.

"What's the other option, "Lienad let out a sigh, "You only told us one of the two options and it isn't a very appealing one."

"Oh, yes," Swidom murmured again, "Well, if you take some water from this lake and use a fairy spell on it you can create a portal. Now leave me ALONE!"

Swidom slammed the door shut and locked the door. Arura dug through her pouches and found an empty vial, which she filled with water from the lake. They walked back to the ship, planning to take a rest while Arura looked for whatever spell she needed for the portal. Though, this rest period did not last long.

"Alright I found it," Arura cheered, "It looks fairly simple and straight forward."

"Great, let's get it going then," Lienad stood up and stretched.

"Not so fast lover," Arura giggled, "We have to wait until the moon is at its highest point in the sky."

"Sweet," Renka exclaimed, "That means we can get at least a little rest then."

"Captain Aero, does this ship have a timer or alarm we can use to make sure we don't sleep too long," Lienad walked over by him, "Oh, guys it looks like he is already asleep. Maybe we should take shifts then?"

"How much time do you think there is until we can cast the spell," Renka looked concerned about whether he would get enough sleep or not.

"Judging by the positioning," Lienad squinted out the window at the sky, "Hmm, maybe somewhere around four to five hours."

"That's enough time for us to take power nap shifts," Arura nodded, "Only one person awake for 30 minutes at a time while the other two sleep."

"Excellent plan babe," Lienad rubbed her shoulder, "Enough to get some rest, but not enough to become too hard to wake. I'll take the first watch, then you, then Renka. We will just rotate like that, sound good?"

They nodded in agreement and started the rotational shifts. Renka was difficult to wake up when it was his turn, even though with Lienad's decided order he got the most sleep to start off with. On Lienad's fourth time on watch, which was roughly four and a half hours into the rotation, he noticed that the moon looked close to its highest point in the sky. He shook Captain Aero awake and ran back to wake up Arura.

"Babe," Lienad sweetly said, "It's time for you to work your magic."

"Mmm," Arura looked at Lienad with groggy yet loving eyes, "Only if I get a kiss first."

"My pleasure, my lady," Lienad caressed both sides of her face and gave her a deep and passionate kiss. They then pressed their foreheads against each other and closed their eyes.

"This is what you woke me up for," Captain Aero let out a thunderous yawn, "It's nice you two are in love and all, but do you really need an audience?"

"Sorry," Arura chuckled.

"Ha, I needed you awake because you're about to have to fly," Lienad stood up and looked at Captain Aero, "Get your wits about you, she's about to open up a portal."

Arura left the ship and went to stand in front of it. Lienad and Captain Aero went up to the front of the ship as well. Captain Aero got set up in his chair and Lienad stood next to him, both watching Arura through the window. She held the vial up the moon, and it looked like she had started to charge the water. The vial began to glow a bright neon green. Once it was strong enough to completely illuminate the area, she removed the cap and through the water into the air. Then she quickly drew her hand back and shot it forward, releasing a blue stream that was almost like lightning directly at the suspended water. As the lightning streamed into the green liquid, it began to morph. Suddenly, it was a giant swirling portal in the sky. It was a circular swirl of a rainbow of colors. There was a well-defined magenta border around it. Arura ran back into the ship as fast she could.

"Go," she was trying to catch her breath, "Not, open, long... Must, fly, fast."

Hearing this, Captain Aero did not hesitate; he didn't even wait for everyone to get settled. He put the ship into full power and barreled through the portal. As they entered, they suddenly felt everything around them warp, contort, and then snap back to normal. The portal really was open for only a fleeting time, as it rapidly closed immediately after they went through it. Captain Aero forcefully pulled the ship back to slow it down, which cause everyone else to fly forward. Then he carefully landed the ship.

"What happened," Renka ran out in a frenzy holding his head, "Are we under attack?"

"BAHAHA," Captain Aero boisterously laughed,

"Looks like someone had a bad wake up call."

"I did," Renka winced as he rubbed his head, "I slammed my head into the wall. What's going on?"

"Calm down," Lienad snickered, "We had to rush through the portal that Arura made."

"A warning would have been nice," Renka pouted, "Did it at least work?"

They huddled around the front looking out the window. It appeared they were in the same spot as before, but obviously in a different time. Where once there were trees, now stood buildings. The animals running around had been replaced with cars driving down a paved road. Instead of a dragon flying overhead, there were planes swooping by. While this was a move in the right direction, they had no way of knowing whether they were in the right time or not.

"Well, we are certainly in a different time," Captain Aero chimed, "But when?"

"Given the Earth's history it's tough to say," Lienad had a disappointed tone, "When the 2035 solar flare wiped everything out and humanity had to reset so much it could be anywhere from the year 2012 to 2125 on Earth based on the building architecture and the types of cars I've seen drive by."

"That's a pretty wide range," Renka hung his head.

"Well," Arura huffed, "We just need to move forward and assume we are in the right time. Swidom said that

next we need to go to the planet of the gods, how do we get there? Even Swidom didn't know."

They sat there, silent, uncomfortable, and anxious for quite a while. Every so often one of them would get up to pace around for a bit. Periodically one of them would look up as if they had a useful thought, but then quickly lower their head back down before uttering a word. If there had been an analog clock in the room, the ticking would have been enough to drive you insane. Finally, after a grueling amount of time, the silence was broken.

"You know, I just remembered something," Captain Aero stood up and started lightly pacing, "There is an old story we were told as younglings about how our species was created, though we honestly just thought of it as a good bedtime story. There is a hidden galaxy among the stars of the Primary Dimension, from which the first Heagowl came to Tesheraf. This galaxy was the beginning of life itself, and there is supposed to be a portal on every planet that will take you there. Though these portals are supposed to be impossible to find."

"That sounds like the best lead we have so far," Lienad nodded with a confident grunt.

"So, how do we find a portal that is impossible to find," Renka questioned, understandably so.

As the group was beginning to discuss their path forward, their voices were drowned out from Lienad. Where once he heard his friends around him, he now

started to hear Remus' voice every so faintly. He closed his eyes and began to try and tune in to hear it better. After a few seconds it was as clear as if Remus was in there with him.

"Lienad, I can sense you, can you hear me," Remus sounded frantic.

"Yes, I can," Lienad felt concerned, "What's going on?"

"I have been trying to reach you for quite some time, but I couldn't even sense you within the universe," Remus spoke in a rapid pace, "I fear I don't have much time, but I had to get a message out to you. Listen, Commander Scenkid cannot be trusted. He was the one who was really behind the attack on Anigav. Do not contact him. And one more thing, this is important. You cannot trust any..."

Remus was cut off in the middle of talking. Suddenly, Lienad was overcome with a feeling as though Remus was no longer around. Not just in his mind, but in existence. Without hesitation, Lienad begins to try and contact Neoshyt. If anyone knew what was going on, it would have to be him. Though the last attempts at this were in vain, this one was not.

"Lienad," Neoshyt chimed, "How good to hear from you. Your mission going well I assume?"

"Yeah, listen, we are on Earth but do not know how long it has been since we went back in time or what time we are in now," Lienad paused, "Can you help with that?"

"Well, based on what I have seen in my room of everything... You are back to a point where it has only been roughly a week since the attack on Anigav," Neoshyt's voice grew suspiciously solemn, "Was that... all you needed?"

"No, Remus has been destroyed and says I cannot trust Commander Scenkid," Lienad's thoughts grew angry, "What do you know about this?"

"Yes, I was worried this would happen. Commander Scenkid officially joined forces with Krind," Neoshyt paused, "Because of this, there is no time to feel depressed. You MUST continue you mission. It is even more vital than ever now."

"Okay," Lienad couldn't help but feel depressed, "We need to get to the planet of gods, how do we get there?"

"Yes, there is one active portal left, it is on Tesheraf," Neoshyt's tone grew serious, "You must seek out the Venar. Now then, enough chit chat; go!"

The session with Neoshyt was rapidly disconnected and he could hear everyone's voices come back in. He opened his eyes and saw that it seemed they may have been in a bit of an argument, but he didn't have time for petty squabbles; they had a universe to save before more friends died.

"The Venar," Lienad shouted above everyone else.

"How do you know about that?" Captain Aero's

feathers on the back of his neck rose up.

"I'll keep this short," Lienad took a deep breath, "Commander Scenkid is bad, Remus is dead, and Neoshyt told me that to get to the Planet of the gods we must seek out the Venar on Tesheraf."

"Do you know what this is?" Arura looked at Captain Aero.

"Well, I thought it was nothing more than a myth," Captain Aero turned his back and looked up, "Legends say that there is a solitary island, surrounded by waters to treacherous to sail. Travelling by sky is no better, as it is shrouded by a constant raging storm. There is supposed to be a cave at the top of the mountain in the heart of the storm. If you can get there, the cave will lead you to the Venar."

"Great," Renka sighed, "Another impossible task."

"Aero," Lienad stood up, "Do you know where this island is?"

"I do," Captain Aero gave a single nod.

"Do you think you can get us there?" Arura nervously bit her fingernails.

"An island impossible to reach, the source of legends," Captain Aero paused for a while, which caused everyone else's anxieties to increase, "BAHA, that sounds exactly like my kind of trip. Buckle up everyone, our next stop is either glory or death!"

24

The Three

The team rushed to a seat and got buckled in, making sure their straps were properly tightened. Captain Aero looked around to make sure everyone was good to go. He hovered his wing under a button above him that they had never seen him press before. As he went to press the button, it was as if time slowed to a crawl; the tip of his wing inched forward slower than any of them thought possible. Once the button was finally pressed, they popped in and out, in the blink of an eye. Before they even knew what happened, they were hovering over the forests of Tesheraf.

"Wait," Renka quickly looked around, "What just happened?"

"Oh, just a special little button to pop home," Captain Aero laughed.

"And pop we did," Lienad shook his head, "Now, let's discuss getting to this island that's impossible to reach, shall we?"

"There's nothing to discuss, I've already figured it out," Captain Aero turned his chair toward the rest of the group, "Though it is dangerous, getting there by air is our best bet. I am, after all, the greatest pilot in the universe and this is the greatest ship. End of story. I will get us through that storm and into that cave. All you need to do is stay buckled up and hold on tight."

Captain Aero turned his chair back around, ending the conversation before anyone could respond, and started flying. The crew watched as they flew over the lush forests, marveling again at just how beautiful the natural landscape was here. Soon, they reached the edge where the trees met the water; they knew they were getting closer. As they flew over the vast ocean, they started to see something come into view far off in the distance. It appeared to be a large mountain, in the middle of the ocean. As they got closer, the clearer it became. It was, in fact, an island made of a large mountain. They stopped to hover, just close enough to get a good look. The waters around the island violently raged, revealing large, jagged rocks around the base of the mountain as the waves pulled back. Running into one of those would be detrimental to any ship, no matter how fortified. Looking up the mountain, the upper half disappeared into an equally violent thunderstorm. Crashing rain, bolts of lightning illuminating the sides of the

mountains, and thunder so powerful it could be felt from within the ship. They paused for just a moment more, bracing themselves before taking on the chaos.

As they flew into the storm, anxieties were racing. Without a moment's notice, Captain Aero was already having to dodge large bolts of lightning, causing them to miss the ship by just a hair. The booming thunder would rock the ship, and the winds were strong enough to push them around. It was a wonder how Captain Aero was able to skillfully navigate through this. The further into the storm they went, the more limited visibility became. Eventually, they had to rely on the lightning strikes see anything. Suddenly, everything was still and silent.

They continued flying in the pitch black, forward being the only way Captain Aero could think to go. The calm of the storm only heightened the stress and worry felt throughout the ship. Were they getting close? Were they out of the storm? No one really knew. Then, in an instant, a large bolt of lightning crashed down, obliterating the right wing of the ship. They started spinning out of control, Captain Aero was desperately trying to balance out his ship, to no avail. As some light started to pierce through, they all had lumps in their throats. They could see that they were spinning, in part, because they were being sucked into a tornado. A strong gust of wind blew them into another bolt of lightning. It was so powerful it caused everyone to get knocked around, hitting their heads and blacking out.

As they came to, and their blurry vision started to focus, they realized they were no lying on the floor of a cave. The sound of the raging storm was completely silenced. The area around them was dimly lit in turquoise light, provided by luminous stones of varying size. Covering the walls they could see some sort of tribal looking markings; they were carved along the only path they could see around them. There wasn't even an opening to the cave they could leave through. They followed the path, as if they really had any other option, and observe the markings they passed. It felt like they told a story, but no one was able to fully make it out. But one thing was clear, these were faded relics of an ancient time.

At the end of the path, they found a medium-sized pond nestled within an alcove. Instead of the luminous stones that had lit their way through the cave, the pond radiated with patches of bioluminescent algae, their ethereal green shimmers pulsing across the water's surface. On the wall behind the pond, they saw some extremely specific looking markings. In order there was: what looked like a cave, a circle, a pointed squiggle, a star with rays coming from its points. The crew stood there in silence for a while. They felt confused, relieved, nervous, and everything in between all at once. I could tell it was uncomfortable for them.

"I see," Arura sounded confident as she walked over to the markings, "I think I know what this means."

"Good, because I have no clue," Lienad chuckled.

"If I'm right about this, and I really believe I am," Arura put her left hand up to the markings, touching them as she spoke, "Inside the cave, there is water, within the water you reach the stars."

"Okay," Renka, sounded even more confused, "But what does that mean?"

"Well," Arura turned back around and stared into the pond, "It means this pond must be a portal and all we have to do is jump in."

"I don't know," Renka placed his hand on his chin, "I don't see it. Are you su—."

Before Renka could finish his question, Arura jumped into the pond. She slowly disappeared as she hit the water, until there was nothing left but rippling water. The rest of them quickly got up and looked around, she was nowhere to be seen within the pond. Either she was right, or she was horribly wrong. As they tried to figure out their next move, her hand peaked out of the water and waved; though there was no body they could see attached to it. Clearly, she had to be right. Unless, of course, the hand was some evil creature luring them to their death. Since none of them had this thought, they followed her lead and jumped into the pond one after the other.

I don't know if the others had the same experience, but when Lienad jumped in, it was incredible. It was like entering into a vortex of time and space warping around you for but a blink of an eye. On the other side of the portal, they were in a candle lit room filled with various doors. Each door was marked with a unique symbol, which must have represented what has behind it. In the center of the room was a tall, archaic looking, stone tablet. When they first looked at it, they couldn't understand what it said. But, as they stood there, it seemed to transform into a language they could understand.

Upon the tablet was a directory, like one you would find in a large marketplace. It had the symbols on each of the doors listed, with the names of different theological beliefs next to them. It seemed that behind each door were the beings for a specific belief system, and the list was extensive. It was as though this was a central hub for every idol from every religion that existed in the universe. They weren't sure which one to go through to 'meet three' as the engraving told them to do, so they looked around at the doors. I'm fairly certain they were getting ready to just pick one and go through it. Then, Arura started walking over to one to them and points at it.

"Hey," she shouted, "I don't remember seeing this one. Is there a description for a symbol that looks like three brains?"

"Um," Lienad scanned the stone tablet thoroughly, "I don't see that one here actually."

"This has to be the one," Arura motioned for them to join her, "I can't think of any other reason it wouldn't be included if not for this."

Lienad, Renka, and Captain Aero sauntered over to join her in front of the door. While they all had confidence that she was right, they were still reluctant to open the door. Lienad reluctantly inched his hand onto the doorknob and paused. He grasped the knob and gulped a lump down his throat. He didn't know what would happen when he opened the door, but he had this daunting feeling that it would be the beginning of the end. But the end of what, he did now know. He hesitantly turned the knob and pushed the door open. As it creaked open, a large off-white stairway was revealed. With measured steps, they ascended the stairs. The area around them was nothing more than an uncomfortably bright white, no scenery at all. At the top of the stairs was a gazebo-like structure with three floating brains around it, arranged in the shape of a triangle.

"Lienad, Arura, Aero, and Renka," all three brains pulsed with a dim yellow light as a multilayered voice reverberated, "We have been waiting for you."

"You... knew we were coming?" Lienad asked, filled with unease.

"Yes. It was. After all. Us who created Neoshyt," the brains seemed to take turns pulsating and the voice seemed the echo out in varied single layers this time, "He acted on our behalf. He was linked to us."

"What do you mean was," Lienad grew even more uncomfortable.

"The link was severed. But we know not how. Very

recently, it was."

"Did something happen, is he dead," Lienad began to lightly tremble.

"That is of no consequence. His knowledge was limited. Protection. In the event of his compromise."

"Dang, all thought no emotion," Renka mumbled. Though I'm surprised he would care, having never met Neoshyt himself.

"You are correct, Renka," The Three pulsated in unison again, "We are the very essence of thought itself. There is no room, nor any need, for emotions."

"You don't care about Neoshyt, got it, moving on," Lienad rushed, "We need to get the star key. How do we get it?"

"Neoshyt was a valuable tool and nothing more. You do not weep when a hammer breaks," the voice of The Three was exceptionally dry in this moment, "As for the star key, while it is essential for your mission we do not believe you are prepared for the cost."

"Whatever the cost, I will pay it," Lienad closed his eyes and gritted his teeth, "It's something I have to do."

"Even if you are not the only one who must pay?"

Lienad looked at the group, each of them giving him a nod of agreement. Though, Renka's looked as though he was uncertain.

"Yes," Lienad was firm in his resolve.

There was a long moment of deafening silence. The Three began to pulsate with an orange glow that grew faster. The glow slowly turned to a green hue, at which point it remained steady. Then, the glow rapidly died out.

"If this is your desire, then so it shall be."

"So, what is the price for the key?" Lienad had a stern tone.

"This will be revealed, when the time is right," The Three had a cryptic tone become prominent within the layers of their voice, "But know this, the key can shatter just as much as it can heal in the universe. It may also unlock something that was meant to stay hidden. Is it still your wish to proceed?"

This made everyone pause for a moment. The thought of it shattering the universe was counterproductive for their mission. Was this really a chance they wanted to take? Lienad looked around at the group and could see how visibly uncomfortable this thought had made them. But he knew, there was only one thing they could do here.

"Unless there is another choice," Lienad's tone grew solemn, "Then I have to keep on this path."

"There is not," The Three's voice grew quiet and serious, "Engulf the room of doors in darkness, only then will the door be revealed to you. Behind the door of the star, you will find the path to the key."

"Great," Renka scoffed, "Another riddle."

"Renka," Arura hit his arm, "Now isn't the time, plus that's not even a hard riddle."

"What about the land of lore, from the second half of the engraving," Lienad motioned his right hand to get Arura and Renka to be quiet.

"Behind the door of the star, you may not return from whence you came. The key will port you to this planet's core. There you will meet the one known as Erortac; from him the rest of your journey will become clear."

"It sure would be nice if we could get all the answers at the same time for once," Renka leaned his head back, exasperated, "It's a none stop go here and then go there, only getting partial answers each time."

"Renka," Arura hit his arm again, "You chose to come, no one forced you. If you don't have anything useful to add then shut up."

"Thank you," Lienad slightly bowed his head in respect and the group turned to head back to the room of doors.

"Wait," The Three's voice boomed, "Only two may enter for the key. Also, Lienad, if you can still contact Neoshyt he will be of no use. Where Erortac resides even he cannot see, nor does he even know it exists."

"So, what should the two who don't go through the door do then," Lienad was stressed about there being

another hurdle in this.

"They can go anywhere, as long as it's not staying here. Erortac can rejoin the group."

"Yeah, um, not sure how that's gonna work out," Captain Aero chimed in, "In getting here my ship was destroyed. Plus, we don't even know how to get out of here."

"In the room of doors. Return through the portal you entered," The Three once again began taking turns speaking, "You will be whisked away. Into your ship. Fully repaired. Hovering safely. Outside the storm. Go anywhere. We do not care. Just go away from here."

The group turned and walked back down the stairs into the room of doors. Lienad felt like the last statement from The Three was oddly rude. He also found it odd that if the portal took them back to the ship, and Erortac could bring them back together, that the two who don't go couldn't just wait in the room of doors. He shrugged it off, but I didn't; I too was a bit troubled that this may have meant something more heinous. Sadly, I am not allowed to intervene; regardless of how much I may want to at times. I can only observe and report.

They arrived back within the door of doors and gathered around the stone tablet. Arura reached down and clasped Lienad's hand, making it known she was staying with him. There was no argument, everyone seemed to understand the assignment. Lienad and Arura would trek on, while Renka and Captain Aero returned to the ship. Renka

gave Lienad, and even Arura, a tight hug. Captain Aero gave Arura a courteous bow, and he gave Lienad a formal salute.

"Good luck," Captain Aero asserted, "I feel like you may need it."

"Same to you," Lienad returned the salute.

As the group parted ways, no one had a pleasant feeling about it. It was as though an impending doom was beginning to hang over head. They all knew, though, that they had to brush it off and continue forward. The fate of the universe rested on their shoulder. A burden that had become increasingly heavy as this mission progressed. Lienad and Arura watched as Renka and Captain Aero jumped through the portal, hoping all was as they were told it would be. For now, they chose to believe that the two were safely in the ship as they were told. They then turned and gazed deeply into each other's eyes. You could almost see the love from one piercing into the other.

"Well, love of mine," Lienad said as he stepped closer, "Are you ready to do this?"

"As long as I am with you," Arura leaned in, "I am ready for anything."

They held each other tight and kissed passionately, which seemed to momentarily quell their anxieties. It was powerful, possibly even magical. Though I knew they were filled with fear, this moment of love gave them strength and peace—as if they really could take on anything. Through my time watching, I have grown to somewhat understand their love for one another. For the first time, I understood why humans long for this so much. To care for someone so much that you would dive headfirst into the unknown and be willing to risk it all is something spectacular. This moment was so intense, I could swear I felt the spark between them. I just wish I knew what they would be risking next, I'm sure they did as well.

25

The Star Key

Lienad and Arura held each other tight for a while longer. Neither of them wanted to admit it, but I knew they were both worried about what would come next. They wanted to delay the coming unknown, the fear that they may lose one another forever. But they both knew that they couldn't stay in this moment forever, no matter how badly they desired to.

"So," Lienad still held Arura tightly, leaning back just enough to look into her eyes, "Let's get that riddle figured out."

"I did that a long time ago," Arura giggled, "We are supposed to engulf the room in darkness. The obvious way to do that is the blow out all the candles, since they are the light source here. Then the door we need to go through is

supposed to be revealed to us."

"Okay," Lienad reluctantly pulled away, "Let's do it then."

Hand in hand, they from candle to candle. While splitting up would have completed this much faster, they chose to think with heart rather than brain. When they finally got to the last candle, they paused and stared into each other's eyes. As if they had just had a telepathic conversation, they gave each other a nod of agreement. Then Lienad blew out the last candle, engulfing the room in complete darkness. The ground began to rumble beneath them and a faint light became visible in the distance. When the rumbling ceased, they started walking toward the faint light.

A pit grew in their stomach, growing deeper the closer they got to the light. By the time they reached the door, they were uncomfortable and uncertain, filled with anxiety. This was it, the door with the star. Shakily, Lienad reached forward and opened the door. As it slowly creaked open, a dimly lit stairway was revealed. Like the previous room, the lighting was more candles. They walked up the stairs, with their hands still clasped tight. The stairway felt as though it would never end, which only made their worry worsen. The candles would only light up as they grew closer, leaving the full scale of the stairway unknown. With no end in sight, they walked on and on.

Eventually, they reached another door at the top of

the stairs. They opened the door, this time without hesitation. This was probably due to how over this stairway they were. Behind the door, much to their relief, was not another stairway. Instead, it was a candle lit room that was like a replica of the room of doors, minus the doors. In the center of the room there was a white basin atop a silver pedestal, like certain styles of what they call bird baths on Earth. They walked up to and saw it was filled with a clear liquid. This was not what either of them had expected to see, though they never really knew what to expect to begin with.

"What now," Lienad looked over to Arura, "I don't remember anything about this in that riddle, do you?"

"No, I don't," Arura glanced around the room, "Maybe we should look around for clues?"

"Yeah, I guess so," Lienad hesitantly let go of her hand and pointed to the left, "You check this side, and I'll check over here."

Before they split up, Lienad pulled her in close and gave her a long kiss. They split up and started looking for clues, but it was to no avail. As they walked around, all they came across were walls and candles. Lienad decided he should check the ceiling, since nothing else seemed useful. As he was looking up, he slowly walked around. This caused him to bump into the basin. He quickly grabbed the side to make sure it didn't fall over, though his bump didn't make it move at all. When he did this, a sound like wind chimes reverberated throughout the room. Arura nudged Lienad to

look over at the wall opposite of the door. A message was slowly being written with a glowing light. It read:

BY FATED THREADS, TWO SOULS ENTWINED.
HEARTS WITH ONE BEAT, TRUE LOVE'S BIND.
TO CLAIM THE KEY, A COST YOU WILL FIND:
LOVE'S LIFEBLOOD SPILLED AND COMBINED.

As they are reading the message they notice a silver blade appeared, hanging off the edge of the basin. They take a moment, pondering what this message could mean. They both knew it had to be instructions on how to get the key. It mentioned the cost, which The Three said would be revealed to them. A message appearing out of nowhere definitely counted as something being revealed. I was surprised it took them a while to figure it out. When I read it, it seemed straightforward to me. Naturally, Arura figured it out first.

"I got it," she snapped her fingers, "Using the information from the riddle, and the fact that a knife appeared, I believe we are supposed to spill our blood into the basin. Giving it my best guess, I think it will have to happen at the same time."

"Yeah," Lienad tried to sound like he also figured this out, but he didn't, "My only question is, how much

blood do you think we need to spill out?"

"Well," Arura paused, "I don't know. It doesn't specify an amount. Maybe we just try a little bit at first and see if that's enough?"

"That's a good a plan as any," Lienad nodded.

They walked up to the basin and looked at the knife, lumps in their throats. They looked at each other, more nervous than they had ever been. Lienad began reaching for the knife with his free hand when Arura grabbed his shoulder, stopping him. He looked back at her, slightly relieved that she had stopped him. She moved her hand up to his face, caressing his cheek. She stroked his face with her thumb and mouthed the words 'I love you'. He grabbed the back of her neck and pulled her in for a kiss. They kissed as if it were the last thing they would ever do. In that moment, as far as they knew, it might have been.

Lienad grabbed the knife and cut across his hand. Arura took the knife and did the same. They clasped their cut hand together and held it over the basin. As the blood dripped, nothing was happening. This caused the fear to bubble up that it would need to be a lot more blood, possibly even a fatal amount. As the blood continued to drip, the liquid started to rapidly bubble and steam as if it was boiling. It started to evaporate, and a golden glimmer began to appear in the bottom of the basin. By the time the liquid was completely gone, a small golden key had taken form.

"Look," Lienad gasped. "It worked!"

"We got the key," Arura gave a few quick bounces up and down.

They were both relieved that this part of their journey was over. It was also a heavy weight taken from them that an excess of their blood wasn't required. Even I was worried that may have ended up being the case. Now that was over, they had to keep moving forward on their journey. First, they took a moment to revel in their lack of stress and anxiety. Then, they braced themselves for even more unknown.

"So, I guess we just grab the key now," Lienad said with uncertainty.

"Yeah," Arura squeezed his hand a little tighter, "The Three said this would transport us somewhere else to get the rest of our mission."

"Are you ready," he looked into her eyes.

"As I'll ever be," she smiled with confidence.

They held each other close, tight enough to make sure they couldn't fall apart. With closed eyes, Lienad reached into the basin and grasped the key. As he touched it, they felt a swift rush of swirling wind. It was almost as if there was a miniature tornado forming around them. Suddenly, the wind stopped. They opened their eyes and saw they did, in fact, get whisked away to another place. They were in a small room with two doors and two chairs. One of the doors was broken, with a pitch-black darkness behind

it. The other, and intact brown wooden door, had the sounds as if someone was tinkering on something.

"I wonder which door we should go through," Lienad quickly glanced at them both, "With how this journey has gone, maybe we do have to jump into that black pit."

"Or," Arura turned his face towards her, "Maybe we don't have to do something so crazy and should just see what's behind the normal door."

"Heh," he chuckled, "I suppose you're probably right."

They looked at each other, smiled, and giggled. Though, I don't really see what was so humorous about it. This felt like one of those times where someone says, "you just had to be there". The only problem was that I was here, and I still didn't get it. They stopped their unnecessary giggling and leaned in for yet another kiss, something they didn't seem to think they did enough of. As this was happening, the intact door began to slowly creak open and the sound of the tinkering had stopped.

26

The Creature

When the door fully opened, a very strange, yet oddly gentle looking creature emerged. It had a thin and wispy mane of white hair. Some of the strands floated around, while others caressed its face. There were two large pointy ears poking off its head at an angle. If you looked at them closely, you could see them slightly twitching. The creature's face was remarkably similar to that of a goblin. If you have never seen one before, it is rounded with sharp angled cheekbones, a flattened nose, a mouth that almost appeared to have a constant sly grin, and large eyes. Within the white of each eye was a soft brown iris, magnified by rounded glasses. Its clothes consisted of a worn brown jacket, an old white shirt, and black pants. Both hands had three long, bony fingers that ended with sharp points for nails. It had short, stubby legs with three fat toes each.

Behind the creature was a long, dragon-like, tail with purple spikes running down it. Its skin had scaly patches and was painted with varying hues of green, blue, grey, and white. Despite this bizarre appearance, its gaze was oddly warm with a scholarly gentleness to it. To make it simple, this was a weird yet approachable looking creature.

Lienad and Arura were, understandably, taken aback by what they saw in front of them. Obviously, this had to be the creature known as Erortac that The Three mentioned. At least, that's what they had hoped. Otherwise, who knew what they were about to be in for. Though, since they knew nothing about Erortac, no one knew what they were in for even if it was him. So, filled with questions, they silently stood there with their mouths slightly gaped open.

"You're finally here," the creature's eyes glimmered with joy and its voice had a soft-warm tone to it, "I've been waiting for this moment."

"The moment that someone would come," Lienad questioned with caution, "Or the moment we specifically would come?"

"You specifically, Lienad," the creature smiled, which was not as comforting as it may have thought, "It was always going to be you. Arura as well, of course."

"More of this while destiny stuff like what Neoshyt said," Lienad wasn't surprised, "Does this mean you are Erortac?"

"It does mean that, yes. You being here means you have the key, congratulations."

"The Three said we would get the rest of our mission from you," Arura chimed in.

"Oh, yes," Erortac's mouth curled into a less than inviting smile as it slowly spoke, "You will indeed get the rest of the mission from me."

"Well, great," Lienad got excited, he didn't notice the smile like I did, "What all do we have left to save the universe?"

"Saving the universe, of course, yes," Erortac turned and walked over to the chairs, its voice grew darker in tone, "Why don't the two of you have a seat. It may take some time to tell you everything, I would be remiss if I wasn't thorough. Your legs may get tired, and we wouldn't want that."

Lienad and Arura looked at each other, neither of them really thought much of it. I, on the other hand, did not trust him. I suppose they had been blinded to too much suspicion at this point. They walked over and sat in the rigid wooden chairs, which Lienad clearly did not find the least bit comfortable. Arura also looked as though she was attempting to mask some discomfort.

"Got any cushions for these things," Lienad let out a strained chuckle, attempting to make it sound as if he was joking, even though he wasn't.

"Haha," Erortac let out a hoarse laugh, "I apologize that my amenities are not the most welcoming. It's not like I get a lot of guests here. No, I do not have cushions."

"That's, fine," he looked over at Arura, "I'm sure we will manage. So, let's get this word party started and get this last part of our mission. Which, hopefully, will be the last part of it."

"Oh, this will be the end of your mission. I can assure you of that," Erortac let out a chuckle with the faintest hint of menace behind it.

"Well, that's good," Arura grabbed Lienad's hand, "This has gone on for what feels like forever, and it just seems to keep getting longer."

"Well, as I said, this won't be short." Erortac closed its eyes and took a deep breath. "Let me start by telling you about myself. To do that, we must go back to the beginning of everything in this universe. As you know, or at least have heard, in the beginning there was Ganel and Velid. Ganel was responsible for creating the different dimensions and the planets therein. Ganel is often referred to as the mother because of this, though Ganel had no actual gender so to speak. Regardless, for streamline this, at least a little, we will refer to Ganel as she and Velid as he. Anyways, she was nice and pure; a real sweetheart you could say. She was ever loving of her creations."

Erortac stopped to take a breath. "He was, however, not. He was filled with anger, hate, and jealousy of her. He did not have the same powers of creation as she did. His jealousy led him to develop a plan to twist her creation, though he was unsuccessful. It seemed as though he would always be her second fiddle, if you will."

"Wait," Lienad interrupted, "Neoshyt said that Velid corrupted the Gretualin species form being pure, like me."

"Yes, I know what he said," Erortac slyly smiled, "We will get to all of that in a minute, for now let me get back to this story; if you please. He was prepared to give up, and he did. But his negative emotions continued to fester and boil. They began to assume his very essence. Eventually, he was no longer the same celestial being he used to be. He, himself, had become twisted and corrupted. His mind became obsessed with trying to find a way to not only become better than her, but to ruin all her precious creations. It was from this boiling pot of obsession and negativity that I was accidentally created."

"Wait," Lienad's heart started to race, "So you... you were created by Velid? The one known to be extremely evil?"

"Yes," Erortac let out a very menacing laugh, one that was so obvious that even Lienad and Arura couldn't ignore it, "Again though, he didn't mean to."

"No," Lienad quickly stood up. "Arura, we need to get out of here, I don't think we can trust this thing."

"Oh, you poor soul," Erortac rase its hand as Arura

also started to stand up, "There is no getting out of here unless I say so. Considering the fact that I didn't say so, I implore you to SIT DOWN!"

Erortac waved its hand down, causing Lienad and Arura to be forced back in their chairs. Once they were fully seated, straps appeared around their wrists and ankles, locking them in. This made the chairs even more uncomfortable than before, though that was the least of their concerns at the moment. Lienad tried, with all his might, to struggle against the straps; but it was of no use.

Erortac laughed, a deep and vile laugh, at his feeble attempt to break free. Every bit of approachability and gentleness I originally saw in Erortac had disappeared completely. Even its form had become more grotesque. Where there was once wispy white hair, was now a variety of small spikes. Behind its glasses were now coal black eyes with blazing red pupils. Its once short and stubby legs had become long and slender. The spikes along its tail double in size. Large spikes now protruded from its elbows. Large and sharp canine teeth now peeked through its upper lip. This was now a beast like none had ever seen before.

"Now that we are more comfortable," Erortac's voice was now a snarling growl, "Perhaps I can get on with the rest of my story."

"Let us out of here," Lienad yelled as he continued to attempt getting out of the straps.

"I don't believe I will. You see, I need you; at least

for a little while longer."

"What could you possibly need from me," Lienad's heart sank, and a painful pit grew in his stomach.

"In due time, Lienad," Erortac's snake-like tongue flicked quickly in and out of its mouth, "This will be revealed to you, among many other things. All you have to do is sit tight and listen. The first one should be quite easy for you now. Can you keep your mouth shut long enough to hear what I have to say, or do I need to strap that closed too?"

Lienad stopped struggling and looked over at Arura, who was completely frozen in fear. It tore him to pieces inside that there was nothing he could do for her. He was beginning to become filled with rage, but he knew that wouldn't help the situation. So, he did the only thing he could think to do. He sat there quietly and gave Erortac a nod.

"Good boy," Erortac bellowed with a shrieking laugh, "Looks like you can be smart. Now then, shall I continue my tale?"

27

The Real Truth

There was a heavy moment of silence, thick with discomfort. Lienad and Arura had given up trying to break out of the straps that bound them. They had tried so hard that their wrists had started getting rubbed raw. Erortac looked pleased at their admitted defeat. The beast looked as though it was reveling in this moment, soaking in his success at suppressing their will to fight. Once again, as much as I wanted to help, I was unable.

"Now that you're being unwillingly submissive, I'll continue my story," Erortac sneered, "As I already told you, I was an accidental creation of Velid. I was also the root of his demise. I was born with a lust for power and control. So, I absorbed my father and took his power for my own. It was I who corrupted the Gretualin species. They were her first, it only seemed natural that I should begin there as well," Erortac paused with a look of pride upon its face.

"While I waited for my corruption to take full form, I created The Three, believing they would one day come in handy—and how right I was. They went on to create the false gods and Neoshyt, as I'm sure they told you. Everything ended up going so well. The corruption of the Sparebryr got so intense, they started slaughtering their own just for being born differently. Eventually, nothing was left but the corruption," Erortac smiled a most grimacing smile and softly chuckled.

"By this time, Ganel had started to catch on to what I was doing; at least some of it. She wasn't aware of my testing grounds; you know them as the land of lore. I had been secretly stealing humans from earth, putting them into it, and testing on them. From this I create many a monster. The humans called them by many names, such as vampires, werewolves, mermaids, and zombies. I found the names to be quite dull, but the havoc they wreaked was glorious. It was so easy to do as well, the Earth was largely ignored by Ganel. I could basically do anything I wanted to them."

A flicker of resentment crossed its face. "Eventually, however, Ganel ended up deciding enough was enough. She stepped off her proverbial throne and came for me. Unfortunately, I wasn't strong enough to take her down at that time. She strapped this locked shackle around my ankle, binding me to this room and suppressing my powers. But not before I was able to absorb a piece of her. This gave me

just enough power to resist the shackle to continue my work creating monsters. Since then, I have created the perfect incarnation of evil."

Erortac's gaze sharpened as it leaned forward and brushed the back of its fingers across Lienad's face. "Now that you are here, I will be able to break free and finish my original mission of corrupting the entire universe. I'll also be able to complete my new goal, getting rid of Ganel; permanently. Not that anyone would notice, seeing as to how she has secluded herself and stopped caring."

Erortac stepped back and spread its arms open in a mocking gesture. "Now, I'm sure by this point you may have some questions. I'm not horrible enough to refuse answering them for such adoring fans. Let's say I'll allow one at a time."

"None of this explained how you could have known I would come," Lienad grunted through gritted teeth.

"Oh, but it does," Erortac placed its hand on its chest, "You see, because I absorbed a piece of Ganel, I had gained a limited access to her thoughts and memories. I knew she had created a key for this blasted lock. The key could only be obtained by a pure Gretualin, free of my corruption, that had found their soul mate. So, I had The Three engineer and deploy a new DNA alteration that would allow for pure Gretualin to periodically be born. However, they made me so proud and continued to kill the odd ones out." Erortac wiped a tear of joy from its eye.

"I knew I had to do something and do something I did. I had The Three manipulate Neoshyt's mind into believing this fantastical tale, the one he told you that led you on this mission. Because he believed this, he kept watch over Sparebryr and was able to convince your parents to rescue you from certain death. They then watched you and molded your steps to eventually lead you to this point. Of course, you almost got away when you had Remus erase your mind."

"Wait," Lienad interrupted, which visibly irritated Erortac, "That still doesn't explain the engraving, the orb, or any of the other steps to the mission."

"You really are an idiot," Erortac had a low and guttural growl as he spoke, "If you wouldn't interrupt me, I would be getting to it. How rude you are, stopping me in the middle of a glorious tale. I set all of this up. I had the engraving created in a language that few knew. Using Ganel's memories, I knew about Swidom and how to find him. I had the orb placed for you to find. How else would you have gotten to Neoshyt? You see, if you pay attention, it all makes sense."

"No, it doesn't," Lienad retorted in a snarky tone, "This doesn't explain anything about Krind, Arura's fairy powers, or the specific team members I needed. It also doesn't explain how I was able to get to the key at all. I mean if Ganel created the key, why would she have kept the door to it in a place you created?"

Erortac began to boil up with rage. Not only was Lienad interrupting, but he was also giving attitude as well. Erortac huffed and snarled while stomping around. Lienad took some satisfaction in being an irritant, but also worried about what it would mean next for them. The only thing that brought him comfort was the belief that Erortac still needed him, for now at least. Erortac continued the tantrum for a little longer before stopping and quickly walking towards Lienad. The creature leaned forward, pressing its face right in front of Lienad's.

"Well, with all your stupid questions it sounds like you want me to tell you the full story. You just can't keep quiet long enough to HEAR IT," Erortac's voice was strained, and teeth were tightly gritted.

"You're absolutely right," Lienad was filled with sarcasm, "Please do continue."

"Not that I need your permission, or your attitude, I will," Erortac stood up and let out a heavy breath, "I am grateful to your parents. Not only did they preserve you, but they also gave birth to my perfect Gretualin. Your brother Krind is exactly how I envisioned the species going. His hate, thirst for power, and blood lust are a thing to be admired. Without even knowing it, he is paving the way for me. As for your team, Neoshyt hand selected them based on the needs he understood from the mission."

Erortac took a deep breath and started to speak slowly. "If you remember, I absorbed some of Ganel. I knew where the key was and The Three were able to create a pathway. She didn't create it near me, I just outsmarted her in finding a way to get there. Though I may hate her, I cannot call her stupid; just not as smart as I am. As for Arura's powers, I cannot take credit for that. That was all on her parents. But since I knew you would need fairy powers for parts of this quest, I made sure unlocking their full potential was a part of it. Though her meddling parents somehow started to learn a little about the true history behind Sparebryr. Had they dug too deep they may have ended up learning about me. Since I couldn't have this, I had them disposed of. I still don't know what prompted them to start digging, it's a shame because I would have liked to have known. Regardless, they were removed before they could even scratch much of the surface."

"You," Arura screamed out, "You are the reason I had to grow up without them?"

"Oh, Arura dear," Erortac reached forward and caressed her face with its bony hand, "I did you a kindness. You were better off without those pesky parents of yours."

"What about all the other stuff Neoshyt showed me," Lienad interjected to try and get the subject changed, he could see how horribly it was affecting Arura, "How the universe was created, all of the different universes, and stuff like that?"

"All just a fantasy," Erortac let out a vile laugh, "Even he believes that lie. If there were other universes, don't you think I would have gone to one of those instead to start my, soon to be endless, reign of terror? As far as I am concerned, Ganel has always existed and created this universe, which is the only one out there."

"Another thing," Lienad had a puzzled look on his face, "How did you guarantee Arura, and I would be soul mates?"

"Ah, yes, that," Erortac paced a bit, "That was something that I had to take a risk on. I must chalk the fact that it worked out to pure luck. I have never been a believer in soul mates or true love. That was Ganel's fantasy. But you two sure did prove me wrong. For instance, had it not been for her coming to get you the PROTM never would have been reversed. Then I would have had to wait for another pure Gretualin to be born and groomed for my purposes. So, in a sense I suppose I do owe her a lot of thanks for unknowingly making sure my plans could be completed."

Erortac maniacally laughed at this. But Arura's wide eyes grew hollow and distant. I could tell this made her feel destroyed, like it was really her fault they were in this. If I could have, I would have tried to comfort her. Lienad looked at her, feeling her pain as he saw it on her face.

"Hey, don't let this thing get to you," Lienad leaned over and softly whispered to her, "It's not your fault. I bet this would have happened somehow regardless. You can't blame yourself."

"How touching," Erortac said in a smug tone,

"Comforting her is of no use. It's not like you have much time left anyways."

"WHY ARE WE STILL HERE TO BEGIN WITH," Lienad couldn't hold back his rage, "If all you needed was the key, why haven't you just killed us and taken it? Why do you feel the need to tell us all of this?"

Tears rolled down Lienad's face. He was heartbroken at how hurt Arura was. He also couldn't believe that it all came down to this. What started as a mission of hope to save the universe had been nothing more than an evil plot they were roped into. In the end, his agreement to go on this mission is the real cause. In his mind, this was all his fault. Plus, with the truth being revealed he shuddered to think about the true fate of Renka and Captain Aero.

"Where's the fun in just killing you and taking the key," Erortac's face grew a terrifyingly evil expression, "By telling you all of this, I get the pleasure of completely breaking you down. I wouldn't get that if you're dead. Besides, I have something far more fun planned for you than death. Well, fun for me anyways. But you do remind me of an important fact."

Erortac patted Lienad down checking all his pockets and folds. When the key was found, Erortac held it up and admired it. Next, it was lowered down into the shackle, the only line of defense against this impending doom. As the key was slowly turned, it created a shrieking grind of the metals against each other. It felt like a long and hideous scream. Then the lock clicked open, releasing a blast of air so powerful it rocked Lienad and Arura's chairs. Erortac took a deep breath in and gave a loud roar. Its bony figure slowly filled in with muscle and the various spikes grew. The creature, now more grotesque than ever, grew taller. Its presence loomed, an overwhelming shadow of malice. It was clear that its power had grown to an immense degree that caused physical changes.

"There it is," Erortac let out a long sigh of relief, "I can feel my former self being restored, I finally feel alive once more!"

Erortac lifted the shackle and crushed it in its hand with ease.

"I must thank you," Erortac turned its gaze to Lienad and Arura, "You have given me my freedom. Now let me give you something in return."

Erortac waved its fingers upwards, causing Lienad and Arura's chairs to slightly levitate off the ground. Their eyes darted left and right, scanning the ground beneath them with dread. At this point, they knew they were done for. They didn't know what torment Erortac's earlier threat implied, 'something far more fun than death'. But they knew it couldn't be anything less than a true horror. They just hoped whatever it was would be quick and painless.

"It's been fun, for me at least. In the end, that's all that really matters," Erortac let out a snarling laugh, "Do say hello to your friends for me, if they are still alive."

Erortac quickly waved its hand, sending them flying through the broken door and into the pitch-black darkness.

28

<u>The End</u>

Lienad and Arura plummeted through the darkness, still strapped to their chairs, unable to see anything—not even their own hands. In an instant, pure terror seized them as they tried not to think of what unspeakable horrors awaited them. It was a sickening paradox of weightlessness and violent descent, like being yanked in every direction by a chaotic tangle of unseen strings. Then, without warning, the drop surged faster—violently.

Lienad tried calling out to Arura—again and again—but no sound left his lips. He even tried screaming—but still, nothing. The silence around them swallowed everything. With how fast they were falling, he expected to hear wind roaring past his ears. But there was nothing, not even that. With each breathless second, they slipped further into a fear-fueled madness. Then, just before their minds were

lost, they crashed into the ground. Their chairs shattered beneath them, wood and metal scattered, freeing them from their binds—and yet, not a scratch. They were completely unharmed—not even a bruise to prove they'd ever fallen.

They stood up, dusted themselves off, and scanned the area for any clue of where they were. High above them, centered in the sky, hung a large white moon. To their left stretched a lake in front of a tall mountain range—its peaks were lost in a silvery mist. To their right was a patch of woods, filled with a low-hanging fog. In front of them ran a river, just before a large stone wall lined with evenly spaced lookout towers—it had the feel of a city's outer defenses. Looking back, the fog obscured everything but the outline of more trees.

"Are you okay?" Lienad wrapped his arms around Arura, "That was one hell of an event just now."

"Physically, I'm fine," Arura said, pausing with a slight shudder. "Mentally—still stands to be seen."

"I know, but don't worry—at least we are together," Lienad gently rubbed her back.

"Do you... do you have any idea where we are?"

"If I'm being honest..." Lienad took a deep breath and blew it out through pursed lips, "I was kind of hoping you would know. Considering that you're the smarter one between us, after all."

"Yeah," Arura giggled, a welcome sound in the moment, "That's true. But I have no clue. Maybe it's another part of Earth in the medieval times? No... the moon's too big. I really don't know, babe."

"Well, if I had to guess..." Lienad said, taking another look around. "I would say we are probably in the land of lore—or, as Erortac called it, the testing grounds."

"I think you're probably right about that," Arura swallowed a lump in her throat, "Which, if you are, doesn't really feel all that comforting."

And I believe he's right. This area doesn't seem familiar to me either. Which is unusual considering I am from the Grand Universe Archives—the one place that holds knowledge of all known realms. I have never seen this land, nor read any tomes that describe it. I don't even know if I can transmit my writings back from here. Unfortunately, I must now stop writing and test the connection. But I will immediately resume documenting. Even as I write these final lines, two figures approach Lienad and Arura from the direction of the stone wall.

Pronunciation Guide

Below is a pronunciation guide for select words featured in this work. This guide was created by the G.U.A. and is included for the benefit of all readers. Some of these words may be unfamiliar to those that may open this tome. We believe the inclusion of this guide will allow the book to be more inclusive and allow for a better reading experience.

Planets:

Earth (**ERTH**)

Anigav (**AN**-ih-gav)

Sparebryr (**SPARE**-brye-er)

Tesheraf (**TESH**-er-af)

Pecoaphlyly (Pe-co-ah-**FLEE**-lee)

Cerulyt (**SE**-ruh-lit)

Friyaldan (**FREE**-all-dahn)

Species:

Human (**HU**-man)

Bonel (**BO**-nel)

Smeglin (**SMEG**-lin)

Snuln (**SNUL**-in)

Pixie (**PIK**-see)

Fairy (**FAIR**-ee)

Heagowl (**HEGG**-owl)

Sterimy (**STER**-ih-mee)

Gretualin (**GRET**-u-a-lin)

Serpisapion (**SER**-pi-sa-pi-on)

Individuals:

Lienad (**LEE**-en-ad)

Arura (**UH**-roo-ruh)

Remus (**REE**-mus)

Renka (**REN**-kuh)

Aero (**AIR**-oh)

Erortac (**EHR**-or-tac)

Scenkid (**SKEHN**-kid)

Krind (**KRIND**)

Nereg (**NEH**-reg)

Neoshyt (**NEE**-oh-shit)

Cri (**KREE**)

Stol (**STOHL**)

Fyrnip (**FUHR**-nip)

Ganel (**GAN**-el)

Velid (**VEH**-lid)

Peetnum (**PEET**-nuhm)

Zidral (**ZIH**-drall)

Swidom (**SWEE**-duhm)

Ladnarmesa (**LAD**-nar-may-suh)

About the Author

Daniel J Wright is a Texas-based author that specializes in Fantasy, Science Fiction, and Children's Books. A writer since age 11, Daniel competed as a writer through high school and won various academic awards. His passion for storytelling is fueled by his love of the macabre, magic, mystery, and outer space. He aims to craft immersive worlds that blend emotion, intrigue, and the occasional plot twist.

Beyond writing, Daniel is an accomplished artist, musician, and IT professional with multiple degrees. He has toured the United States as a musician. To this day he still creates music from death metal to electronic. He is a lifelong learner and avid reader, thriving on exploring new ideas and pushing creative boundaries.